WHITE WOLF'S FEUD

Jim Allen — small, freckled, and riding a horse named Apple Pie — seems a harmless innocent to those not in the know. But this youthful-looking drifter with the sweet tooth is the philanthropist outlaw known as the White Wolf: dextrous with his guns, generous with his ill-gotten gains, and worth twelve thousand dollars to any bounty hunter who can fell him. Now he is on the trail of Quong Lee, a skilled knifeman and ruthless leader of a dope-running gang. Meanwhile, Jim's twin brother Jack, a sheriff, has been tasked by the United States secret service with investigating the same dope ring. Their headquarters have been traced to El Crucifixo, an outlaw town where a lawman's life isn't worth a plugged nickel. The only way Jack can safely enter is by passing himself off as the White Wolf . . .

SPECIAL MESSAGE TO READERS

THE ULVERSCROFT FOUNDATION
(registered UK charity number 264873)
was established in 1972 to provide funds for research, diagnosis and treatment of eye diseases. Examples of major projects funded by the Ulverscroft Foundation are:-

- The Children's Eye Unit at Moorfields Eye Hospital, London
- The Ulverscroft Children's Eye Unit at Great Ormond Street Hospital for Sick Children
- Funding research into eye diseases and treatment at the Department of Ophthalmology, University of Leicester
- The Ulverscroft Vision Research Group, Institute of Child Health
- Twin operating theatres at the Western Ophthalmic Hospital, London
- The Chair of Ophthalmology at the Royal Australian College of Ophthalmologists

You can help further the work of the Foundation by making a donation or leaving a legacy. Every contribution is gratefully received. If you would like to help support the Foundation or require further information, please contact:

THE ULVERSCROFT FOUNDATION
The Green, Bradgate Road, Anstey
Leicester LE7 7FU, England
Tel: (0116) 236 4325

website: www.foundation.ulverscroft.com

WHITE WOLF'S FEUD

HAL DUNNING

First published in the United States by Chelsea House

First Isis Edition
published 2018
by arrangement with
Golden West Literary Agency

A catalogue record for this book is available from the British Library.

ISBN 978–1–78541–554–8 (pb)

Published by
F. A. Thorpe (Publishing)
Anstey, Leicestershire

Set by Words & Graphics Ltd.
Anstey, Leicestershire
Printed and bound in Great Britain by
T. J. International Ltd., Padstow, Cornwall

This book is printed on acid-free paper

Contents

CHAPTER ONE

Start of the Trail

"You ain't fit to die," Jim Allen said softly. The man, who crouched against the wall of the canyon, shivered and broke into incoherent pleadings. He was a thin man of twenty-three, with a white, pasty face. There was nothing of the desert or mountain man about him, and he looked strangely out of place in that desolate, barren country.

"Don't shoot. Don't kill me," he whimpered.

"You ain't fit to die," Allen repeated.

His strangely shaped eyes were filled with a mixture of contempt and loathing as he gazed at the terrified man before him. With a lightninglike movement he returned his two guns to their holsters, then placed his hand on the mane of his lean, gray colt and leaped lightly into the saddle. He reined the gray about and looked down at the other.

The man's face was alight with the new hope and joy of a condemned man who has received a last-minute reprieve.

"Tom Mann, that's your name. But you was sure named wrong, 'cause you ain't a man, only a worm. I reckon Sam Brown and that chink, Hop Sing, is the real coyotes, even if it was you what pulled the trigger and presented old Jim Sterns with a harp. You can tell them friends of yours that the 'Wolf' sure figures any gent what runs dope over the border or peddles the stuff is lower than a sidewinder. So tell them I plans on puttin' my heel on their necks. The gent what got you started usin' dope is the one what really killed old Jim."

The tattered little figure on the gray, having finished his speech, shrugged his shoulders and trotted off down the canyon. He seemed to realize that the wretched creature on the ground lacked even the courage of a cornered rat, and would not dare to chance a shot at his back, for never once did he look behind him as he continued on down the trail.

Slowly the color returned to Tom Mann's face. He remained in the same position until Jim Allen had vanished around a bend in the canyon, then rose to his feet. His hands were still trembling as he mounted his horse, and his face wore the dazed expression of a man who, as yet, was unable to believe his own luck.

Allen had taken the trail north, so Mann turned south in the direction of the border. He spurred his horse into a fast run, for he wished to put distance between himself and the little outlaw in the quickest possible time. Also, he knew that if any officer of the law overtook him, he would not escape a second time.

He felt that there was danger in passing on Allen's warning, but it had to be done. Unless the Wolf were trapped, he would surely track down the members of the gang. The news would get out that he, Mann, had squealed, and then his end would be certain.

It was past midnight when he halted on the outskirts of Dry Creek, a small town about fifty miles from the border and the outlaw town of El Crucifixo. He left his horse concealed in a clump of bushes some distance from the trail and crept forward through the darkness on foot. He slipped cautiously through an opening between two houses, listened for a moment at the window, then scratched quietly on the pane.

There was a moment's silence. Then a voice called out softly: "Who's there?"

Tom gulped and quavered: "It's me — Tom Mann."

Again there was silence. Then he heard the bolts of a door on his left slide back. He had an impulse to flee, to rush for his horse and race across the border. But he checked himself, for he knew there would be no safety for him in Mexico.

He had never seen Quong Lee, the leader of the dope ring, but he knew him by reputation. To betray Quong Lee was suicide. His agents and killers were everywhere. Mann had heard many times of men who had attempted to break away from the organization, and he knew that their end had invariably been the same. They had been found in some alley with a knife thrust through them, or had been killed in a saloon brawl by white gunmen.

No, there would be no safety for him in Mexico, and if he attempted to hide in the United States, he would not only have Quong's men to fear, but the law as well. Then, too, there was Allen. The little outlaw might change his mind, and Mann shivered with fear as he recalled the yellow flare in the Wolf's strange eyes. There was nothing to do but face Sin Wang and "Black Steve" and give them his warning — and hope and pray that they would not guess that he had let out some names under Allen's questioning.

The door creaked open, and the space was filled with yellow light. Mann's knees trembled as he advanced toward it. At a guttural command he entered. The door swung shut behind him, and he was pushed into a brightly lighted room. He blinked his eyes for a moment, then fixed them on a wizened figure that sat behind a desk at the far end of the room. His heart turned to water.

The man's face was like ancient parchment. His head was bare as a billiard ball. His eyes were long, narrow and half concealed by heavy, drooping lids.

Tom Mann had never seen him before, but he knew instantly that this sinister figure was the dreaded Quong Lee himself. He would never have entered the room had he suspected that Quong would be there. Mann rather prided himself on his ability to lie, and he was convinced that he could have deceived Black Steve and Sin Wang. But there was no deceiving Quong Lee.

Quong wore the brilliantly colored, beaded robe of the mandarin. His hands were concealed within the folds of the wide sleeves. He was apparently unarmed, but Mann knew that the old man could throw back the folds of his robe and fling a knife that bit into its victim with the quickness and sureness of the deadly cobra. He had heard much of the sudden death dealt out by this ancient, wrinkled Chinaman.

Mann knew now that he was securely within the spider's web, and that if he failed to convince Quong of his innocence, he would be dead in five minutes. He had no chance against this man, and there were, besides, two other men in the room, both of them killers.

Sin Wang, a short, powerfully built Chinaman, could break a man's back with his bare hands. Moreover, he carried a sawed-off, double-barreled shotgun which he could use as deftly as a gunman does a Colt.

Black Steve, the third man, whose aquiline nose and small, beady eyes told of a mixture of Apache and Chinese blood, was also ruthless, and as cruel as the worst of his savage ancestors.

"Why did you come here?" Quong Lee suddenly rapped out.

"We had to kill Jim Stearns," Mann stammered. "He found — he found where we cached the stuff up near Salt Spring."

Quong Lee's wrinkled face remained as inscrutable and emotionless as that of a carved Buddha. Only his eyes seemed alive. "Any one see you?" he asked in his singsong, toneless voice.

"No — I mean — well, no one but Jim Allen."

"The Wolf? He saw you?" Black Steve exclaimed.

Mann licked his lips and nodded.

"I know the Wolf. If he saw you, why are you here?" Quong Lee asked.

"Why, you see, he trailed me and warned me that he intended to crush you all."

"He told you that, did he?" Black Steve growled, as his hands caressed the butts of his two guns.

Mann nodded again. He moved uneasily, and shuffled his feet as the two Chinamen and the half-breed stared at him in silence. He sensed the hostility in their gaze. At last Quong broke the silence, and Mann jumped as if stung.

"The Wolf — he caught you, knew that you had assisted in the murder of Jim Sterns, knew that you were a member of a dope-running gang — and then let you go. Why?"

"He — he said I wasn't fit to die," Mann stammered, then added hastily: "He let me go so I could warn you all."

"So you told him about us! You talked!" Sin Wang took a menacing step toward Mann.

"No! No!" Mann shrieked.

"A coyote yaps because he is afraid," Quong said softly. "Why did the Wolf send us a warning if you did not talk?"

The trapped man's face was ghastly white. His eyes were glassy as he glanced about wildly. He moved with jerky steps toward Quong and thrust out his arms appealingly. "I didn't blab. I never mentioned you. He was goin' to kill me, but I never told the Wolf your name."

"But you spoke of Hop Sing and Sam Brown," Quong interrupted.

"No, no, I — I —"

"Why are you afraid, if your tongue did not deceive you?"

"Don't you see I came here to warn you so you could trap the Wolf?" Mann shrilled.

"The Wolf is like a lion, yet the lion falls into the trap of pointed sticks." Quong's heavy eyelids lifted and revealed two pools of black fire that glittered like the eyes of an angry snake.

Mann shivered and tried desperately to speak, to think of some excuse which would save him, but his brain seemed to be paralyzed, and he could only stare like a hypnotized bird into those evil, deadly eyes.

"Thy ancestors await thee. A man may not talk from the sky."

Quong's voice was like the pur of a cat. Suddenly his gorgeous robe became a blur of color; a clawlike hand flashed into view. A streak of silver light crossed the room, and Tom Mann clutched at his throat with both hands. He uttered one horrible sound like the cry of a mute, swayed for a moment, then, as he started to topple to the floor, Sin Wang caught him in powerful arms, lifted him easily and carried him out a rear door.

Black Steve laughed throatily. "Quong, you're sure fast with a knife," he commented.

"A knife may travel faster than a bullet," Quong said quietly. But his words were both a statement and a challenge.

For a second, Black Steve hesitated. Like all killers and gunmen, he prided himself on his speed with guns. He knew that he had but to deny Quong's statement, and the question would be settled there and then, for he was certain that Quong had other knives concealed about his flashing robe. For one brief instant, his eyes met those of the aged Chinaman, then his ugly face split in a grimace, and he shrugged. "Yeah, I reckon you are faster," he mumbled.

The rear door opened, and Sin Wang entered. He padded across the floor and laid a knife on the desk before Quong Lee. Its blade had been cleaned, and it reflected the light from the lamp.

"The Wolf?" Sin Wang questioned.

"While the earth is covered with darkness, Black Steve must ride and warn Hop Sing and Sam Brown." Quong's heavy lids almost covered his eyes. His face was expressionless, like that of a man asleep. His voice was a singsong whisper. "Words are the color of blood; a whisper can bring on a war. Quong Lee values the skin of the Wolf beyond price."

"Quong need say no more. A clever man understands a nod," chanted Sin Wang.

The two, Black Steve and Sin Wang, stood there for several minutes and waited. Then, when Quong did not speak, they understood that he wished to be alone, and softly slipped away, leaving him sitting there like some withered, evil idol.

When the door had closed behind them, Black Steve drew a deep breath of relief and swore feelingly. "He ain't human! He gives me the shivers. Reckon now that

Quong is after him, it means the end of the trail for the Wolf."

"The Wolf is brave, but Quong is wise," replied Sin Wang softly.

CHAPTER TWO

First Blood

On the following morning, Jim Allen turned his gray horse into the faintly defined trail that led from Dead Hills to Dry Creek. Twice the gray shied at the bleached bones of a long-dead steer.

"Shucks! You ain't very old, and this is your first trip out of the valley where you was born," Allen chided him, "but that ain't no excuse for you to go cuttin' up like a yearlin'."

This horse was the son of Princess, Allen's favorite mare. He was three years old and looked much like the rest of the grays raised in that hidden valley close to the center of the Painted Desert. He was gaunt, with a small head and vicious-looking, bloodshot eyes. For months Allen had trained him to stand under rifle fire, to come at a whistle, and to do all the other tricks which Princess had performed for years. Since Honey Boy had been returned to Jim's brother, Jack Allen, the colt Apple Pie, so-called because of his fondness for that delicacy, had become Jim's favorite.

"Look a here, Apple Pie, you behave yourself, 'cause if I ain't mistaken, you're sure goin' to need all your wind to hit the breeze pronto. That there town, Dry

Creek, is the home of a homicidal gent called Black Steve, who's sheriff of this county because there ain't another gent what has the nerve to be sheriff. 'Cause why? 'Cause this here county, layin' so close to El Crucifixo, is plumb full of bad hombres."

Apple Pie pricked up his ears as though he listened, then swung his head and nipped at one of Allen's feet. The little outlaw's freckled face split in a broad grin.

"You askin' why we's headin' for Dry Creek if it's so darn full of bad gents? Then, I'll elucidate. We got to get some chuck, and there ain't another town between here and El Crucifixo. Besides which, these tracks of Hop Sing and Sam Brown is sure headin' for Dry Creek, and we got to follow them coyotes plumb to blazes to stamp on their heads. Why? So's they won't be gettin' other kids to usin' dope and turning them from decent kids into raging devils."

After Allen had left Tom Mann in Sky Blue Canyon, he had returned to the scene of the murder and picked up the trail of Hop Sing and Sam Brown, and had followed it through the Dead Hills to his present position.

When he turned the gray down the single street of Dry Creek, he was as alert as a wild animal traveling in a strange country. Though he appeared to be careless and at ease, he was still following the tracks of Hop Sing and Sam Brown. Several times he leaned forward and stroked Apple Pie's neck — an excuse to scan the road before him carefully.

He pulled up before a restaurant and glanced at the sign which read:

SIN WANG
GOOD EATS

For a second, he hesitated. For him to remain in town any longer than necessary was sheer folly. He had intended to buy supplies at the grocery and cook himself a meal in the security of the hills. But two things now decided him to have his meal at this restaurant. First, he had not had a decent meal in more than two weeks. The second and more important reason was that the men he had been following had apparently stopped there.

This was a Chinese restaurant, and one of the men he was pursuing was Chinese. That made the risk worth while. It was possible that this Sin Wang was also a member of the dope-running gang.

Allen gave a quick glance up and down the street, then slid from his gray. Giving a sharp order to Apple Pie, he pushed open the door and stepped inside.

The only occupant of the room was a tall, lean man seated at the counter, noisily engaged in eating a bowl of stew. The man turned and looked sharply at Allen, who glimpsed a thin face, covered with a week's stubble of beard. Then the man attacked his stew again, while Allen searched his memory and tried to place him. He knew that he himself had been recognized — the man's nervous manner was proof of that — but try as he might, he could not recall ever having seen the fellow before.

He could hear singsong voices somewhere in the rear. But minutes passed, and no one appeared to take his order. He grew impatient. Each minute he lingered in Dry Creek increased his danger. Then he noted a bell on the counter and rang it sharply.

The thin man leaped to his feet. "Them chinks is asleep, stranger," he mumbled. "I've finished my chow and got to pay 'em, so I'll call 'em for you."

With that, he dashed precipitately around the end of the counter and vanished through a door at the rear. Instantly Allen was alert. The man's manner had not deceived him. He was not the type who would go out of his way to do a stranger a favor. He must have a reason for running to the kitchen, and Allen could guess what this reason was.

His instinct warned him that he had better leave at once, but he disregarded the warning, for he felt that he was close to an important clew in his search for the dope runners.

He tiptoed to the rear partition and placed his ear against it. He could hear a gruff voice which he guessed was that of the thin man, and the soft voices of two Chinamen. He could not distinguish the words so he moved along the partition to the door, but, as he reached it, the voices ceased. A moment later he heard a rear door slam, then there came the sound of hoofbeats which quickly died away.

Hastily he retreated to the front and waited. Every sense was alert. He knew that the man with the thin, stubbled face had gone for help; still he waited. Unconsciously, his hands dropped to his holsters and loosened his guns.

Suddenly his expression changed. The tense look left his face, and his lips split into a broad grin. His eyes became greedy as they rested on a china bowl filled with lumps of brown sugar. He stepped forward eagerly, reached out a hand and thrust a bit of sugar into his mouth. For the moment, he was off his guard, for sugar and all sweet things were an obsession with him. For years Jim Allen had ridden the long trail, outside the law. He had been denied all those things which go to make up the normal man's life, and it was almost as if his passion for sweets had grown until his desire for them unconsciously represented the things of life he had missed.

He was still cramming his mouth with the sticky mess when a Chinaman glided through the door at the rear and moved toward him behind the counter. The man was old. His hairless head and his face were like yellow, wrinkled parchment. His manner was bland and courteous, and he seemed harmless and ingratiating.

Allen grinned at him and licked the corners of his mouth. Then, in a flash, he was once more alive to his danger. He must not betray that his ears were strained to catch the first sound of movement, either on the street outside, or in the rear of the room. Even as he watched the old Chinaman, he had one eye on Apple Pie, through the window. He knew the horse would warn him of men outside.

"Hello! You Sin Wang?" he greeted.

"No, me Quong Lee."

"All right, I'm plumb starved. S'pose you rustle me a steak and pie." Then Allen added carelessly, his eyes glued on the masklike face before him: “You know a chink what rode in this morning?”

Quong Lee’s impassive face did not change expression, but Allen caught a shift in the old man’s eyes. They sparkled venomously as a snake’s beneath their heavy lids.

“Me no know. Why you ask?”

Allen’s face was as guileless as an infant’s, and he might easily have fooled Quong, had the latter not known who he was.

“Nothin’, only I was following his trail this morning an’ picked up a pocketbook full of stuff with funny marks on it which I figure is chink writin’,” he said.

Again Allen caught that venomous glitter in the Chinaman’s eyes, and in his own a little yellow spark grew to a flame.

“Give it to me,” Quong demanded sharply, as he thrust a clawlike hand across the counter. His other hand remained concealed beneath his wide-sleeved gown, and Allen knew that it contained a weapon of some sort. His whole air had changed; it was now menacing, threatening.

Allen had invented the story of finding the pocketbook, but he grinned and shook his head.

“Not any, ’cause you just tole me you didn’t know the chink.”

For a moment, Quong Lee’s face ceased to be a mask and became the incarnation of evil. His drooping lids lifted and revealed his black eyes that glittered like those of an angry cobra. For one second — for ten —

the two men's eyes clashed. An infuriated cobra, ready to strike, coiled facing a yellow-eyed desert wolf.

But suddenly the cobra vanished and gave way to a bland Chinaman. He slid along the counter to the rear door and, as he opened it, turned and murmured: "All lighty, you wait little time, Quong bring big steak and pie."

"He was gettin' ready to go on the prod, but he decided to draw in his horns," Allen said to himself, as he stood there, listening. "Sort o' looks like he figured it would be better to wait until other gents blew in. Wonder how come he got heated so sudden like? Reckon he must be one of these here coyotes what is runnin' in dope."

The murmur of voices reached him. Two Chinamen seemed to be having a heated argument. When the voices died away, Allen slipped through the front door and glanced up and down the street. But he saw no one, save two or three Mexicans lounging in the strip of shade before the grocery store.

For a moment, the little outlaw stood there in doubt. The store reminded him that he was badly in need of provisions, but to wait to get them would be folly. Then he grinned broadly and ran back into the restaurant. He reappeared a moment later with the sugar bowl, which he stuffed into one of his saddle pockets. As he placed his hand on Apple Pie's bridle, the horse pricked up his ears and pointed his nose toward the corner of the building. Allen knew then that some one was skulking there.

He listened for a second. Then, with a little run, he leaped around the corner. He landed on his feet, catwise, some ten feet on the other side. As his feet touched the ground, his hands flashed to his guns, and they belched fire and smoke. There came the answering bellow of a double-barreled shot-gun, and a heavy charge of buckshot tore into the wall of the restaurant.

Through the smoke Allen saw a huge Chinaman pitch forward on his face. The smoke still curled from his own guns, as he leaped to the back of Apple Pie and spurred the gray on a headlong run down the empty street and out of town. He kept up the pace until he was sure he was not pursued. Then he pulled Apple Pie to a walk. One glance at the trail convinced him that the men he had been following were still ahead of him. But the signs of a galloping horse made him pause.

"Wonder if the gent what was on that there horse was the one eatin' stew, and if so, for why the darned hurry?" he asked himself, halting.

The trail which led to El Crucifixo was broad and well marked. For years it had been the main underground route leading to the border and the outlaw town. Allen brought Apple Pie to a stand on the crest of a swell from which he could easily see the trail as it wound its way down the slope between great mounds of loose rock and patches of brown mesquite.

The little rider squinted his eyes and focused them, Indian fashion, on the spot where the trail started to climb the farther slope. Soon he nodded, for he had picked out a faint dust haze and then another one a couple of miles ahead. He knew that those dust clouds were made by horsemen, for the country clear to the border was a barren waste, a desert, and lacked the necessary fodder for even the tough, wiry, longhorn steer.

Like all men who live alone in the waste spaces, Jim Allen had the habit of expressing his thoughts aloud and addressing his horse. Now, after a moment's thought, he leaned forward in his saddle and tweeked Apple Pie's ear as if he would attract the horse's attention.

"There ain't no doubt that that first dust cloud is made by the two gents what I've been trailin'. They're headin' for El Crucifixo, sure, 'cause there ain't no other place for 'em to go." He grinned broadly and slapped the gray's neck. "Here, open your ears, you fool kid hoss, an' you'll learn somethin'. Now, I figures the other dust cloud is made by the skinny gent who must be part hog, from the way he drinks his stew. He's hittin' the breeze to catch them other gents. Now I'm askin' you what the others will aim to do when he catches them?"

He paused and leaned forward as if waiting for the gray to answer. Then, when Apple Pie shook his head, Allen grinned and nodded.

"Sure, you're plumb correct. Them gents will be waitin' for us, hid behind some rocks or brush. Supposin' we fool 'em and light out for El Crucifixo by the Goat Trail. All right, then, get goin'."

The gray swung away from the main trail and took a fork to the right that followed the crest of the watershed. As he topped a swell, Allen looked back and saw the town of Dry Creek glimmering in the heat. The distance was too great for him to distinguish anything clearly, but he could see people, like small lead soldiers, moving about here and there in the streets. He lingered there, watching for signs of pursuit, longer than he would have, had he known that a pair of heavily lidded eyes were scanning that particular part of the trail through powerful binoculars. Also, he was unaware that, the moment he disappeared over the swell, two smoke signals arose from the roof of the restaurant.

CHAPTER THREE

Premonitions

About three miles from where the Goat Trail branched from the main road to El Crucifixo, it dipped sharply from the watershed and followed Sheer Rock Canyon. At times it wound around the rim of the canyon; at others it dropped and followed sheer walled ledges which were so narrow that Allen could peer down the dizzy abyss to the floor of the canyon a quarter of a mile below, while his stirrup scraped the perpendicular wall. Few men, even hard-pressed outlaws, would choose this trail deliberately, and fewer still would straddle a horse while following it. It was equally dangerous to man and beast, for time and weather had chipped the edges of the cliffs and covered them with loose shale which had fallen from the inner wall.

Yet Allen turned Apple Pie along the treacherous path with a carelessness born of complete confidence in the sure-footedness of his gray. From the time Apple Pie had been weaned as a colt, he had been trained with the wise old Princess and the other grays to travel the roughest trails in the Painted Desert, so that by the time he was strong enough to bear a saddle, he was as agile as a mountain goat.

"Hey, yuh darn idjut, stop that! Now don't be tellin' me you're scared of fallin', 'cause you've took trails worse than this at a dead run."

Allen spoke sharply. Twice Apple Pie had attempted to turn on some wide part of the trail, and the gray showed increasing reluctance to proceed. He would stop, prick his ears, and go forward again only at Allen's sharp command.

"You darned fool!" Allen cried with a grin. "You're actin' as skittish as a high-school gal."

Apple Pie snorted and balked for several seconds, refusing to advance until urged by Allen's knee and a resounding smack on his rump. He was as nervous as a green colt. No one knew better than Allen the danger of having a panicky horse on that trail, so although his voice was at times sharp and angry, and at others pleading, not once did he betray the slightest sign of nervousness.

"Huh," he scolded, "you tryin' to tell me it would be plumb disastrous to be bushwhacked along this trail? Well, I'm agreein' with you. Only there ain't no danger 'cause nobody savvies we took it."

The gray went forward for another half hour, then again stopped and snorted. Allen kneed him forward until the trail widened, then swung to the ground.

"So it was them tracks what was bitin' you," he grumbled. He stooped and examined carefully the marks in the sand. "Well, you don't have to worry about them gents, 'cause they're real desert rats. I can tell from the way they plants their feet. That funny feelin' you had that some gents was layin' for us is plumb crazy." He grinned at the gray and tweaked his ear. "I'm curious as to why they come this way, but just the same, Apple Pie, you is mistook. No desert rat is goin' to corral us." Then he sniffed. "Huh! So that's what you smell — coffee and bacon! I reckon them gents has camped a little bit ahead."

He rubbed his dust-begrimed eyelids and peered down the trail. A doubtful scowl settled on his sunburned, freckled face as he considered the advisability of pushing on and joining the prospectors. He would certainly be able to procure a meal, and they might even be willing to sell him some coffee, bacon, and sugar. He was woefully hungry, for he had had nothing but some weak coffee and cold flapjacks since the previous day.

But his instinct warned him that it would be wiser to trail them and wait until he reached El Crucifixo before he satisfied his hunger. All men spelled danger to Allen. Loneliness, eternal vigilance, distrust of every one, dexterity with his guns and the speed of his grays — these were the price of liberty. He was fair game to every officer of the law, and he always risked sudden death from the guns of some outlaw looking for the reward or the notoriety of killing the Wolf. Dead or alive, he was worth twelve thousand dollars to the man who could drop him from the back of his gray. It was a fortune to tempt the greed of most men, and there had been friends in the past who had been unable to resist the temptation to try to collect it. Hence Allen instinctively avoided all travelers when he was on the trail.

But he was hungry, and his stomach clamored for food. The odors of coffee and frying bacon were highly tantalizing. As a rule, all true desert rats were his friends. The desert plays strange tricks with men. It accentuates the good or bad that lies deep in their hearts. The silence, the vast distance, the lonely nights, are hard on a man's conscience, and only those men who are simple-hearted and fear God may abide for long in the silent wastes. Allen knew that if the men ahead of him were true prospectors he was safe; for although they dared death in their search for gold, it was not the gold itself that urged them on, but a desire to find the end of the rainbow. The reward offered for him would not tempt them, for they lacked the lust for money that grows in the heart of the city man. Under ordinary circumstances, he would not have hesitated to approach their camp, but conditions were unusual. Why, he speculated, had these men taken this particularly dangerous trail? What was their business in Skeleton County? And why were they approaching El Crucifixo from the rear door? At length his misgivings were overcome by his hunger, and he swung about to face Apple Pie.

"All right, you old pie eater. If you insist, we'll join these gents."

He flipped his rifle from the boot beneath the saddle, glanced at the breach, wiped the dust from it, and, carrying it in the crook of his left arm, walked down the trail. When he was fifty yards ahead of the horse, he stopped and whistled softly. Apple Pie, who had been watching him anxiously, immediately started to follow, but he made no effort to close up the distance which lay between him and his beloved master. Allen had taught him to follow, by night or day, at just that distance, and the trick was well worth the time and patience it had taken to teach it. Now it enabled Allen to approach the prospectors silently, without the chance ring of a steel-shod hoof to betray him.

About five hundred yards farther on, he peered around a sharp curve in the trail and saw the two prospectors a little ahead of him. They had unsaddled and made camp in a wide box canyon which was cut in the inner wall. The men were clad in dirty, tattered old garments. One of them had a long white beard and ponderously heavy body, while the other was tall and lank.

"Darn me if that old gent with the whiskers who is doin' the cookin' ain't 'Pop' Casey," Allen murmured, with a delighted grin. "And there's Mary Anne, his old mule. But tother gent I ain't never seen before."

Old Pop Casey was kneeling, frying pan in hand, with his back to Allen, while the lanky man, whom Jim was shortly to know as "Skinny" Hinks, was busy with the packs at the other side of the fire. Allen approached quietly and was within fifteen feet of the two before Hinks spotted him. The prospector's first reaction was one of alarm, and he jerked himself upright while casting anxious glances around in search of his gun. Then when he remarked Allen's freckled face and broad, friendly grin, his fear gave way to annoyance.

"You dang fool, don't you know better than to sneak up like that? You might hev got hurt."

Pop Casey looked up at Skinny and demanded: “Who you callin’ a fool, you danged old catawampus?”

Jim Allen grinned, then threw back his head and loosed the fierce yet plaintive cry of the lone desert wolf. The old prospectors jumped as if a bomb had suddenly gone off at their feet. Skinny, scrambling backward, grabbed up an ax and stood glaring about as if expecting to see a real wolf. Pop Casey tipped over sideways and dropped the contents of the frying pan into the fire as he clawed ineffectually at the weapon he wore on his hip.

Then his bleary old eyes fixed on Allen. He blinked without recognition for a moment, then his mouth gaped open as if he were staring at some strange apparition. Finally his eyes gleamed, and his rusty old joints creaked as he hastily arose to face the little outlaw. “Gosh all hemlock, if it ain’t you! Hello, Jim! You remember me?” he croaked.

“Sure do, and I knows that old mule of yours, too,” Allen answered, as he thrust out his hand.

The old prospector seized it in his gnarled and calloused one, and his tanned and wrinkled face lighted up with pleasure. He grinned with delight as he glanced over his shoulder at his partner.

“That old sour belly is Skinny Hinks, but you ain’t got to pay no attention to him ’cause he’s just naturally disagreeable like a rattler.”

“What you mean makin’ a gent spill good victuals by playin’ the kid and howlin’ like a wolf?” Skinny growled wrathfully.

"Shucks, I'm sorry, mister, but I was only callin' my horse," Allen replied innocently.

"Callin' your horse!" Skinny cried.

There came the sound of hoofs clanking against rock, and Apple Pie flashed around the bend, charged toward the group and came to a sliding halt beside Allen. Skinny shook his head. Words failed him. He was angry and astounded that any man should call his horse in that manner.

"He's got a permanent grouch, so don't mind him at all," Pop chuckled. "Jim, I'm right glad to see you."

"That goes for me, too," Allen replied. "What you two old-timers doin' down in this God-forsaken country?"

"Why, we —" Pop glanced at his partner and broke off, adding feebly: "Nothin' at all."

Allen noticed Pop's confusion and decided to ignore it. "You figure you could feed me?" he asked.

"You bet. And we'll make a feast of her." Pop invited enthusiastically.

"I'm hollow as a balloon," said Allen ruefully. "I'll fix that billy goat of mine, then."

They watched Allen water the gray and lead him to the entrance of the box canyon, where he staked him out.

Pop chuckled. "What do you think of the White Wolf?" he asked Skinny.

Skinny turned and squinted at Allen. "You always was a liar, and now you tryin' to tell me that kid there is the Killer Wolf?"

"I never said he was the Killer Wolf," Pop cut in quickly and heatedly. "What I said is he's the White Wolf. The gents in El Crucifixo calls him the 'Killer Wolf,' but not gents like us. You savvy how a gent says the wolf's at the door, meanin' he's plumb out of luck, and how the Navajos twist it other side first and says the white wolf is with 'em, meanin' their troubles is over? Well, there's many an old desert rat like us and many a starved old woman what was out of luck and due to cash, when the White Wolf shows up and fixes things. So don't you go callin' Jim-twin Allen no killer wolf, or I'll bust you open proper."

Skinny glanced suspiciously at Pop. "You ain't funnin'? You sure it's him?"

"Yep, I knows him well. And didn't he howl like a wolf?"

This seemed to erase Skinny's last doubt, for he glanced hastily at Allen, who was returning and was within a few feet of camp, then whispered huskily to Pop:

"Let's make this a real bang-up feed!"

CHAPTER FOUR

In Wolf's Clothes

At half past nine on Tuesday, four days before Jim Allen turned his gray along Goat Trail, a man descended from the smoker of a train when it halted at Santa Fe. He was a small, undersized man of about twenty-eight. His hat, with an extra-high crown, was the finest grade Stetson; his boots, custom made of patent leather, had abnormally high heels; his shirt was of silk and knotted with a loose black tie, and silk-faced lapels adorned the long-tailed frock coat of his black suit.

He stood for a moment pulling at his dark beard and gazing about the station. Then he entered the depot and checked his bag. In a few moments, he secured an ancient horse cab and was driven to the Sad Night, a small Mexican café not far from the Plaza.

He pushed open the door and entered the bar of the café. He had been told that if he were not met at the station, he was to wait at the Sad Night until a messenger came for him. His curiously shaped eyes swept over the crowd of Mexican and American laborers that thronged the place. After a brief glance he decided that his man had not yet turned up, and he began to speculate as to why there was need for such great secrecy in this meeting with one of the heads of the department of justice.

He had been there for nearly half an hour when a big, burly looking ruffian entered and forced his way to a place at the bar by the little man's side. Realizing that the big man was drunk, the stranger ignored his shoving.

"Greasers and runts get out of my way, for I can lick my weight in wild cats," the big man shouted belligerently. "I'm pure wolf, and this is my night to howl."

Several of the more timid ones near him edged away, and the man took advantage of the confusion to turn toward the little stranger.

"If your name is Allen, follow me when I go out of here," he whispered. Then, raising his voice to blustering tones, he ordered drinks for the house.

When they had been served, he tossed some coins on the bar, turned and staggered out. The little man waited a few minutes, then he, too, made his way outside. A voice called softly to him from the darkness.

"This way. Follow me."

The diminutive man whose name was Allen, allowed his guide to proceed some thirty feet before he followed. Keeping at that distance apart, the two wandered up and down narrow lanes, circled the plaza, then turned up a tree-bordered street which led behind the government buildings. Here the guide went down a narrow passage and entered a small door.

When the little man had joined him, the guide introduced himself as Tim O'Brien, and as they shook hands, he added: "I'm sure glad to meet you. I've heard a lot about you. The chief will explain the reason for all the secrecy."

Entering a room at the far end of a large hall, Allen saw a thin, stoop-shouldered man with snowy hair, seated at a desk beneath a brilliant lamp. Allen knew the man by reputation. He ranked high in the United States secret service and was known as a shrewd and fearless operator.

"Chief, this is Mr. Allen," O'Brien introduced; then, turning to Allen: "This is Chief Weatherspoon."

Allen bowed and waited expectantly.

Chief Weatherspoon regarded him silently. His first impression was one of acute disappointment, but as his blue eyes met Allen's, his hasty opinion changed. He was a keen judge of character and knew better than to condemn a man because of the peculiarity of his clothes.

"You're Jack Allen." It was a statement rather than a question.

"Jack-twin Allen," the little man corrected.

The chief nodded approvingly. He understood that by adding the "twin," Allen meant to make clear to the world that he was not ashamed of the fact that he was the twin brother of Jim-twin Allen, the most notorious outlaw of all times.

"I have heard of you. We will dispense with compliments. It is sufficient to say that had what I heard been unfavorable, you would not be here now." The chief spoke briskly. "Now, to business. You, in your capacity as marshal and sheriff, are aware of the horrors connected with the dope traffic. You have seen the evil it causes and realize that the men who are engaged in this thing are lower than beasts."

Jack Allen nodded again and waited. He was a man of few words, but his manner of flipping open his coat and displaying his guns was more eloquent than language.

"For some time," the chief continued, "we have been aware that a large and powerful dope ring was operating in this neighborhood. We have managed to trace them to El Crucifixo — you've heard of that outlaw town. Their headquarters are down there, but we have not been able to find it or the men who are at the head of the organization. I sent for you to ask you to go down there and try to locate it for us. In one way you are particularly well fitted for the task. I'll explain that later. We have already sent four men down. Three simply vanished off the face of the earth without a word. The fourth, Jack Cutbill, got word to us that he was sure he was suspected and asked us to send some one to him immediately. As we could not wait for your arrival, we sent an operator, Dick Martin. Cutbill says that he is positive that there is a leak right here in this office, and I am inclined to agree with him, for that would account for the disappearance of our men the moment they arrived at El Crucifixo. That is the reason for the secrecy with which I am meeting you. No one knows that you are here but O'Brien and myself, and that is a combination which can be trusted."

O'Brien stood to Allen's left, a little to the rear of him, and as he listened to the chief's explanation, Allen watched the big man in a looking-glass which hung behind the desk. He noticed a fleeting smile flash over O'Brien's face, as the chief made his final remark. There was something crafty about that smile — something contemptuous and slightly triumphant. The chief resumed his explanation, and though Allen did not miss a word, he was surreptitiously watching O'Brien and speculating as to the meaning of that smile.

"It is needless to warn you of the dangers you will meet with in El Crucifixo," Weatherspoon went on. "They have no law there, and the moment you appear, every one will turn on you like a pack of wolves. If you consent to go, I have thought of one disguise in which you will be reasonably safe, and I hope you'll be able to help us rout out this gang and unearth the traitor in my office."

Again Allen caught that fleeting smile on O'Brien's face. He perked his head and looked squarely at the big man who was momentarily off his guard. Almost instantly the man's face hardened, and he smiled straight at Allen. Allen's face was impassive as he again turned to the chief.

"And this disguise?" he queried.

The chief hesitated. He was obviously embarrassed, and when he spoke, his words lacked their usual crispness. "You'll excuse me, but I've heard the story of how, when you were laid up with a broken leg, your brother grew a beard and took your place until you recovered."

Allen grinned cheerfully. "He made a good job of it, too."

"Well, I was wondering, as he once impersonated you, if you would be willing to shave your beard and go down there and impersonate him. As Jim Allen, the outlaw, you would be safe."

Jack realized that the chief's plan was a sound one. The mention of his brother's name caused a cloud to pass over his eyes, but the smile did not leave his lips. "Without my beard you can't tell us apart," he said. "That's why I wear it."

"And" — the chief cleared his throat nervously — "your brother being what he is, there will be no danger of the impersonation being discovered by your lack of knowledge as to his past adventures. Well — will you do it?"

"On two conditions."

"Name them. If it's a question of money, I'll pay any price you ask."

Allen shook his head. "It's not money. I'll take the pay of your regular operators. My first condition is this: If I play the part of my brother, he is to get the credit in your report."

The chief was surprised. He glanced at O'Brien and shrugged his shoulders.

"I fail to see what good that would do the Wolf. It would take a lot more than that to wash him clean," interjected O'Brien.

He spoke with a laugh, but there was something about his words that made Allen swing about to face him. They held a covert sneer. As he glimpsed Allen's face, O'Brien involuntarily recoiled. It was a mask of diabolical fury.

"Excuse me," O'Brien muttered. "I didn't mean anything."

"Don't be forgettin' — ever — that Jim is my twin brother," said Allen coldly. He had intended to tell the chief the reason why Jim had started to ride the long trail, but now he decided to wait until he was alone with him.

"I'll grant that condition," said the chief hastily.

"All right, we'll let the second go for the moment. What if Jim is down there?"

"We have word that Jim left two weeks ago to return to the Painted Desert," Weatherspoon replied. "I have the necessary clothes for you in the next room, and your gray horse is in a stable near by."

"Then that's settled. I'll start to-night. Glad to hear that Honey Boy arrived safely."

The chief took two photographs from his desk and handed them to Allen. "The first is a picture of Jack Cutbill, and the other is Dick Martin. Study them carefully so that you will be able to recognize them when you arrive."

Allen glanced at the photographs and handed them back. He had an excellent memory for faces. "If you'll get my horse, I'll be shavin' and changin' my togs," he said abruptly.

The chief smiled and decided that although Allen might be small and insignificant looking, he did not lack decisiveness.

"I'll get the gray at once," O'Brien said cheerfully.

But Allen held up his hand. “Wait,” he commanded. “I want you to tell me something about the trails down there. Chief, suppose you get Honey Boy. It’ll save time.”

The chief was startled. He recalled the wordless clash between Allen and O’Brien, and was disturbed at the request, for he sensed something antagonistic between the two. O’Brien was frankly surprised, but Allen gave neither of them time to object.

“Where are my things?” he queried briskly. “You have a razor, of course.”

The chief threw open the door leading to an inner room and pointed to a heap of clothes lying on the bed. He showed Allen where he could find a razor and some stain for his face as well, then reëntered the larger room.

“He’s dangerous. Be careful not to get his claw up,” he warned O’Brien hastily.

The big man shrugged. “I won’t mention that killer brother of his again.”

When the chief had left him alone, Allen turned his attention to the clothes on the bed. He inspected the faded and tattered shirt and jeans with every evidence of disgust. But he knew that these were the kind of clothes habitually worn by Jim, so he would have to don them. He pulled off his shiny boots and threw off his coat, and began to clip his beard with a pair of scissors. Once he tiptoed to the door and peered through a crack. O’Brien was sitting at Weatherspoon’s desk, intently scanning some papers. But, after all, Allen reflected, that might be part of his business.

Ten minutes later, minus his beard, Allen grinned at his reflection in the mirror. He had applied the stain to the part of his face which the beard had covered, and the change in his appearance amused him. Then he slipped quickly out of his clothes and donned those on the bed. He pulled on the moccasins, placed the battered, felt hat on his head and carefully adjusted his cross belts, tying the holsters to his thighs. Then he quietly opened the door and stepped noiselessly into the other room.

O'Brien was seated at the desk writing, and so absorbed was he in his task that he failed to hear Allen until the latter was within a few feet of him. When he did look up, he stared in amazement, and the color drained from his face. He sprang to his feet, thrusting the paper he still held in his hand into his pocket.

"Gosh, you sure scared me! I thought you was the Wolf. You look as like as two peas." He forced a laugh.

Jack regarded him silently. Then he demanded bluntly: "What you scared of the Wolf for?"

"Why — I — you — I'm not scared of him," the burly man stammered. "I never saw him. You just sort of surprised me."

"If you never saw him, why did I scare you?"

O'Brien let the question pass unanswered. With a desperate effort he summoned a sickly smile to his face. He fumbled in his pocket, brought forth and lighted a cigarette and blew a cloud of smoke through his nostrils. Allen watched him, puzzled by his actions. He had noticed the spasm of fear that had flashed across the man's face at sight of him in his disguise — a fear so great that it had temporarily paralyzed the man's mind — and he wondered what had caused that fear. And what had been behind that fleeting, satirical smile he had caught reflected in the mirror? The little gunman was sure that O'Brien had had some contact with Jim — a contact that made him fear the outlaw as cowards fear death. He was convinced, too, that O'Brien was the traitor in the chief's office, but he had not an atom of proof. There was nothing that he could lay before Weatherspoon, and although he might draw and force the operator to submit to a search, he did not believe that O'Brien would be careless or stupid enough to carry any manner of incriminating evidence on his person.

Yet, if O'Brien were the traitor, how was he, Jack Allen, to get to El Crucifixo without the knowledge of his coming reaching the gang? A plan leaped suddenly into his mind, a plan which he thought might succeed. He put it into operation, when the chief returned, by announcing that he had changed his mind and would not start out that evening. Though Weatherspoon was surprised, he offered no objection, for Allen was a free agent and did not come under his jurisdiction.

A few moments later, Allen requested to speak to the chief privately, and when O'Brien had left the room, he informed the other of his suspicions. As he had anticipated, Weatherspoon scoffed at them.

"I've tested O'Brien over and over again, and I'd stake my life on his integrity," he said, but there was no reproof in his tone, for he did not take Allen's accusations seriously.

"O'Brien knew about the first three men you sent down there, didn't he?" asked Allen. "But did he know about Cutbill and Martin before he heard you mention them to-night?"

The chief frowned, and his face was thoughtful as he shook his head.

"I'm not askin' you to believe me," said the little sheriff. "I don't expect you to. But I've hunted men, and been hunted by them, and I reckon I've developed a sixth sense like animals have. It's saved my life many a time in the past, and I'm trustin' in it now. Now I ain't askin' you to lock up O'Brien, 'cause I may be mistaken. But my life is at stake, and I got the right to ask you to help me fool him. I want you to tell him that I showed my hand, that all the talk I made about not wantin' money was only a bluff, that I asked so much you couldn't pay it, and that I'm goin' back North. Tell him you figure I'm just yellow and scared to go down there, and make him think you're mad. Now I'm askin' you to make a good job of it, because it's my life that's being risked."

The chief agreed, and when, a little later, O'Brien was called in, Allen could find no fault with the way Weatherspoon played his part. The chief acted both angry and disgusted, but offered no explanation, and it was not until Allen had again donned his own clothes and swaggered from the room without even saying good-by, that Weatherspoon explained the situation to his operator.

O'Brien listened in silence while the chief succinctly told him his opinion of Jack-twin Allen. Not until the chief had finished, did he speak.

"Huh!" he sneered. "I knew the minute I laid eyes on him that he was a four-flush, just like that killer twin of his."

CHAPTER FIVE

Ambushed

"How come you took this trail, Jim?" Pop Casey inquired.

"Oh, I figured some gents was too anxious to see me on the other one," Jim replied, rolling a cigarette.

"You savvy who they is?" asked Pop. " 'Tain't none of my business, but —"

"Sure, I been foolin' with 'em for a couple of days," Allen replied. He was silent for a moment, staring into the fire, then he looked up and asked: "You ever see a gent what takes dope?"

"Yeah, I did," said Skinny. "My brother Ed's kid got to takin' it. He warn't really Ed's kid, but Ed adopted him and his baby sister. The kid was a nice enough feller till he started takin' the stuff, then he changed complete. He went broke one day and didn't have any stuff, so he tried to rob a gent to get the money to buy it with. But he was nervous and killed the gent. He got catched and locked up, and they was gettin' ready to stretch his neck when Ed got back to town. Ed was the sheriff and a two-handed fightin' fool, so plenty of gents hated him and figured they'll get even by stretchin' the kid. Ed made the kid tell him who sold him the dope and went and blew blazes out of the gent. Then he got a couple of hosses, put the kid on one and shot his way out of town, droppin' a couple of gents in the get-away.

"The kid was hit and died, and 'cause Ed was the sheriff and dropped them gents, the governor says he's got to be caught and made an example of. But Ed got clear. That was a long time ago, and Ed's still ridin' the long trail just 'cause some coyote started the kid to takin' dope."

As Skinny finished his narrative, Pop glanced at Allen and read the sympathy in the little outlaw's eyes. Skinny was frankly wiping a tear from his tanned face with the back of a calloused hand.

"You know a gent what goes by the handle of 'Kid Bell'?" he asked Allen.

"Sure, I know him." Allen was about to add that he had never known anything good about the old outlaw, but a sudden idea struck him, and he was glad he held his tongue. He glanced from Pop to Skinny, then stared into the fire.

"This Kid Bell's your brother Ed?" Allen asked Skinny, after a pause.

The old prospector nodded. "He's sort o' gone bad since he hit the long trail," he said miserably.

"He's all right. He's a friend of mine," Allen lied glibly, and was glad of the lie when he saw how Skinny brightened. "I knows Mary Bell, too."

"She's the reason we're headin' into El Crucifixo by the back door."

"Yeah?" Allen exclaimed in surprise. "How come?"

"Mary Bell heard Kid was plumb sick, an' afore I could stop her, she lights out for El Crucifixo to nurse him. About two weeks ago, we gets a letter from Kid Bell, askin' us to come down and fetch her, 'cause it ain't safe for him to try an' bring her back. He also warns us he's afraid some gent will try and drop him an' run off with Mary Bell."

Allen was thoughtful. He had speculated as to why the girl was in Crucifixo. Only a month ago, he had encountered her there just as an outlaw called "Shanghai Pete" had insulted her. At a word from Allen, Pete had slunk away, and Jim-twin had escorted the girl back to Kid Bell's house, though he and the old outlaw were not friends.

"I sort o' passed the word around that I'd take it personal if any gent bothered her," Allen said carelessly.

"Huh, she's a right pretty gal; but if you said that, I reckon that no hombre will get fresh with her." Pop chuckled grimly.

"Maybe so," said Skinny, "but Kid Bell tol' me in this letter that there was a chink that was makin' eyes at her. My brother run him off the place, but he was some worried 'cause the chink is a member of some gang. An' if he's worried, it means that other gents would be scared to death."

"A chink!" said Allen quickly. "What's his name?"

"He's an educated chink; been to college an' wears store clothes. Shucks! What was his name?" Skinny wrinkled his brow and pondered. "Charlie Quing — Quang — Quong, or somethin' like that."

Allen frowned. Quong — where had he heard that name? Of course, that was the name of the old Chinaman in the restaurant in Dry Creek! But that couldn't be the man. Must be another of the same name.

"Gents, I don't mind tellin' you that there's a chink with the gents I been trailin'. You say this Charlie is a member of a gang which is so poisonous that even old Kid Bell acts careful. I wonder if the hombres I'm trailin' is in the same gang. If so, I got to let 'em live till I finds the head of the gang."

Pop, who had been preparing the meal, now looked up curiously and inquired: "What these gents done to make you trail 'em?"

Until that moment Allen's face had been that of a serious, troubled boy, but now it changed for the flash of a second as he answered, "Sellin' dope."

Skinny gasped as he glimpsed that momentary flash of yellow fire in the outlaw's eyes, but it was gone almost immediately.

"Let's eat," said Pop.

They had crisp bacon, beans, tomatoes, coffee, and hot bread — a real meal, and a feast when eaten in the desert. Time after time all three refilled their plates, and Allen, in spite of his size, managed to put away more than the other two.

Shortly after they had finished, Allen was saddled and ready to leave. The old prospectors urged him to wait over the night, but he shook his head.

"Nope, I've got to be in El Crucifixo this evening. I can't wait until to-morrow. Now don't be forgettin' —

about five miles the other side of where Goat Trail hits the one comin' in from the west, you'll see a black rock. Turn off into the mesquite there, and you'll see where I stopped a cut through the brush with some dead stuff. Pull it out, go through and follow the brush and you'll come to a cabin. You two stay there, an' I'll bring the gal out to-morrow. So long."

"So long, Jim!" Pop cried, but Skinny only nodded his farewell.

They stood and watched Allen ride down the box canyon and swing the gray along the trail. Pop grinned as he saw the gray balk, but Skinny shook his head, and his wrinkled face was serious. Twice the horse swung about and refused to enter the trail, but the third time Allen forced him into it, and horse and rider disappeared around the corner.

"Dang me," Skinny grumbled, "I feels funny like the night I was goin' to visit 'Big-foot' Jackson an' finds him full of Apache arrows. You betcha that gray has a feelin' he shouldn't follow that trail."

"Quit bein' a grave digger," Pop grunted. "Nobody's goin' to get Jim. He's too wise."

Pop spoke positively, but even to himself his words lacked conviction. The two men seated themselves on convenient packs, filled their pipes and smoked in gloomy silence. They seemed to be waiting, for every few minutes they craned their necks and listened. A half hour passed, then an hour, but still they sat, almost expectantly. The base of the canyon wall was covered with deep shadows, and in the east the first star had appeared, when suddenly the silence was broken by a far-off double *boom*, followed by louder and sharper crashes.

The old prospectors sprang to their feet, and their faces were drawn and white as they looked at each other. The echoes of those shots resounded back and forth across the hills and slowly died away.

"The first two was from a Colt. Tothers was rifle shots," Skinny muttered softly.

"Do you reckon them gents what was waitin' for Jim circled around and got him?" asked Pop with a break in his voice.

They picked up their rifles, and with strained eyes searching the growing dusk, walked side by side down the trail and turned along it.

Twice after Jim-twin Allen had succeeded in forcing Apple Pie to leave the box canyon, the colt had shied at some imaginary enemy.

"What you think you are, a bashful gazelle?" Allen chuckled.

To all appearances the diminutive outlaw was carefree as he rode along the trail. He lounged in his saddle, smiling to himself, and kept up a running flow of low-toned conversation with the colt. Nevertheless, he was as alert as some wild animal. As he talked, he kept swinging his head from one side to the other, listening almost unconsciously. No bird fluttered in the bush beside the trail, no lizard scuttled across the path that he did not hear. Once he checked his horse, and the two stood like a statue as Allen listened. Then, satisfied, he again urged Apple Pie forward.

The sun, a giant ball of copper fire, hovered for an instant over the knifelike peaks of the Dead Men Mountains, then slid down from sight with a rush. A brilliant, painted banner was flung across the sky; it changed to fantastic shapes and faded. Purple shadows on the canyon floor swallowed up the thread of the river and crept upward, blotting out the sheer walls.

"We got to hustle, or we'll get catched on this ledge in the dark, Apple Pie," warned Allen.

The gray swung around a sharp bend in the trail and again shied. He rose straight up on his hind legs and snorted in terror, as a loose ball of white fluff, part of a cactus bloom, was caught by the light breeze and blown toward him.

Some twenty yards ahead the trail widened out and was bordered by thick clumps of mesquite and cactus, but at the spot where the gray reared it was so narrow that when the horse attempted to swing about, his forefeet clashed against the inner wall. As Apple Pie pawed at this wall in his desperate effort to turn, his hind feet were within a few inches of the edge of the abyss, with its sheer drop of a thousand feet.

Allen still thought that the gray was frightened by a bit of fluff, for the horse had been nervous and skittish all day. Had he realized the truth, he might have followed a different course of action. Twice he swung the gray around, but each time Apple Pie's forefeet had barely touched the ground when he would again rear and attempt to turn. The edge of the cliff crumbled, and one of the colt's hind feet slid downward. Poor

Apple Pie snorted in terror, and with a tremendous effort managed to scramble again to firm ground.

The men who lay hidden watching and waiting for a clear shot at the little outlaw, caught sight of his face and marveled. There was nothing in his expression to betray the fact that he was looking at death — a death that would have driven most men into a gibbering panic. Quietly he leaned forward, talking to the struggling horse.

The colt swung about a bit more, and it was then that Allen's eye caught something in the brush where the trail widened out. His voice came to an abrupt halt, and, guided by reflex action, his hand flashed to his gun. It had boomed twice, even before his conscious sense told him that the glitter he had caught was the barrel of a rifle, and the blurred spot behind it the figure of a man.

In immediate answer to the crash of his Colt there came the whiplike crack of three rifles, speaking simultaneously. Apple Pie leaped into the air, snorted and swung about so that he was headed straight back the trail. Allen threw himself sideways toward the inner wall, as another rifle cracked. For a moment, Apple Pie balanced precariously on the edge of the cliff, then with a heart-rending scream of terror he vanished. There was the clink of metal, as Allen's heavy Colt struck the stony trail. As he fell, his hands clawed for a moment at the rim of the cliff. For a brief minute, his fingers clung to a piece of rock, then that broke away, and the trail was empty.

The echoes of the shots were still booming back and forth from wall to wall of the canyon, when there came floating up the sound of a far-away crash. Then all was still.

There was a moment of complete silence, and the trail remained deserted. Then the head of Black Steve appeared above a clump of brush, and he stepped out onto the trail. He was followed by How See, a tall, stoop-shouldered Chinaman, and two other men. Gingerly the four stepped along the trail to the spot where man and horse had disappeared, and peered over the edge. They could see nothing down there, for night had already crept in to hide all signs of the tragedy. Their faces, with the exception of the impassive one of the Chinaman, were strained and drawn.

Black Steve was the first to recover. He laughed harshly and a little hysterically. "Well, that's done, and I'm dang glad I don't have to do it over again."

"Me, too. If Quong wants any more wolves killed, he can do it hisself," Tom Haggart, a heavy-set, burly man, spoke fervently.

"He's sure a quick-thinkin' cuss. He could have got clear if he hadn't tried to save that gray hoss. I never even seen his hand move when he pulled steel," stated "Little Billy," the fourth member of the crew, with admiration and a touch of awe in his voice.

"Man does not take gold with him into Heaven, neither his skill with guns," chanted How See and pointed into the canyon. "The Wolf is now more harmless than a child, for there is nothing to fear from dead men."

"You're sure correct, How See," cried Billy recklessly. "I'm sure glad we made a good job of it, 'cause while I ain't none scared of his ghost, I wouldn't hanker to have the Wolf on my trail."

"Where's 'Lanky'?" demanded Tom Haggart suddenly.

They looked at each other in surprise, then walked back to the clump of brush. There they found Lanky, the man who had been eating stew on the morning when Allen had entered the Dry Creek restaurant. The man lay flat on his face, quite dead. Both of Allen's bullets had struck him in the breast.

"Dead as a mackerel," announced Black Steve, after a brief examination. "That feller was powerful fast and sure, and ridin' a buckin' horse when he pulled, too."

"What'll we do with him?" asked Haggart. "Lug him back?"

The Chinaman stooped and quickly rifled the dead man's pockets. Then he said in his singsong voice: "The Wolf got him; let him keep the Wolf company."

Black Steve laughed, and he and Haggart picked up the corpse and heaved it over the cliff. They stood and listened until they heard the body strike.

"Well, let's get goin'. I got a thirst like a camel," Haggart stated.

The four outlaws started down the trail to where they had left their horses. They had gone about twenty yards when Little Billy suddenly turned and hurried back to the spot where Allen had gone over. He dropped to his knees and groped about in the dark. At last he found it — the Colt that Allen had dropped.

“It’ll make a darn good souvenir,” he muttered with a grin, as he hurried after the others.

The clatter of hoofs died away in the distance. The ledge was once more silent and empty. The moon rose, serene and cold, above the peaks, bathing the desert with its light and turning the tips of the Dead Men Mountains to silver. It softened the edges of the canyon walls, cut through the black shadows and silvered the stream that tumbled along the canyon floor. Moon rays lighted the path for the two old prospectors as they trudged along the trail, and caught and flickered on two empty rifle shells which lay close to the brush.

The old men’s faces were grim and sad, as, with rifles held ready, they came around the bend in the trail. It was Skinny who first noticed the empty shells. He pointed to them, wordlessly, and the pair turned and back-tracked for a short distance. Both were old-timers, and to them the signs were as plain as if they had been printed. They looked at each other with drooping shoulders. Old Pop’s tanned cheeks were tear-stained, as he leaned forward and peered over the edge. The sheer drop was even more terrifying by moonlight than by the light of day. He staggered back and clutched Skinny with a trembling hand.

“Dang the coyotes! He’s down there!” he cried in a voice which broke with grief.

CHAPTER SIX

El Crucifixo

The morning after Jack-twin Allen parted from Chief Weatherspoon in Santa Fe, he left the Rio Grande and turned westward into the foothills of the San Luis range, where he picked up the outlaw's underground trail to the border. It twisted and turned to avoid all villages of size, and a man could follow it for miles without encountering another human being. Those he did meet would circle him as carefully as he did them.

Honey Boy had traveled far during the night, but Jack was impatient and did not make camp until noon of that day. By dusk he was again on the road. As he rode beneath the bright moon, he sang snatches of song to himself, for strangely enough, though he realized that he was starting on one of the most dangerous missions of his life, he felt unusually cheerful and light-hearted. It seemed almost as if with the clothes of Jim — which he had again donned — he had assumed some of the other's heedless character. He felt freer than he had in years.

"Honey Boy, Jim don't have such a bad life, after all. He ain't got a darned tie in the world, he can drift wherever he darn pleases and don't have to worry about duty." Jack chuckled.

But Jack Allen was soon to realize that his brother's life was not altogether to be envied. On the morning of the third day after leaving Santa Fe, he entered Quarta, a small Mexican hamlet on the border of Death Mesa, to replenish his supplies. He pulled up before a little grocery store and glanced up and down the sunlit street. Almost directly opposite him, on the other side of the road, several saddle ponies were at the hitch rack in front of a saloon. As Allen glanced over them, the door of the bar banged open, and a big man stepped outside. The first thing that Allen noticed about him was the star pinned to his waistcoat. It conveyed nothing particular to his mind, certainly not a warning of danger, for ordinarily he had nothing to fear from sheriffs. He had momentarily forgotten that not only was he playing the part of the most notorious outlaw in the West, but looked exactly like him. The sheriff quickly reminded him, however, that if he were to play the part of Jim, he would have to take the consequences.

The moment the officer's eyes rested on Allen, he went into action. Without warning, he grabbed at his Colt and sent a slug within a few inches of the little man's head. That automatic sense of Jim's was almost as keenly developed in Jack so that, even before he had recovered from his surprise, he had slapped Honey Boy with his heels and sent him flying down the road.

The sheriff's aim was blocked by the horses at the hitching rail, and by the time he had run clear of them, the gray, thanks to his lightning start, was already out of accurate pistol range. The sheriff emptied his gun uselessly, bellowing orders to the men who had run out of the saloon at the first sound of shooting. Three minutes after Allen had cleared the last house, the sheriff and a posse of four men were pounding along in pursuit.

"Darn you, I won't forget you, you shootin' fool! I'll come back with my whiskers on and learn you to cut loose on a gent without warnin'," Allen spluttered angrily. But gradually his rage left him, and he chuckled to himself. "Guess we was sort o' mistook in sayin' Jim's life wasn't a bad one. Come on, Honey Boy, we got to lose them gents back there."

But Jack was to have the disagreeable experience of learning that this was easier said than done. Unknowingly, he had stumbled on one of Jim's most relentless pursuers. The little outlaw had nicknamed him "Hopeful Harry" because of his tenacity and stubbornness in sticking to a trail. On one occasion he had followed Jim for over six weeks before giving up the pursuit, and the chase had passed through three States. At that time, Hopeful Harry had summoned to his aid half a dozen other sheriffs and a troop of cavalry, and it was only by the aid of an unexpectedly heavy blizzard that Jim had eluded him.

Jack Allen naturally had had more experience in playing the hound than the fox, but many years of work had taught him all the tricks that help to hide a trail. He tried one after the other in the hope of throwing the sheriff off. He back-tracked, crossed stretches of sand where he knew the breeze would soon broom out his trail, cut across lava beds and followed streams, but Hopeful Harry hung on like a bloodhound. It was well past midnight when Jack finally turned his gray up a game trail that zigzagged across the almost perpendicular wall of a high-flung mesa, and shook the sheriff off his trail.

The posse attempted to follow, but when one man had received a broken leg and another had been badly shaken up because of their horses falling, the sheriff gave up trying to scale the mesa. When he and his men had at length found another way up, Jack was far to the south and close to the outlaw country.

Without knowing it, he entered the town of Dry Creek some six or seven hours after Jim had clashed with Quong Lee. Jack, too, pulled up and looked wistfully at the Chinese restaurant, which was now closed. He reached the fork in the trail at sunset, and as Jim had done, stopped to study the land before him. He examined the well-marked trail down the slope and picked out a faint dust cloud which moved up the far side of the valley. He knew that he was within striking distance of El Crucifixo, and guessed that the dust cloud was made by a group of men also headed for the outlaw town. Although they were several miles ahead of him, he decided that it would be prudent to allow them to increase the distance, so he sat cross-legged in his saddle and gazed at the panorama before him. As the sun rushed down, the shadows cast by the cactus and the mounds of loose stone seemed fairly to race across the ground.

There came faintly to his ears the far-off reports of rifles. He sat listening for a moment, then chirped to Honey Boy, and the gray trotted down the slope.

"Those shots weren't fired at any game, 'cause there was a volley of 'em, so I reckon they was pottin' some gent. They must have got him, too, seein' as how he didn't shoot back. But it ain't any of our business, is it, Honey Boy?"

The moon had been up for several hours, and Jack Allen had been riding what seemed to him an endless distance along the winding trail through a jungle of mesquite, pear and cactus plants before he saw ahead of him the lights of El Crucifixo.

He had no plans, for his future movements depended on chance. He realized the peril in attempting to impersonate another person. Jim-twin Allen had a few friends and many enemies. How was he, Jack, to distinguish them? Then, there were many men along the border who would shoot at Jim on sight, as the pursuing sheriff had done. Jack shook his head and sighed. The nearer he came to the border town, the more difficult his task appeared. Being unable to tell Jim's friends from his foes, he would have to wait until the latter announced themselves by opening fire. A pretty prospect!

Then there was the difference in the mannerisms of the two brothers. The resemblance between them was remarkable, but whereas Jack seldom smiled, Jim usually wore a cheerful grin on his face. Well, he would simply have to leave it all to chance, Jack reflected, and locate Martin and the other operator as soon as possible. Perhaps they could give him some hints as to Jim's special pals, if the little outlaw had any.

El Crucifixo had once been a Spanish mission town. When it had been built, the Spaniards had thought of the future, and the magnificent cathedral, the monastery and other religious buildings and the government houses had been constructed to take care of ten times the population the town had. Then the Apache had struck — horribly and fiercely. The people had been massacred, and the town fired. The Spanish influence had waned, and El Crucifixo had never been rebuilt. The gaunt skeletons of the buildings remained untenanted, except by a few Mexican herders, until a band of passing outlaws discovered the place and turned it into a refuge for their fellows.

Most of the town was smothered by the ever-encroaching jungle of mesquite which covered the entire mesa and surrounded the town. Here and there single houses or groups had been cleared of the growth and made habitable, but the work had been very haphazard. El Crucifixo had a floating population of about two hundred outlaws, each with a price on his head, and about an equal number of Mexicans who ran the saloons, restaurants, and stores. There was no law, nothing that even approached it, and the town was a veritable outlaw paradise.

As Jack Allen rode Honey Boy through the openings in the mesquite which choked the broad streets, he looked about him at the tall ruins that raised their heads through the thick brush. Bathed as they now were in the moonlight, they looked weird and uncanny, and gave him a disturbed, uneasy feeling. There was no sound, save the soft thud of Honey Boy's hoofs in the sand, and the heavy silence increased his feeling of unreality.

He knew that he would find the main life of the settlement on the other side of town, clustered about the ancient plaza. He pulled up and studied the situation, for it was well to have a general knowledge of the buildings, as well as the exits, should he find it necessary to leave in a hurry.

The plaza was a large oblong, bordered by the old cathedral and the principal buildings of the former mission. Directly opposite from where he stood were two saloons. Apparently the night life of the community was in full swing, for the strumming of guitars, snatches of song, screams, shouts and oaths made the night hideous.

Allen secreted Honey Boy behind a clump of tall brush and crossed the plaza on foot. He remembered that Jim had spoken of hanging out in a place called the Bucket of Blood, run by a man named "Scarface," a mulatto and ex-sailor, sometimes called "Sailor Joe." Allen decided that that would be the place for him to make his first appearance, but as neither of the saloons possessed a sign to distinguish it, he had no way of knowing which was the one he sought. As he stood there, undecided, he heard the sound of running horses, and in a few minutes, four horsemen swung into the plaza and pulled up in front of the nearer saloon.

Jack slipped back into the shadows and watched the men dismount.

"Tom Haggart, you're elected to take the horses to the stable," he heard one of the men say gruffly.

The man addressed broke into a volley of protests, but his companions only jeered, and still grumbling, he led the horses diagonally across the plaza toward the ancient cathedral.

"I'm goin' in the back way, 'cause it ain't good sense to let that bunch see me down here," grunted the man who had first spoken.

"Yeah," sneered one of his companions, "there's some gents might think it queer if they knew Black Steve, the terror of the bad hombres, was visitin' a outlaw town."

"Little Billy, I'm tellin' you you're too damn mouthy," snarled Black Steve.

Little Billy, without replying, pushed open the door and, followed by the fourth man, entered the saloon. Black Steve also vanished from sight down a narrow alley.

"Black Steve, huh?" muttered Allen to himself. "Reckon you'll stand watchin'. Reckon I might as well follow them and take a chance on this bein' the Bucket of Blood."

He examined his guns carefully, wiping them free of dust, then raised his hand to push open the door. But as the sound of voices babbling in Chinese reached his ear, he once more drew back into the shadows and looked across the plaza.

CHAPTER SEVEN

The Ghost of the Wolf

The building which Sailor Joe, otherwise known as Scarface, had appropriated for his saloon had been originally built to serve as a trading post. It consisted of a long, high-ceilinged room with wide doors at the front and rear. The rear door opened on a narrow passage, flanked on both sides by fair-sized rooms. Most of these had been fitted with rough cots and rickety furniture, and were littered with the belongings of the untidy outlaws. Chaps, saddles and wearing apparel hung on the walls or lay where it had been kicked into the corners. The tables were littered with cigarette stubs, empty bottles, and cracked, dirty glasses.

At the far end of the passage was a suite of three rooms, and passing into these, you left behind the degenerate West and stepped into the effete East. The walls were hung with dragon panels, the floors covered with priceless rugs. There were teakwood tables, chairs, stools and low couches covered with silk and piled high with cushions. The narrow windows had been blocked with adobe, and no sound within the room reached beyond the inclosing walls. The only means of ventilation were through small holes cut in the roof, and the air was heavy and oppressive with incense. It was a bit of exotic China in the midst of the American desert.

In the first of these three rooms were two slant-eyed, heavy-set men who squatted in low chairs, holding sawed-off shotguns across their knees as they watched the door leading to the hall. In the second room, the largest of the three, Quong Lee sat on a cushioned stool and puffed at a scented cigarette. Beside him was a carved table which was cluttered with red papers, paint brushes and a brass bottle of ink. He was dressed in a robe of heavy black silk, embroidered in gold with a sleeping dragon which seemed to stir and quiver like a living thing as Quong leaned forward to flick the ash from his cigarette. His parchmentlike face was expressionless, but from time to time his glance would go to the outer door, and his thin, clawlike hands tapped impatiently on his knee. His whole appearance gave the impression of a man trying to subdue his impatience. At last he heard a faint knock on the outer door and looked up eagerly.

One of the two guards in the other room entered and singsonged a question. At a nod from Quong, he vanished, and a moment later, How See, followed by Black Steve, appeared. Quong waved them to chairs. Black Steve was obviously both impressed by and ill at ease amid the splendor of the room, and he squirmed uneasily during the heavy silence which followed their entrance.

"The Wolf has wings; he has flown away to join his ancestors," chanted How See at last.

Quong Lee's black eyes flickered, and he permitted himself a faint, malignant smile. "Good. You are sure? Your brain has not been blinded by the brilliance of your own intellect?" he purred softly.

"No, we ain't blinded by our own brilliance," cried Black Steve positively. "We are plumb sure the Wolf is dead. I know he's hard to kill, but he'd have to have nine lives like a cat to live with three or four .30–30 slugs in his carcass and a drop of a couple of miles into the canyon, besides."

This was a slight exaggeration, for Black Steve suspected that the horse, not Allen, had received the rifle fire. The animal had reared just as they fired. That did not matter, however. The important thing was that the Wolf was dead, and Black Steve had no qualms on that score.

"You have the Wolf's pelt?"

"Didn't I just tell you he tumbled into the canyon?" replied Black Steve. The big sheriff was irritated. He both hated and feared that saffron-faced statue with its malignant eyes and cruel smile. It went against his grain for him to have to take orders from a Chinaman, and it filled him with shame and a fierce resentment to admit that he was afraid of this yellow devil. He opened his mouth to pour out a stream of abuse, but when he met Quong's cold, deadly eyes, his own fell, and he left his complaints unspoken.

Having subdued Black Steve with a glance, Quong lighted another cigarette and puffed at it in silence.

How See waited impassively, and Black Steve wriggled nervously, pulling at the stained handkerchief about his neck.

"There was a bounty on the Wolf's pelt," Quong reminded them coldly.

Black Steve gaped and scratched at his mop of hair. "A bounty! I get you. I'll say there was — twelve thousand dollars, dead or alive!" he cried, understanding at last. "We was so danged set up at droppin' him and still bein' in the land of the livin' that we clean forgot his scalp was worth a fortune."

"To-morrow at dawn we will return and search," said How See hastily.

"There were five of you. You were each to receive one thousand dollars in gold —"

"The Wolf got Lanky afore we nailed him," interrupted Black Steve.

"Then you are to receive four thousand for his pelt," continued Quong imperturbably. "He was worth twelve thousand. If you do not recover it, you four will owe me eight thousand."

Black Steve gasped and swore silently, but he made no comment. "All right, to-morrow I'll go look for him."

Quong vouchsafed no reply.

Black Steve, anxious to break the silence which again pervaded the room, pointed to the plates of pungent and fragrant Chinese delicacies which reposed on a long table. "Somebody gettin' married?" he asked with rough joviality.

Quong blinked, and for the first time Black Steve caught a glimpse of something that was not sinister in his eyes.

"No," he replied, "my son, Charlie, come back to-day."

"But he only went away a week ago," protested Black Steve.

"May not a son return to his father? He sent word that he had important business." Then, suddenly realizing that it was not dignified to answer a subordinate's questions, Quong again relapsed into silence.

Black Steve felt as if he were choking. He was unaccustomed to the heavy incense. He longed to leave, but he knew from past experience that the old Chinaman would be offended if he made a move to go before being properly dismissed, so he sat there, raging, and thinking with envy of his pals at the bar outside.

"The honorable pursuer of the men who sell the flower of the lotus is stubborn and refuses to speak," chanted Quong drowsily.

"You mean the secret-service gent, Cutbill?" Black Steve inquired.

"None other. He has wisdom, yet he is a fool, for he has chosen torment rather than speech," Quong explained.

Black Steve shuddered and edged farther away from the Chinaman as he glimpsed the gleam of evil in the old man's eyes. He knew from Quong's remark that the government agent had been tortured in an effort to make him divulge some information, and had refused. "What you goin' to do with him?" he asked shakily.

"To-morrow Charlie will place him on a hill, and when he finds himself going down the hole, atom by atom, he will realize his folly in pitting his brain against that of Quong."

Black Steve felt nauseated. By "hill" Quong referred to an ant hill, and he knew how those terrible, saw-toothed insects would literally devour a man alive.

"What of the new one — Martin?" murmured How See.

"He is a fool, blinded by his own vanity," replied Quong. "He is precious to me and must not be harmed."

Black Steve had to admit that the old devil was clever. The wise operators he removed; the harmless fools he permitted to live.

There came a knock at the outer door, and a moment later two Chinese glided into the room. One was a stranger to Black Steve, the other was Charlie Lee, Quong's son. He was about twenty-one or two, of medium height, with plump, yellow cheeks and full lips. He had inherited all of his father's vices and none of his brains. Black Steve listened without understanding to the volley of words which the three Chinese hurled at each other. Abruptly Quong brought the discussion to a close by raising his hand.

"You must return to college. You are your father's son," he cried sternly in English. "Let us eat and have done with words."

But Charlie, who affected American clothes, had, in acquiring Western manners, lost his Oriental respect for his parents. "Don't forget I'm past twenty-one," he said in a voice that was a mixture of snarl and whine. He pointed to the man who had entered with him. "Sin Yet, here, wants to quit the Mexican end. Well, I want to go down there and run it for you. I'm going to do it, and I'm going to take the girl with me."

"What has woman to do with the sale of what we have?" Quong asked, as he sighed and shook his head.

Charlie laughed rudely. "The truth is that you are afraid of what might happen if you kidnaped the girl."

Black Steve jumped. So that was the trouble. Charlie was after Mary Bell again. There had been a big row about her only the previous week, and Quong had apparently settled the question, but Charlie had returned to the attack. Black Steve knew that it would be madness for these men to kidnap the girl, the niece of old Kid Bell, for there were dozens of men in the town who, though they were guilty of every crime in the calendar, would yet make it exceedingly uncomfortable for any man who turned over a white girl to a Chinaman. For, strangely enough, every outlaw in El Crucifixo who had one drop of white blood in him, was dominated in certain matters by that drop, and claimed to be white.

"Why are you afraid?" Charlie cried passionately. "Because she is white, and I am your son? You, my father, shame your ancestors, for you agree with those men out there that because I am a Chinaman, I am not worthy of her."

"This business which brings in much gold is not to be cast aside for the quickly tarnished charms of a woman."

"I would as soon be an ant on a hot rock as to have gold that will not buy what I desire," said Charlie scornfully. "The Wolf —"

"The Wolf has but lately ascended the dragon of immortality," Quong interrupted softly.

"Then we have nothing more to fear. Men are angry for a day, then quickly forget," shrilled Charlie.

"My son, an intelligent man recognizes the will of Heaven. I surrender. I am glad that you have been frank with me. False humility is genuine arrogance. You may replace Sin Yet in Mexico, and your rose blossom shall go with you."

Black Steve swore silently. He knew that Quong had made a decision which might land them all in trouble, but it was useless to protest.

"Kid Bell is out in front. The girl's alone now," Charlie pleaded eagerly.

Before Quong had time to reply, there came an excited hammering on the outer door, and the muffled sound of a shrill voice. The door of the room was yanked open, and Little Billy appeared. His face was white, his eyes were round with fear, and he was shaking with excitement. His terror had lent him such strength that he dragged with him the big guard who had tried to bar his way.

"The Wolf — his ghost is out there!"

His listeners failed to grasp the import of his words, but his fear was so vivid and real that they all, even

Quong, glanced apprehensively at the door. As they stood there, waiting and listening, for they knew not what, there came to their ears the double roar of two Colts.

"*There* — the ghost has started on Haggart!" Little Billy screamed.

CHAPTER EIGHT

Trapped

Jack-twin Allen's entrance into the Bucket of Blood had been interrupted by the appearance of Charlie Lee and his fellow Chinaman, and he had reconsidered his original plan. He decided to delay his entrance until he had more thoroughly reconnoitered the adjoining buildings. His first move was to explore the alley down which Black Steve had vanished. He discovered that the building was fully forty yards long, and that about halfway down, the alley was blocked by a wooden fence. He pushed open the gate and passed through to the other side. Close to the rear wall he found a narrow path which had been cut through the heavy growth of mesquite. The moon was shining directly on the wall of the saloon, and he noticed that several of the windows in back had been blocked up, while the ones in front were open.

"Sort o' makin' the place air-tight," he reflected, and stopped in front of a door and tried the handle. It was locked. "I wonder if that Black Steve gent went in this way? I'm plumb curious as to why they cut that trail through the brush. They must have wanted a back door bad, 'cause that was a man's job, and took a heap of time. Now if they was to lock the door in that fence, a man could come and go in here without bein' spotted by any one out front. That's sure it. But who done it and why? Looks suspicious."

He slipped back through the door in the fence and glided out into the plaza. Leaning against the front wall of the saloon, he listened to the babble which poured from the open door and tried to think. He knew that the moment he stepped inside he would be in a position where the chances of winning through were ten to one against him, but the risk had to be taken. Jack had not been a sheriff and United States marshal for ten years without learning that boldness was half the battle. Better to go in and face the music before some one saw him skulking outside and warned the brutes. Having made his decision, he squared his shoulders, pushed open the door and stepped inside.

Scarface had utilized the old counter of the mission's trading post for his bar. It ran two thirds of the way down the room, and was on Allen's right as he entered. To his left there were some small tables occupied by men who were drinking and gambling. At the rear the floor was cleared, and several couples were dancing to the music of the three-piece Mexican band. The room was lighted by three enormous oil lamps and reeked with the odor of stale tobacco and the fumes of rank whisky and unwashed humanity.

There were fully a hundred men in the place and a score of women whose blood ran from pure Indian to mixtures of white, Negro and Chinese. The men were of all ages and sizes. Some had pleasant, though reckless faces, some were coldly sneering, while still others were brutal and bestial; but Jack knew that whatever their outward appearances, they were all from the same mold and were all "wanted."

Allen hesitated by the door. Suddenly he caught the eye of a heavy-set, grossly fat man, with small ratlike eyes, whose barrellike middle was circled by a once-white apron. He was serving drinks to the crowd of jostling men around the bar. His face was disfigured by a livid scar which started in the roots of his hair and ran diagonally across his face to his neck. Allen knew instinctively that this was the proprietor that Jim had told him about.

Scarface blinked at him for a moment and failed to respond to the cheerful grin which Jack threw at him, but finally he jerked his head in acknowledgment, and Allen drew a breath of relief. He had passed the first hurdle.

Allen glanced again down the long bar. He noticed that some of the men stood alone or in couples with a kind of detached grandeur, while the general mob avoided them and crowded into the remaining space. Allen grinned to himself. It was easy to pick out the real and dangerous gunmen. He marked one man who was given even more elbow room than the others — a small man, wizened and almost bald. His eyes were like glittering, blue marbles, his nose was thin and hooked like an eagle's bill, and his thin lips curled with a kind of sardonic cruelty.

Allen placed him in a flash. He was Ed Bell, who had been nicknamed "Kid" because of his age. He was wanted in five States for bank and train robberies and murder, and had the reputation of possessing a cool, calculating nerve, and a terrible ferocity when cornered. Allen was thinking what pleasure he would derive from turning the old scoundrel over to the authorities, when he became aware that the man's shoe-button eyes were fixed on him. He had no way of knowing whether the Kid were a friend or enemy, but as the old gunman had not gone for his gun, he decided to take a middle course and nod without smiling.

Kid Bell returned the nod, then shifted his eyes along the bar to a man standing alone at the farther end. He laughed crookedly, but mirthfully.

"Don't you want somethin', Jim?" called a voice.

Jack Allen turned and saw the bartender grinning at him in patronizing fashion. "I'll take some beer," he replied easily. Then he had to suppress a laugh, for as if by magic a way was opened for him through the jostling crowd to the bar. "Might almost think I had the plague," he thought with amusement. Even those killers who had been standing apart, avoided by the crowd, edged farther away. There was no doubt but that Jim put the fear of the devil into these outlaws.

Little by little, conversation ceased, and the various groups of men swung around to stare curiously at Allen. It was evident that they recognized him at once and were dumfound to see him in their midst. Most of the faces showed no hostility, only a kind of astonished dismay. A few stared at him with both hate and fear in their eyes, but no one attempted to draw a gun. Then one by one they began to look away, and soon the buzz of conversation recommenced.

Although puzzled, Jack had no way of determining the cause of the attitude about him, and it both worried and perplexed him. He felt that something was afoot which he did not understand.

Rumor and gossip never travels more rapidly than among wanted men. They are inveterate gossips, especially where one of their kind is concerned. Some one had seen Black Steve and his companions arrive in El Crucifixo, had seen Black Steve and How See vanish down the alley, and noted the semihysterical satisfaction displayed by the other two. Later on, Little Billy had become too free in his talk about the Wolf, and when warned that he had better shut up, had boasted that he was no longer afraid of the outlaw. Little by little the gossip grew, until it bloomed into a positive belief that the Wolf had ridden his last trail. Men were discussing it openly when Jack entered the saloon, which accounted for their dismay at the first sight of him.

Almost immediately, however, they saw the humor in the situation, and it gave them a ferocious pleasure. Here was Little Billy at one end of the bar, loudly declaiming to the world his scorn of the Wolf; there was the Wolf, unbeknown to Billy, quietly sipping beer not twenty yards away. It was not long before the temptation to break the bad news to Little Billy became too strong to resist.

Scarface waddled down to the end of the bar and, placing his fat hands on the rail, leaned over and whispered hoarsely: "Hey, Billy, stop your yap."

"Heck, I'm through talkin' soft and pretty when this Wolf person is about," Little Billy boasted arrogantly.

"Suit yourself. He's right down there." Scarface chuckled horribly.

As if stung, Little Billy whirled about and faced down the bar. Sensing something, the intervening men hastily slid aside, and Billy found himself face to face with the man whom he was positive he had seen fall over a thousand-foot cliff a few hours previously. His first reaction was one of surprise, which quickly gave way to sheer horror. His face blanched, and his mouth gaped open as he stared incredulously. Then he uttered a strangled cry of abject terror, clasped both hands over his eyes, turned and dashed to the rear door, and clawing it open, frantically, vanished.

The spectators' faces were pictures of blank amazement. Although most of them had expected to see Billy draw in his horns and wilt before Allen, they had not expected him to play the part of the craven coward.

Allen was as astounded as the rest, and for the moment frankly nonplused. His eyes ranged around the semicircle of onlookers until they came to rest on Kid Bell. He saw that the Kid was smiling broadly, so when he met his eye, he winked and grinned. Instantly the smile vanished from Bell's face. He walked across the room, straddled a chair and, tilting it backward, watched Allen with a puzzled expression.

It was scarcely a minute after Little Billy's precipitate exit that Tom Haggart stepped in from the street. It was the sudden hush that fell over the room which warned

Jack. When Haggart caught sight of him, his first reaction was identical with that of Little Billy, but the outcome was entirely different. Instead of fleeing from the room, he made a desperate grab for his gun, and as Allen was totally unprepared for this action, Haggart's gun actually went off at the same moment as his own.

The double concussion of the big Colts caused the lamps to flicker, and one of the glasses behind the bar fell to the floor with a crash. Allen stooped and peered through the drifting smoke. Haggart staggered backward, clutched at the door jamb and steadied himself. His gun hung loosely at his side, a thin stream of smoke still issuing from the muzzle.

No matter how skillful an actor a man may be, under stress of excitement he will revert to his normal self. So now for one moment Allen forgot the role of the Wolf and became the officer of the law. "Drop that gun!" he ordered sharply.

Haggart stared at him for a second, then let the weapon slip from his nerveless hand. The stricken man started to sag, straightened himself by a super-human effort, then slumped to the floor with a crash.

At the first boom of the gun the music had ceased, and two women had screamed hysterically. Now there was complete silence, broken only by the wheezing sound of sharply drawn-in and exhaled breaths.

"Well, that's that," Scarface's deep voice broke the tension like a clap of thunder. "Drag him outside, some of you fellows."

A dozen men leaped to obey, and having dragged the dead man outside, they stripped him of valuables.

"Is it all right, Jim?" the bartender asked jovially. Then when Jack made no reply, he added apologetically: "You know the custom."

Jack swore silently. He didn't know the custom, so he nodded at Scarface and let it go at that. He noticed the look of surprise in the fat man's face and blessed his brother's reputation, for Scarface promptly let the matter drop. But some thirsty customer at the far end of the bar was of a different opinion.

"Hey, Scarface! Jim nodded, so get busy and hand out the stuff," he called.

The bartender looked again at Jack for confirmation, and when the latter nodded, hastily slid out several bottles and enough glasses for everyone in the saloon. Then Jack understood that the Bucket of Blood had the playful custom that after a shooting the survivor put up drinks for the house. He paid for the round, then stood there alone, wondering what the next happening would be.

A voice at his side brought him back to the present, and he turned to find Kid Bell next to him.

"How 'bout goin' some place and gettin' some grub?" the Kid asked, his lips twitching nervously.

"Sure, I'm so hollow my ribs are touchin'," Allen replied.

Bell was obviously in doubt. He hesitated as if debating his next words. Something leaped into his little eyes, but before Allen could determine what it portended, it had vanished again.

"Shanghai Pete's suit yuh?" he queried.

Allen nodded absently. He was worried, and his sixth sense warned him that there was something beneath the Kid's offer and that he had best go easy until he learned what it was. He berated his impetuosity. He should have kept to his own society until he had found the chance to see either Martin or Cutbill. They at least could have told him whom he was supposed to be friendly with. Well, it was too late now. He had taken the plunge, and it was up to him to swim. "Sure, let's hit Pete's," he replied carelessly.

Bell gave a wolfish grin and flicked a glance around to see if any one had overheard their conversation. "No, let's go up to my shack, an' I'll make my gal cook us a real meal," he suggested.

Was this a trap? — Allen wondered. He glanced at the Kid, but the weather-beaten old face was quite guileless. To refuse would arouse suspicion, and besides he was desperately hungry, so he nodded and followed the Kid outside.

The moment they had gone, a buzz of comment broke out in the room.

"When did them two get so chummy?" some one inquired.

"When I sees 'em talkin' so friendly, you could have knocked me down with a feather!" another cried.

"Why, only last week Jim wouldn't speak to the ol' devil. Said he thought he would be more use fertilizin' the mesquite than walkin' around pollutin' the air," a third man cut in.

And in the back rooms, Quong, Black Steve, and the other members of the gang, were discussing the unexpected return of the Wolf. The ancient Chinaman scoffed at Black Steve's and Little Billy's belief that Allen's ghost had returned, and roundly berated them for having failed in their task.

"Tom Haggart is dead, but they were not ghost's bullets that killed him; they were lead pills. Your fear blinded you. This afternoon on the ledge you were like frightened children. You closed your eyes, and he escaped." Quong quivered with rage, disappointment and fear. He drove them all from the room, refusing even to listen to the pleas of his beloved son.

When Jack Allen followed Kid Bell out of the Bucket of Blood, he was alert for the first sign of treachery. He knew that there were few men along the border who were the Kid's equal with a gun, and also that the old outlaw was as trustworthy as a snake. So he carefully arranged that the other walk ahead of him across the plaza, and as he followed, his hand was always close to his gun.

As they started along the narrow trail cut through the mesquite, Jack suddenly remembered Honey Boy, and, putting his fingers to his lips, he gave a long, shrill whistle. The horse neighed in reply and charged toward them from his place of concealment. Kid Bell turned and gaped at the gray.

"Danged if it ain't Honey Boy," he muttered as he gazed doubtfully at Allen.

Jack looked at him in some surprise. The old outlaw had a puzzled frown on his face.

"Why shouldn't it be Honey Boy?" Allen asked, with an amused grin.

Kid Bell muttered something unintelligible and turned again along the path. He did not speak again until he reached his house, which proved to be a rambling affair set in the midst of a clearing some way from the main trail through the brush.

"Mary's still up," he remarked shortly.

He rapped on the door and replied gruffly to the query of some one within. Then there came the sound of some one fumbling with bolts, and the door swung open. A small girl, slightly shorter than Allen, stood framed in the doorway. She had a perfectly proportioned figure, and the light from within the room tinged her wavy-brown hair with gold. She rubbed her blue eyes with the backs of her hands like a sleepy child and smiled brightly.

"I was reading and fell asleep," she said.

"I got a friend with me. Do you figure you could get us some supper?" the Kid demanded. He led the way into a plain but comfortable room, whose general air of cleanliness and tasteful furnishing told of a woman's care.

When Mary Bell saw Allen, she shrank back, and one hand flew to her throat. With an effort she recovered herself and gave him a doubtful little smile. "How do you do, Mr. Allen?" she faltered, then turned to the Kid. "Of course, uncle, I'll get you some supper."

Jack Allen watched her, tongue-tied. So Jim knew her! For the first time in his life he was unreasonably jealous of his brother. He sat like an abashed schoolboy, and watched the girl as she set the table and deftly prepared their supper.

He ate the meal in silence, and though it was temptingly cooked, had no idea of what he was eating. He was wondering just how well Jim knew this girl, and why she had looked so startled at sight of him. Women were not as a rule afraid of the little outlaw; he had a wistful air which touched their hearts. Jack was so occupied with his thoughts of the girl that he forgot his suspicions of the old gunman, and even when the Kid followed her into the kitchen and held a whispered conversation with her, he felt no alarm. His sixth sense seemed to have been lulled to sleep. At last he could restrain his curiosity no longer and addressed her directly.

"Why was you so scared when you first saw me to-night?" he asked bluntly.

"Why —" the girl stammered. Then she tried to laugh. "You must admit you were rather frightening the last time I saw you."

"Yeah?"

"I don't blame Shanghai Pete for being scared when you looked at him with your eyes all yellow like that. Of course, I want to thank you for telling all the men in town that you had taken me under your protection. Since that day I've been able to go around, and no one even glances twice at me," she ended breathlessly.

"Shanghai Pete," Jack muttered to himself. Then, in a flash, his sixth sense leaped into play again. He understood now why Bell had suggested that they go to Shanghai Pete's. It had been a trap, and he had blundered into it. Kid Bell, then, must have seen through his impersonation, and that being the case, he had better find out whether the old outlaw were a friend or enemy. He became cool and calculating. The Kid was directly behind him. He must manage to turn and face him before he revealed the fact that he had been tricked. He leaned forward carelessly, helping himself to another piece of cake, then started to rise from his chair. But he was too late. He froze as he felt something cold and hard digging into his back.

"Stay put," the Kid snapped. "Put your paws on the table."

Allen obeyed. There was nothing else to do. He felt his guns drawn from their holsters and heard them thud, as Bell tossed them across the room onto the couch. Allen was overwhelmed at his stupidity. He had been trapped as easily as a boy, and his cheeks burned with shame. He glanced at the girl and felt a foolish sense of relief, as he saw that she had not wittingly tricked him. She was staring at the Kid wide-eyed, and was obviously as surprised at the turn of events as Allen himself.

"Don't be scared, gal. This ain't nothin' but a little business talk, which I figures will be more comfortable if this gent don't have his guns," said the Kid gruffly. "You run on to bed and let us talk."

The girl left the room obediently, and Allen rejoiced when he noticed that her eyes were filled with a dismayed pity.

CHAPTER NINE

An Unexpected Ally

As soon as the door had closed behind her, the Kid faced Jack and looked his prisoner over. "You sure look like the Wolf, but you ain't him. Now who are you?" he snapped.

"What makes you think I ain't Jim?" Allen replied with a grin. His eyes were roving about the room, seeking a way of escape, but he saw none.

"Shucks, that's easy. A couple of weeks ago, Jim rides me for keepin' Mary down here." His lips split in a sardonic smile. "An' when Jim talks, he uses words that an idjut could understan'. He was right insultin'. I talked back to him an' tol' him to mind his own business, but afterward I drawed in my horns and took water.

"But the Wolf ain't like you, an' no gent ever sees his back. So when you spoke to me, it sort o' shocked me, an' then when you winked, I was sure floored. But I watches you. You made a neat draw when you downed Haggart — fast as blazes, considerin' as you was took by surprise — but Haggart near beat you to it, and he wouldn't have done that to the Wolf. Besides which, Haggart is in Jim's book for what he done to a Mexican gal, an' I see right off that you don't know Haggart. When you ordered him to drop his gun, it sounded more like a sheriff than the Wolf.

"When I saw Honey Boy, I was sort o' stumped," continued the old outlaw, "but when I caught you makin' moon eyes at Mary, I knew you was a fake. Now who are you? And what you doin' here?"

Allen shrugged. "What's the diff? I'm a fake. Let it go at that."

He saw a flicker of indecision in the old man's eyes, and when next the Kid spoke, it was more to himself than to Allen.

"Danged if I want the Wolf trailin' me. If I only knew that what they was sayin' to-night was true! But they've said them things about Jim afore." He glared at Jack and demanded sharply: "Come on, who are you? Are you Jack-twin Allen, the United States marshal?"

Instinctively Allen knew that the truth would serve him here, so he nodded affirmatively.

"An' who you down here after?"

Jack's mind worked rapidly, and he decided to lay his cards on the table. He knew that he was taking a chance, but it was his only hope.

"I don't know who they are, but I'm lookin' for some coyotes who use this town as a headquarters to run dope into the country," he explained.

He was totally unprepared for the change in Bell. "You're lookin' for dope runners here in town?" the Kid exclaimed.

"Yes — an unscrupulous, brainy gang, too."

Bell straightened and slipped his gun back into its holster. His face was contorted with fury, and he shook his two fists in the air. Allen had never heard a man swear as the old outlaw did now. Suddenly he sank, shaking, into a chair. With an effort he gathered himself together.

"Dang all the coyotes that run dope! If it hadn't been for them devils, I'd never have ridden the long trail. They got my kid to usin' it, an' —" He broke off abruptly, and when he again spoke, it was more quietly. "There's no use thinkin' about what's done. I'd like to help you, though; it would kind o' help wipe out the past."

His eyes were actually pleading as he made his request, and Allen knew that miraculously he had acquired an ally, who, though he was not a respectable citizen, would, nevertheless, be invaluable. Quickly he sketched the story and told Bell of his suspicions concerning the Bucket of Blood saloon.

"We'll look at that trail through the mesquite to-morrow," said the old gunman when Jack had finished his swift recital.

They talked for hours discussing the various men whom Bell thought might belong to the gang, but the older man decided to say nothing about the rumor of Jim's death, for he was afraid that Jack would at once give up his pursuit of the gang and set out to avenge his brother.

When Jack tumbled sleepily into bed in the small hours of the morning, he reflected with pleasure on the outcome of the night's events, but in spite of his enthusiasm, his last thoughts as he drifted into sleep were of the girl, Mary Bell.

The following morning, Jack was leaning against one of the porch pillars, smoking and listening to the sound of Mary's voice as she sang over her work. He felt peaceful and happy, and thoughts of the gang he was after had been almost driven from his mind by his peaceful surroundings. The Kid had gone to town to see if anything were happening and had left Allen there to watch over the girl. Through the open door of the kitchen he saw Mary, standing on tiptoe in a vain effort to reach a shelf just beyond the tips of her fingers. He turned and entered the house. As the girl heard his footsteps, she glanced over her shoulder and smiled at him.

"I'll get it for you," said Jack grandly. He reached up and just managed to grasp the can she wanted. His fingers touched hers as he gave it to her, and their eyes met. It was the first time in his life that Jack had not had to tilt his head backward to look at a girl, and he felt suddenly strong and protective toward her.

"You don't act at all the way you did that day you scared Shanghai Pete. You seem much different," said the girl suddenly.

"In what way?" asked Jack quite eagerly.

"Oh, I don't know. You don't treat me as if I were a foolish child. You're more dignified, and I'm not afraid of you," she said shyly.

It was on the tip of Jack's tongue to tell her the truth, but before he could blurt out the words, a bell tinkled in the yard. The path through the mesquite almost circled the house before it entered the cleared space, and about halfway around it was blocked by a big branch of brush. Through this the old outlaw had cleverly threaded a thin cord with a bell attached, so that it was impossible to move past the obstruction without ringing the bell. When he himself passed it, he always rang it a second time as a signal to Mary. Now, as the two in the kitchen listened, the bell tinkled again.

"There's uncle," cried Mary, and ran out of the house.

Allen watched her through a partly shuttered window, and as his eyes were on her, he did not see who it was that had entered the clearing.

Charlie Lee was well aware that his father, Quong, would not let him kidnap Mary Bell until the Wolf's reappearance had been solved, but as his permission of the previous evening had not been canceled, the pudgy youth decided to act first and notify his father later. He had seen Kid Bell go into the Bucket of Blood, so he expected to find the girl alone. With him was How See, and before the girl realized their intentions, they had darted between her and the house, cutting off her escape. They grabbed her and started to drag her toward the opening in the mesquite.

"Jim! Jim!" she screamed in terror.

In answer to her screams, Jack Allen dashed to the porch. How See, startled by her cry, glanced apprehensively around in time to see Jack appear.

"The ghost of the Wolf!" he screamed and bolted.

Charlie had been too much occupied with the struggling girl to grasp the situation at once, and when he did, it was too late. It was Jack's mood of physical superiority, so recently acquired, that impelled him into the fight without his guns, and he attacked Charlie with his fists. He was like unchained lightning compared to the Chinaman, and before the other knew what it was all about, he was being pummeled with fists like pistons. The fight lasted only a few minutes, and when it was over, Charlie had been reduced to an incoherently sobbing wretch. His eyes were puffed, his lips swollen, and two front teeth were missing, when Jack inspected his work.

"Fan the breeze, now, and don't you never get fresh with a white woman again," Allen cried sternly, and helped him on his way with a well-directed kick. Had he known the man's motives, it is doubtful if he would have let him off so easily.

Charlie went rapidly. The girl ran to Allen and looked up at him anxiously.

"You're not hurt?" she questioned.

Jack assured her grandly that he was not, but she insisted on doctoring his bruised knuckles and swathing them in heavy bandages. He did not have the heart to tell her that they would make it impossible for him to draw if he needed to, and she was still fussing over him when the Kid returned.

When he had heard the story of their experience, his face was a mask of fury. "Why didn't you sieve that dang chink?" he raved.

And when Jack had learned the man's intentions, his rage equaled that of the old outlaw.

"I'm goin' to the Bucket of Blood an' make it plain that I aims to kill that chink on sight," Bell stormed.

"Me, too. Let's get goin'," replied Jack.

They ordered Mary to keep the house locked until they returned, and started out through the brush. The old outlaw was consumed with mirth when he spotted Jack's hands.

"You ain't goin' to town with them fool bandages on, is you?" he chortled. "Why, every gent there could beat you to the draw with them things on."

Reluctantly Allen stripped off the yards of linen and hung them on a bush. He intended to replace them before returning to the house.

Side by side they entered the Bucket of Blood. It was Jack who laid down the ultimatum, for, as the Wolf, it was his prerogative. There were a score or more of men around the bar.

"You gents can tell the chink, Charlie, that I aims to wolf him on sight," he told them softly.

"And you can say that it goes for me, too," Bell added.

"Guess that'll sure make the chink hard to catch," remarked one of the men, when the two had departed.

A few minutes later, a short, burly man slipped unobtrusively away from the bar and sneaked through the rear door. He hurried along the passage to Quong's room and repeated Allen's message to one of the guards, then sought the bar again.

★ ★ ★

When Charlie returned from his encounter with Jack, Quong had been coldly contemptuous. He looked at his son's battered features with disgust and heard the whimpered tale of the fight without sympathy. "I have fathered a donkey on two legs," he said cuttingly.

"Fate plans for a fool, but action is the father of luck," retorted Charlie angrily. "What are you going to do — wait? Remember, a patient rat can bring down a tall tower, and if you do not destroy this Jim Allen, he will bring your organization down about your ears." Charlie lacked the Oriental calm of his father, and his desire for revenge was almost suffocating him. "I would like to stake the Wolf out on a hill, as I did that other this morning," he stormed.

Quong flicked a glance at Little Billy, who lounged against the door, then turned again to his son. "Did the chaser of men cry out with surprise when he found himself disappearing down the ant hill?" he asked.

"He was as one already dead, and died quickly," Charlie responded. There was keen disappointment in his voice, and Little Billy shivered. He had witnessed the death of Cutbill, and it had left him weak and shaken.

One of the guards opened the door and said something in Chinese. Little Billy could not understand what the man had said, but by Charlie Lee's expression he knew it was important. The yellow youth's pudgy face became the color of bleached parchment, and terrible fear leaped into his eyes. He tried to speak, but the cords of his neck seemed paralyzed, and he only frothed at the lips. Quong sat impassive, but his eyes flashed with hate. Finally Charlie managed to speak.

"Quick! Send some one to the Wolf and tell him he can have the girl. I — I must get out of here," he panted heavily.

"If you leave here, there will be none to carry on the glory of the Lees'. A rabbit is safe in its own burrow," responded Quong. He looked at Little Billy, and there was more of an appeal than a command in his voice. "Tell them Quong will pay his weight in gold for the Wolf's pelt."

Little Billy blinked and started to speak, but changed his mind and left the room in silence. He passed down the hall and entered another large room where three men were playing cards. He knew them all — Black Steve, "Lily" Joe, a coal-black Negro, and Shanghai Pete, a tall, big man in whose veins ran a mixture of Chinese, Apache, Indian, and Celtic blood. He and Black Steve ranked as the fastest gunmen along the border, and it was generally conceded that they could beat the Kid, and came next to the Wolf himself.

Little Billy told them with a sneer of Charlie's terror and repeated Quong's offer of gold for the Wolf's body.

"The Wolf came in a while back and said it plain that he'd down Charlie on sight," said Lily Joe, in a rich, sonorous voice.

"Oh, so that's what the guard told 'em!" Billy laughed. "No wonder they was so done up!"

"Me, for one, ain't gunnin' for Jim Allen again," Black Steve said, with an oath.

"Me an' Black went out this mornin' an' searched every foot of Sheer Rock Canyon an' didn't find hide nor hair of the Wolf," Shanghai Pete informed Little Billy.

"His hoss was there, dead, but he warn't," Black Steve added.

"Then it ain't his ghost — it's hisself," Little Billy cried.

"Maybe so, but a gent what can take a few .30–30 slugs an' then fall a couple of miles down a canyon an' come sailin' up again, ain't human," Lily Joe said slowly.

"I sees 'Bottles' Keating and his two brothers — you remember they warn't no slouches with guns — cut loose unexpected like on the Wolf, an' he was close enough to be an easy mark, an' not one of the shots hits him. An' then he dropped all three of them," volunteered Shanghai Pete.

It was stories of this type that cloaked the Wolf in a mantle of superstitious fear which defeated his enemies even before they started battle. Subconsciously fearing that Jim-twin Allen had a superhuman quality which made him invulnerable, even outlaws with the steeliest of nerves shot hastily and lost their cunning when they faced him.

"Me, I'm plumb glad I didn't have no hand in shootin' the gray off the ledge, 'cause the Wolf sure thinks a heap of them pets of his," Lily Joe rumbled thankfully.

Black Steve laughed nervously and hitched his chair around so that he could watch the door. He picked up a bottle and drained it at a gulp, choking as the fiery liquid ran down his throat.

"To blazes with the Wolf!" he growled. "We're scaring ourselves like a bunch of kids."

When Little Billy reported that the men refused to go gunning for Allen, Quong's face was a picture of baffled fury. His rage quickly spent itself, however, and he began to plan and scheme.

"Send the Wolf word that I don't want the girl," Charlie pleaded.

"Truly the gods are kind, if the Wolf really desires your rose blossom," Quong told him. "A man who is blinded by a woman will follow her into a trap."

"You mean —" Charlie asked hopefully.

"The men who are afraid of the Wolf will still take the girl. She will lead him to me — he will follow." Quong flipped open his robe and revealed the long knife in his hand. "The drinker of blood will make no mistake."

CHAPTER TEN

First Payment for Apple Pie

That night Kid Bell and Jack Allen started out to investigate the path which led to the rear entrance of Scarface's saloon. They found the door in the fence which blocked the alley was locked, but after weary hours of searching through the jungle of mesquite, they at last discovered a path which opened into the one they sought. They followed it for many a mile as it led south from the Bucket of Blood, and just at dawn came into a slide which led to the floor of a canyon. There was little vegetation; the land was mostly barren rock, sculptured by time into many fantastic shapes. As the two men rode down the canyon, the Kid grew more and more excited. Suddenly he pulled up his horse and pointed to a pile of stones surmounted by rude crosses.

"I know where we are now. This here is Monument Canyon, an' there ain't no way out of it till you hit Skeleton Pass which is tother side of the border. Them crosses is where a bunch of Mex soldiers was trapped in here and murdered by the Apaches."

"The gent what cut that path through the mesquite had brains as well as patience," said Jack admiringly,

“ ’cause when he finished, he sure had a private back way into El Crucifixo.”

“Yeah, I’m bettin’ this is the way them coyotes run the dope over,” cried Bell excitedly.

Allen nodded. “Now we got to find who the boss is, an’ how they get the stuff out of El Crucifixo, then we can smash them. How far is it back by way of Skeleton Pass?”

“Fifteen to twenty miles,” Bell decided.

“Then we got to risk goin’ back the way we came. I don’t like leavin’ Mary alone so long.”

“Wish that brother of mine would show so I could send the gal up-State,” Bell grumbled, as they swung back along the trail. “An’ I sure hopes we don’t meet any of the gang in here. It’s a nasty place to have a scrap in.”

Jack agreed, and the two were silent and alert as they made their way back, the way they had come. But luck favored them, and before long they were dismounting in front of Bell’s house.

That evening Jack finally located the first of the two secret-service men he was in search of. He spotted Dick Martin in a Mexican restaurant, and, calling him outside, explained who he was. After several minutes, the little sheriff managed to allay the other man’s suspicions and convince him that they were both on the same mission.

“I haven’t seen hide nor hair of Cutbill,” Martin told Allen in a worried voice. “I guess the gang nabbed him.”

"You got any suspicions as to the traitor up in the office?" Jack asked.

"Nope. If I had, I'd be hunting the dirty rat to choke the life out of him. If the gang got Cutbill, that makes the fourth murder he's to be thanked for," Martin said wrathfully.

Allen looked at the young operator speculatively. He decided that the man had nerve, but little brains or discretion, so he refrained from mentioning his own suspicions of O'Brien. That decision was to have far-reaching results and to bring Allen close to death itself.

"There's no doubt but what the headquarters of the bunch is in the Bucket of Blood," Martin went on. "I figure that a sheriff called Black Steve is in with them, an' if he is, it would be easy for them to get the stuff to the edge of the country. Then, there's Little Billy, Shanghai Pete, Lily Joe, and a Chinaman called How See, but I haven't a suspicion as to the big boss. From something some liquored greasers let drop one night, I figured him to be a chink, but it doesn't seem natural for white men to be taking orders from a yellow one."

Allen agreed with Martin. Then he told him about the trail that he and the old outlaw had discovered.

"So that's how they get it over the border!" Martin grunted. "Now we've got to find how they get it out of town and then follow them to their distributing stations."

Allen arranged to meet the operator at Bell's house on the following morning. Then the little sheriff left the restaurant and joined the old outlaw at the Bucket of Blood.

He repeated the gist of his conversation with Martin and asked the Kid if he had ever heard of a Chinaman who might be the big boss.

Bell shook his head. "Nope. But I recollect now that 'Baboon' Connelly did warn me to watch out for Charlie, that fat chink, 'cause while he warn't very dangerous hisself, he had some pals what was real bad hombres. An' Baboon don't talk loose."

"An' to think I let that chink out of my hands," Allen said regretfully.

"What we got to do is to find a way into those back rooms," Bell suggested.

They waited until they thought the evening uproar in the saloon would drown any noise they might make trying to force their way into the rear, then slipped out the front door and into the alley. The door in the fence was still locked, and as they saw it was impossible to scale the fence, they decided to investigate the building on the other side.

This was built on exactly the same lines as the Bucket of Blood, but it was unused and in ruins. They could see the sky through the gaps in the roof, which had fallen in and littered the floor. It was desperately dark in the old building, and the dense blackness gave both men an eerie and uncomfortable feeling.

Step by step they moved along, groping through the dark with their hands. They came to an abrupt halt as a warning rattle reached them, and stood rigid, scarcely daring to breathe, until a faint, slithering noise told them that the snake had moved out of their path. At last they came to the door which, as in the saloon, led to the passage and back rooms. The place was a regular snake den, but each time they heard the warning rattle, the reptile moved out of their path.

Suddenly Jack grasped his companion's arm and pointed excitedly. "Look," he whispered, "there on the wall."

They were standing in the doorway of a large room and high on the opposite wall they saw the faint outline of light that came through a large crack in the wall.

After a prolonged search they found two timbers which they propped against the wall to serve as ladders. Jack scrambled up like a cat and laid his ear against the crack. He could hear muffled voices, which gradually became clearer until he could make out words and sentences. He listened until the light went out, and he judged the men had retired, then jumped down.

"I didn't hear nothin' startlin'," he reported. "But enough to know that the gent we's huntin' is in there. I hears them say the boss is some scared, and I figures his name is Quong. That means he's a chink.

"One gent, who sounds like a Negro, says that if the boss is too scared to run in some of the stuff they'd better tend to it themselves. So we got to listen here day an' night, an' when they gets ready to run it, we'll nab 'em," Jack finished.

The following morning, Dick Martin arrived at Bell's house. As soon as Jack introduced the handsome operator to Mary, he began to regret it, for he was sure that she would be captivated by his good looks.

Day after day slipped by, and the men took turns listening at the wall of the ruined building, while the two who were off duty haunted the various saloons and restaurants, listening and watching. Their list of suspected members increased, but for over a week their eavesdropping brought no definite results.

Jack Allen, meanwhile, found himself falling in love with Mary. He fought against it, for he felt that he had no right to ask any woman to share his life. He was sure, too, that she was interested only in Martin, and he almost grew to hate the good-looking operator. Had he been more experienced in the ways of women, he might have seen that his chances were more than fairly good, for though the girl also fought against her growing affection for him, there were times when her heart was in her eyes.

At times the girl felt that she understood the little man, and her heart would go out to him in his desperate loneliness, but at others she would remember that he was the Killer Wolf — for she still believed him to be Jim — and recalling tales of his savage ruthlessness, she would shrink away from him.

At first Kid Bell had been the leader of the three men, but little by little Jack Allen had usurped his place, for he was a born leader. Martin felt an instinctive antipathy toward the little sheriff and chafed under his orders, but there was something in Allen's eyes that kept him from open rebellion.

It was Martin who first was responsible for Jack's discovering the report of his brother's death. Mary said something to him about Jim-twin Allen, and the operator replied sneeringly:

"Say, this fellow isn't the Wolf. He's good with a gun, but not in the same class with the Wolf when he was living. You know they shot him off a shelf into Sheer Rock Canyon about a week ago."

Mary caught her breath, and a feeling of huge relief surged through her. So this was Jack, the Wyoming sheriff and marshal, and not Jim, the outlaw. That accounted for many little things she had been puzzled about. A short time afterward, she surprised Jack by laying her hand on his arm and saying softly: "I'm glad you're not Jim."

"Who told you?"

"Dick Martin."

"Why are you glad?" he asked her. "Jim's all right."

Color stained her cheeks, and for a moment she did not answer. "I didn't mean that. But uncle told me about that poor girl, 'Snippets.' You know they've loved each other for years. It must be terrible to love a man that you can't ever marry. And how awful she must feel now that he's dead!"

"What? Jim dead!" He seized her roughly by the arm, and the expression on his face was horrible to see. Then he whirled to face the Kid, who had just stepped onto the porch. "What's this about Jim?" he demanded hoarsely.

"Look here, Jack, don't go off half cocked. I didn't tell you, 'cause I was afraid that you'd drop your work here an' go gunnin' for the gents what did it." Briefly the Kid explained the rumor of how Jim had been shot.

Jack stood like a man in a trance for a minute, then he flipped out his guns and stared at them stupidly. Suddenly he swung about and started for the opening in the mesquite. With a cry, Bell caught hold of him. Martin came to his aid, and between them they managed to hold him. Kid Bell pleaded and argued for an hour before Jack calmed down and agreed to wait until he had finished the dope runners. When he had entered the house, Mary crept to the door of his room and listened, and tears came to her eyes as she heard his terrible sobbing.

Day after day Quong sat in his glorious room, inventing and discarding plans. This time there must be no error, and he tried to think of something that could not be marred by the human equation. He had tried by means both of bribes and threats to get his men to attack Allen, but they had refused.

"This quarrel is personal between Charlie and the Wolf, an' I ain't hornin' in. I've seen gents draw on Allen, an' their mouths is full of dirt," Shanghai Pete declared, and the other outlaws agreed with him. If forced to, they would fight, but not otherwise.

Then something happened that brought a glint to Quong's lusterless eyes. One of his guards entered hastily one day, followed by a small, bow-legged man, and Shanghai Pete and Lily Joe. The small man talked hastily for several minutes.

"Yeah, I seen him next door," he concluded. "I heard some one move in the back room, so I walks back there. A gent lights a match, an' I see that dumb United States agent, Martin. I waits an' see him climb up the side wall an' put his head against a lighted crack. He was listenin' to the boys in their room."

"Let's go nab him," Lily Joe growled.

Quong silenced the Negro with a gesture and rapidly outlined a plan. The burly outlaws listened with growing satisfaction, and when he had finished, they swung from the room to carry out their part. Fifteen minutes later, they returned.

"He fell for it an' dusted out for the Kid's like a scared rabbit," Lily Joe reported jubilantly.

At dusk the following evening, Lily and Shanghai saw Martin, Allen, and the Kid meet about half a mile from town and ride west. Half an hour later, at the head of ten heavily armed but nervous riders, Lily and Shanghai swung along the same trail.

Quong had received the news that a new shipment of opium was to arrive on that same evening, and so jubilant was he at the working out of his plans that he arranged to have Mary Bell kidnaped while his gunmen were out tracking Allen. He sat in his room, smoking cigarette after cigarette, and dreaming rosy dreams. Then, swiftly as an eagle flies, came disaster.

First came a wounded man who had acted as one of the guards for the shipment of opium.

"The Wolf jumped us at the entrance to Monument Canyon. He dropped 'Big Tom' and 'Greasy Steve' afore we knew he was near, then Little Billy goes down, an' I lights out for here," the man explained wearily.

"The Wolf! You are crazy — you dream dreams! The Wolf was here in town at dusk. Is he a grasshopper that he can jump over mountains?" Quong asked coldly.

"I seen the Wolf plenty an' I knows him. I tell you it was him. He laughed that devil's laugh of hisn," the man repeated stubbornly.

"Where is the opium?" demanded Quong with anguish in his voice.

"I tell you, the Wolf got it," the fellow insisted.

Quong's eyes glittered. "Lies are the color of blood," he purred softly.

The man's scream rang out as Quong's robe stirred; there was a flash of silver across the room, and he slumped to the floor.

Quong rose to his feet and recovered his blade from the twitching body. Then he glanced down at it regretfully. "What have you done, drinker of blood? A man may not speak from heaven."

The lost shipment had been worth twenty thousand dollars, and now because of his hasty action in killing the man whom he thought had stolen it, Quong had lost all chance of recovering it, for no torture could make a dead man speak. He was still brooding over the stained blade when the two men he had sent to kidnap the girl returned and reported that, though they had searched all through the house, they had been unable to find her.

"An' we got out just in time, 'cause the Wolf is out front now," the spokesman ended.

Quong staggered and sat down weakly on a chair.

"An' he told Scarface to look in the band stand in half an hour," the second man added. "an' he says to tell Black Steve that he aims to provide wings for all the gents what had a hand in the killin' of his horse, just like he did Little Billy."

Little Billy had been with that shipment of dope. If the Wolf were out there, perhaps the man he had killed had not lied, after all, thought Quong. But it was impossible — a man could not be in two places at once.

But when he heard what it was that the Wolf had left in the ruined band stand, he was filled with the same superstitious fear that had turned his men from ferocious killers into frightened rabbits.

The day after Jack Allen heard about Jim's death, he saddled Honey Boy, and, without telling the others of his intentions, rode out along the Goat Trail. He found the place where Jim had gone over, then hunted around until he found a path down the canyon wall. Painstakingly he searched every crevice, but he could find no trace of his brother's body. Finally he returned to El Crucifixo, where he found momentous news awaiting him.

"The gal's gone," old Bell told him. "My brother showed up, an' he an' his partner is stayin' in Jim's old place which is so well hidden that a million men couldn't find it. Martin went along with 'em, an' he says it's perfectly safe. Mary told me to tell you to come an' see her," he added carelessly.

In one way Allen was relieved, for he had worried a lot about leaving the girl. Nevertheless, he felt lonely.

He was aroused from his thoughts by Dick Martin, who came dashing into the inclosure.

"Get on your saddles, gents, they're goin' to move some stuff to-night," he cried excitedly.

It had been Martin's watch in the old building. He had grown tired of waiting and had descended from his post to seek solace in a cigarette, though smoking had been banned. Just after he had lighted the match, he had heard a muffled footstep in the hall, but as he had listened intently and heard nothing further, he decided that it was a rat. After he had again climbed to the beam, he had heard the mutter of men's voices, which soon became distinct enough for him to make out everything they said.

"It was Lily Joe an' Shanghai Pete. They're goin' to where the border trail crosses the one to Stony Hill. There's a big red butte there where they're goin' to meet the Mexes what's bringin' the stuff over the border. They're to be there at twelve o'clock," he told the others jubilantly.

At dusk the three men left town by devious routes to meet at a given point half a mile away. From there they followed the main trail. Martin wanted to push straight on to their destination and wait near the butte, but Allen, afraid that they might frighten their quarry, insisted on turning off the trail at the first convenient place and hiding in the brush. Shortly thereafter, a group of horsemen dashed by, spurs tinkling and leather groaning. It was too dark for them to distinguish the riders, but they saw that the men looked grim and foreboding.

When they had passed, Allen insisted on circling through the brush instead of following the main path, and though the trails through the mesquite crossed and crisscrossed in a bewildering manner, he picked his way along as surely as a wild animal. As they neared the butte, the little man left his two companions and slipped ahead to reconnoiter. He returned in an hour.

"It's a trap," he reported in disgust. "They've got six men hiding by the trail, and six more on tother side the butte."

The others were dumfounded. "They either knows we was listenin' or they seen us leave town," said the Kid sourly.

They were tired and disgruntled when they returned to town. Jack rode along in silence, his mind bitter and his heart heavy with thoughts of Jim. He was full of impatience to finish this job so that he could start on the trail of his brother's murderers.

As the three reached El Crucifixo, they saw a crowd milling about the ruined band stand in the center of the plaza. Some of the men carried lanterns and by their light were excitedly inspecting a figure which dangled from the roof.

Jack was too weary and dispirited to be curious, and he turned sharply to the right and headed for the Kid's house. His companions, however, spurred across to join the crowd.

They gaped at the figure and read the placard on its breast, then with one accord wheeled after Jack. The Kid was spluttering with excitement.

"Jack! Jack! Dang me, if I ain't tickled pink! That gent what got his neck stretched is Little Billy, an' there's a sign pinned to him what says:

> "Here's one coyote to pay for Apple Pie. It'll take three more to square the bill.

"An' it's signed — Jim-twin Allen!"

Jack stared at the Kid for a moment without understanding.

"Don't you savvy?" the Kid yelled. "Them folks back there think you done it — but you didn't. So it means that Jim somehow got clear an' never went down that canyon. An' he's alive — alive!"

CHAPTER ELEVEN

The Wolf's Help

On that moonlit night when Jim Allen and his gray had been shot off the ledge, Pop and Skinny had stood for many moments peering sadly down at the spot where the two had gone over. Suddenly Skinny cried out and staggered backward. Old Pop seized him, thinking that he had an attack of dizziness, but Skinny shook him off and pointed with a trembling hand down into the depths.

"He's down there," he faltered at last, "stuck on a cholla like a frog."

Directly below the spot where Jim had gone over, the cliff was split by a great crack which time had filled with sand and dirt. A cholla seed had somehow been carried there in years past, and it had grown and flourished until at last, with its roots reaching far into the cliff, it had attained gigantic proportions. Allen had miraculously fallen across the stem of the plant, close to the face of the cliff, and though the shock of his fall had made it sag and tremble, the cholla had held his weight, and its cruel thorns now gripped him as firmly as the tentacles of an octopus.

The two old men called out to him, and at last were rewarded by a faint cry.

"Get a rope, you old galoots, an' stop talkin', I'm all punctured like a pincushion."

"Danged if they can kill the Wolf," Pop breathed, with pride and joy in his voice.

"Stop your gabbin' an' hustle," Allen called and let out a stream of oaths.

"He ain't hurt bad if he can cuss as good as that," Skinny cried gladly, as he trotted off toward the camp.

Half an hour later, he returned with a coil of rope fastened to Mary Anne's back. The task was a difficult and dangerous one, but at length they had a loop fastened around Allen's shoulders, and, with the aid of the mule, hoisted him to the ledge. His face was twisted with pain and showed the color of paper. His teeth were clenched, and his forehead was covered with beads of perspiration. He gave one faint moan, as their friendly hands seized him, then lapsed into unconsciousness.

"Great gosh!" Skinny gasped, as he pointed to Allen's back and thighs.

His shirt was crimson-stained, and his back was literally covered with balls of the poisonous, barbed thorn. The prick of that thorn is more painful than a hornet's sting, and as they are barbed like the quill of a porcupine, considerable force is required to pull them out.

"It must have hurt him like old billy, when we pulled him out," Pop whispered. "I remember when I got my knee full of the dang things, an' I had to drink a quart of liquor 'fore I got nerve to pull 'em out. An' here he's full of 'em an' never peeped."

A swift examination showed them that Allen had received no bullet wounds. After pulling the worst of the burrs from his back, they put him on the mule, and while Pop led her down the trail, Skinny returned to the camp to pack the burro, for they had decided to get off the ledge in case the outlaws returned.

Two hours later, Skinny, driving the burro and packing some of the equipment himself, caught up with Pop. Allen had few periods of consciousness, but during those lucid intervals he managed to direct them along the maze of trails that led to his house. It was close to dawn when they reached it and found the ancient Indian who acted as a sort of caretaker during Allen's absences.

The Indian promptly took charge of the little outlaw. His clothes were stripped off, and then, with the aid of a pocketknife and a pair of small plyers, they started to extract the terrible thorns. As each one came out, a bit of flesh clung to its barb, but the Indian washed the countless punctures and covered them with a green lotion which he had brewed.

"Him heap sick from poison — maybe die. But him heap strong like lobo — maybe live," the Indian said when he had finished.

For three days, the little outlaw raved in delirium, and at times the three men watching over him would choke, and their eyes would fill with tears.

On the sixth day, he tottered to his feet. Fever had reduced him to a mass of muscle and bone, and his back was still filled with tiny, festering wounds that burned like hot needles, but he made no complaint. He recovered from the poison at a rate which was miraculous. On the eight day, the little outlaw held a long conversation with the old Indian, then went to the stable and saddled Princess, his beloved old mare.

"Old Mud-in-the-face tol' me his great grandson tol' him that some gents has cut a trail from the blind end of Monument Canyon through the mesquite to El Crucifixo. I'm ridin' down that way to have a look at it, 'cause I figures maybe that's the way these dope runners get their stuff in," he told the partners.

"You ain't strong enough, Jim," protested Skinny.

"Reckon I am. It's about time I collected for Apple Pie. He was a right nice colt," Allen replied quietly. "Skinny, you go down and get that gal, an' bring her here," he added, as he swung into the saddle.

Skinny departed for El Crucifixo, and with little trouble managed to locate Kid Bell. The brothers' faces were expressionless as they met.

"Ain't seen you for ten years," Skinny said unemotionally. "Still outlawin', you old rascallion?"

"Sure, an' you're still chasin' rainbows in the desert, I see," his brother retorted.

Mary objected strenuously when the Kid told her she was to go away. But the Kid was perfectly firm and explained that any day both he and the two government men — Allen and Martin — might be obliged to take a long trip.

"But I'll send Jack over to visit you right often," he chuckled in parting.

The girl flared up at once. "He needn't come unless he wants to," she said.

It was close to midnight when Jim Allen returned to his house after his ride south. The girl, peering from a window, saw the gray and heard Allen's voice, and reflected with pleasure that it hadn't taken Jack long to visit her.

"Have any luck?" she heard Skinny ask.

"Yeah. Ran into a bunch of buzzards with a lot of dope. One of 'em called hisself Little Billy, an' as he had the gun I lost up on the ledge, I makes him the first payment for Apple Pie," Allen replied carelessly.

Mary knew what he meant by the first payment, and she shuddered at the casualness with which he spoke. She threw herself on the bed and burst into tears, wondering why men were so hard and cruel.

The next morning she found the little man she supposed to be Jack strangely lacking in that dignity she had admired so much, yet he seemed more wistful than usual, and she longed to smooth his rumpled hair and stroke his head.

He rode away after breakfast, and she did not see him again until dark. She noticed that he looked tired and summoned a smile only with an effort. The first time they were alone together, she said in a tone of gentle reproof:

"Jack, you can't fool me. I know you're still grieving about poor Jim."

Jim blinked and stuttered, then suddenly enlightenment came to him. The night before, Skinny had informed him that Jack was in El Crucifixo, masquerading as his outlaw brother. Apparently Jack and the girl were on very good terms. Jim Allen wondered if they were perhaps more than friends, and since she so evidently believed him to be Jack, he decided to have some fun.

"Yeah, you're right. Jim ran with a wild bunch, but he was all the folks I had," he said sadly and let out a heavy sigh. He was glad that the darkness hid the mischief in his eyes, but he felt a little guilty when he remarked the tremor in her voice as she laid her small hand on his arm.

"I know you're alone, but — but — well, *you* shouldn't be ashamed of your past life, you should be proud of it," she ended in a rush.

That sounded as if she were "stuck" on Jack and were trying to encourage him to speak up, Allen thought. He chuckled as he reflected that perhaps he ought to give his brother a boost.

"You mean that my life ain't been so terrible but what I could ask a gal to marry me?" he asked.

"Why, lots of girls —" she began, then quickly changed the subject. "Have you ever seen Jim's place in the Painted Desert? Tell me about it."

"It's a pretty place," he said slowly. "Kind of a sunken mesa, with walls a couple of hundred feet high all around it, an' full of flowers an' grass an' trees. There's a brook with trout, an' lots of deer an' birds. An' there's about twenty gray horses in it, an' two of

’em is the most stuck-up little colts you ever seen. They walk around like they owned the place, an’ you should see ’em eat pie.” Allen had forgotten the pretense of being his brother now, and talked on, more to himself than to the girl.

“It’s sort o’ funny how a fellow will dream about things. Just ’fore you get to the valley, you go through Devil’s Canyon, then you start climbin’ up and up, an’ the moonlight comes down so’s it almost seems as though you’re climbin’ on moonbeams. I never go up it without wonderin’ how a gal would like it, ’cause at the top is the place. But it’s darn lonely, an’ I reckon it would be too lonely for a woman.”

The girl caught the forlorn hopelessness in his voice. It was infinitely sad, yet held no bitterness, and as she listened, the tears came to her eyes, and she timidly closed her fingers about his hand.

“It wouldn’t be lonely there. I’d go with you,” she said softly.

With a start, Jim came back to reality. He had forgotten her in his dreaming of another girl, and now he realized that he had got Jack in deeper than he had intended.

“Shucks, you don’t know me!” he said, with a laugh. “Why, I’m the most conceited, bumptious little cuss. Do you know that I wear eight-inch heels, an’ whiskers, an’ a hat big enough for a giant, to make me look man-sized? Yes, sir, I’m plumb filled with dignity an’ vanity.”

For a moment, Mary was hurt at his quick change of mood, then she laughed softly at him. Allen whistled, and Princess, who was saddled, trotted to his side. He swung into the saddle and looked down at her.

"Now promise me somethin'. You stay right here, an' the next time I see you, remin' me to ask you somethin' about who we was talkin' about to-night."

"I promise, but I think I could answer it now," she replied.

"No, you do it the next time you see me," he said hastily. And before she could protest, he leaned swiftly down and kissed her full on the mouth.

With that he was gone. As he spurred along the trail to El Crucifixo, he reflected that he was almost her brother-in-law, so it was all right.

Arriving in town, the little outlaw went straight for Bell's place, and as he turned down the path, he loosed the thin, wavering howl of the wolf. He grinned happily as an answer came from within the house.

The meeting of the Allen brothers was as casual as had been the one between Skinny and the Kid. Jim slipped from his saddle, and the two looked at each other silently.

"Huh! Heard you was crow bait," Jack cried at last.

"Gosh, you look funny without them whiskers," Jim retorted. Then in mocking reproof he added: "What you mean comin' down here playin' you're me?"

Rapidly Jack explained, then jerked his thumb in the direction of Bell, who waited in the shadow of the house. "He's helpin' me."

Jim nodded coldly at the old outlaw. "That's sure funny, you two huntin' them gents, an' me doin' the same thing," he said. He, in turn, explained his experience in falling over the cliff. Then the three entered the house to compare notes.

"Jim, let's you an' me let bygones be bygones until this here thing is over," Bell suggested, and the little outlaw agreed.

They talked over their plans and suspicions, and at length decided that it would be good strategy to keep secret from every one, including Martin the mystery of the Wolf's ability to be in two places at once. Suddenly Jim chuckled.

"Jack, *she* thinks I'm you, so we got to change places to-night."

Jack looked at his brother suspiciously, but the little outlaw's face was guileless. After he had ridden off, Jim turned to Bell with a broad grin.

"Let's you an' me go up to Dry Creek," he suggested. "I got a feelin' I'd better get out of here pronto. Is Jack sweet on that gal?"

"He sure is. He moons around here like a calf."

"Then that's all right," said Jim, with a sigh of relief, and told the old man how he had helped his brother along. The Kid's chuckles increased as the tale progressed, and when Allen had finished the tears were rolling down his cheeks.

CHAPTER TWELVE

O'Brien's Plan

For three days after the body of Little Billy was found swinging in the plaza, the rear rooms of the Bucket of Blood were in bedlam. Lily Joe, Shanghai Pete, and the other outlaws spent their time in drinking and swearing, while the Oriental members of the gang burned prayer slips and muttered incantations to dispel the evil *fengshui* of the Wolf's work. Fear had reduced Charlie to a gibbering maniac, and Quong had smuggled him out to one of their northern headquarters. He himself intended to abandon El Crucifixo as soon as he could make arrangements for the transportation of the fittings of his rooms, and the quantity of opium on hand.

Hatred of the Wolf had become an obsession with the old Chinaman. In a few short weeks, the diminutive outlaw had brought Quong's carefully built-up organization tumbling about his ears, and the men who, a few days before, had cringed before him, now sneered and refused to obey his orders. But on the fourth day, there happened that which again raised Quong's hopes. As he sat brooding in his room, the guard brought in a raggedly dressed, unkempt man whose hat was pulled low to hide his face. When the two were alone, the newcomer pulled off his hat, and Quong recognized O'Brien. The latter looked at the packing boxes in surprise.

"Why are you leaving here?" he asked.

Quong told him the whole bitter story, and when he finished, O'Brien laughed heartily.

"That's why I came down here," he said. "The Wolf's dead all right. It's his brother that's posing as him. I thought he suspected me and was only pretending to go north again." He explained rapidly the circumstances behind Jack's arrival, and the Chinaman listened in amazement, forgetting the recent mysterious deeds of the Wolf.

"You got four hombres you want to get rid of?" O'Brien asked suddenly.

"A dozen who have been insolent to me in my trouble," Quong replied vindictively.

"All right, pick out four. We'll fix up a lot of tins with burnt molasses to make it look like opium, an' shoot it up to Dry Creek with those hombres as a guard. I'll hunt up Allen an' tell him I'm down here because I've found how you ship the stuff. Then we'll ambush the four, an' wipe 'em out. Sheriff Jack'll think he's captured a big shipment an', since I put him wise to it, he'll forget his suspicions."

Quong mulled the plan over for a moment, then asked: "Why not kill this second Allen at once? When my men find he's not the Wolf or a ghost, they'll tear him to pieces at a word."

"That's just it. If another agent disappears down here, they'll send a troop of rangers to mop the place up. If I get Allen's confidence, I'll get him up in Black Steve's county. Steve, as sheriff, can kill him an' say he thought he was the Wolf."

When O'Brien had left him, Quong smiled contentedly and sent for Pete and Joe. Quickly he explained the situation to them and outlined O'Brien's plan. Shanghai Pete was wrathful.

"I ain't scared of no man but the Wolf," he cried. "An' any gent what scares me like this Jack Allen done has got to pay for it in lead." He was about to start out in immediate search of Allen, but Quong persuaded him to wait and carry out O'Brien's plan.

Jack Allen left Jim and Kid Bell with mixed feelings. He wanted to see Mary, but he also wanted to go with them to Dry Creek. He was suspicious of Jim, for he had caught him looking at him slyly several times and could not fathom his brother's expression.

It chanced that he and Mary had breakfast alone the next morning.

"Do you want me to keep my promise now?" she asked, blushing and smiling.

Jack questioned her with his eyes.

"You remember what we were talking about — and you told me to remind you to ask me something."

"I did?" Jack almost choked, as the truth began to dawn on him.

"And then you talked so foolishly. Why did you say that you were vain as a peacock, and wore high heels to make you look bigger?"

"Did I say that?" Jack stammered.

The girl looked at him in surprise. "Yes, but I don't believe you're a bit conceited, and I don't think you ever wore whiskers. Why do you joke that way?"

"What else did I say?" Allen asked miserably.

"Why, Jack, you didn't say anything, but you — Well, I suppose I ought to be angry, but I'm not."

"If I didn't say anything, I did something. What did I do?"

"Why, I don't think it's nice to kiss a girl, and then pretend you don't remember it," said Mary indignantly.

"I kissed you!" Jack roared. "Darn the little runt, I knew he was up to something. I'll bust his eyes out."

And before the girl had recovered from her surprise at his strange behavior, she saw him going at a gallop toward town.

When he arrived at Bell's place, the old outlaw was the only one home.

"Where's Jim?" Jack demanded.

"Trackin' some gents over in the Dead Men's Hills. What you want him for?" Bell asked.

"To give him the dangedest drubbin' he ever got in his life," Jack replied grimly, and his intention was written on his face.

He returned to Jim's house, and for two days lived in a haze, raging at Jim's nerve, partly because he lacked the courage to imitate him. On the afternoon of the third day, he rode again to Bell's house, but though Jim was absent, he found there some one who drove all thoughts of his brother from his mind.

Dick Martin and O'Brien were with Bell. As soon as Allen saw O'Brien, his eyes grew hard, but the government man stepped forward with outstretched hand.

"I'm down here to work with you," he said cordially. "I gathered that you took a dislike to me in Santa Fe, but let's try to be friends until this job's over."

Allen regarded him suspiciously and said nothing.

"Jack, what's bitin' you? This gent knows how the dope's run out," protested Bell.

"I'll bet he does," agreed Allen meaningly.

O'Brien shivered at the tone of his voice, and his smile was sickly. He knew that he had to convince Allen or his game would be a losing one. Swiftly he began to talk, and although his sentences were jerky at first, he speedily regained his self-confidence. He knew before he had finished that he had duped Martin and Bell, but Allen still regarded him with cold, expressionless eyes.

"Reckon that's the goods," Bell cried when he had finished. "You say they cache the stuff near Chimney Butte? I can find that blindfolded. There ain't nothin' to do but go out an' jump 'em when they dig it up. You say they ship it north every Wednesday night, an' this is Wednesday."

"A Mex in Dry Creek told you about this?" Allen asked, directly.

"Yes, he's been working for us for some time," O'Brien replied. Then he played his last card. "Look here, Allen. I'm giving you straight stuff, but if you imagine it's a trap, suppose you stay behind and let us handle this."

He could have said nothing which would have attained his object more quickly. Jack Allen was not the man to remain behind while others risked their necks.

"All right, we'll go," he said abruptly.

After dinner the four men threaded their way through the mesquite toward Chimney Butte. It was about ten when they reached their destination, and after a whispered consultation they decided to approach the rock from different directions. Bell and Martin were to attack from the west, while Allen, who had chosen O'Brien as his partner, was to come in from the east.

Allen and O'Brien crawled forward across the smooth sand, and presently Allen gave a faint warning hiss. Shortly there came the sound of horses' hoofs beating across the sand. Then the watchers could make out four blurred shapes and catch the guarded talk of the riders. Creaking leather told them that the men were dismounting.

Suddenly Bell's voice rang out through the night: "Give it to 'em!"

The darkness was torn by the roar of Colts and screams of fear and surprise. One of the outlaws managed to reach his horse and fling himself into the saddle, but Jack Allen's gun spoke, and horse and rider crashed to the ground. O'Brien caught sight of one of the men crawling away, and whipping out his gun, fired twice. The figure collapsed and lay still.

"We got 'em all," Martin exulted. "An' there's about twenty thousand dollars' worth of stuff here."

In spite of himself, Allen had to admit that his judgment of O'Brien had been wrong. As Martin had said, there was a fortune in dope here, and had the operator been a member of the gang he would not have helped them capture it. They carried the tins over to the brush and burned them, and since Quong had been clever enough to put a small quantity of opium in each tin, the sweet odor of the burning drug was plainly noticeable.

The following day, O'Brien sneaked into Scarface's saloon and reported his success to Quong.

"Swallowed it — hook, line, an' sinker," he boasted. "An' Mr. Jack Allen's so sorry he distrusted me that he's eatin' from my hand."

"And when does he kiss his ancestors?" Quong purred.

"The sooner the better. He and Bell figure this is the first stage of the underground opium trail, so they're hittin' for Death Mesa to uncover the second. They're going to make their headquarters the other side of Dry Creek and bring the girl up there."

"The rose blossom has vanished completely," said Quong regretfully. "I must have her."

"You want her for Charlie." O'Brien grinned knowingly. "I guess I can find her. Bell and Allen won't tell me where she is, but Martin knows, and I'll get it out of him. You going to use her as bait, too?"

"To lead Jack Allen to Black Steve. After that there will be a very grand wedding, and Charlie will smile again."

After he had left Quong, O'Brien hunted up Martin, whom he found in one of the Mexican restaurants. The burly man ordered a glass of wine, and for a time the two talked of various matters.

"Where does this girl of yours hide out?" O'Brien remarked casually. "How about goin' out to see her this afternoon?"

Martin shook his head.

"What's the matter? Aren't you allowed to go and see her alone?"

"I'm my own boss," Martin declared angrily.

"Don't look like it. Of course, if Allen forbids you, that settles it."

"Like blazes it does!" Martin flared. He was tired of taking orders from Jack Allen, and though he had given his word not to tell Mary's hiding place to any one, he decided suddenly to follow his own wishes for a change. Besides, he argued to himself, O'Brien was a friend. What harm could there be in it?

"Come on," he declared. "I'll show you the prettiest girl in seven States."

As they passed the Bucket of Blood on their way to Bell's house, O'Brien drew a handkerchief from his pocket and allowed it to dangle in his right hand. A Mexican who had been lounging in the doorway of the saloon, vanished at once into the interior, reappearing a moment later with four of his countrymen. They mounted horses at the hitching rack and rode slowly out of town. They hid in the brush until Martin and his companion passed, then started to follow.

Martin had some difficulty in finding his way through the blind trails that led to Jim's house, but eventually he found the right path, and they soon were dismounting before the door.

"What you bring that gent here for?" Pop demanded sharply.

"He's all right," Martin replied, with a carelessness he did not feel. "Where's the girl?"

"Inside," the old prospector replied.

Suddenly a voice from behind them cried out: "Reach for the sky, hombres, queeck!"

The four men faced about to find themselves confronted by five Mexicans, all with guns in their hands. Martin snatched at his gun, but O'Brien restrained him.

"Don't be a fool," he hissed. "Let them have our money. You haven't a chance."

Martin realized that the other was at least partly right, and relaxed.

Swiftly three of the Mexicans began to bind them hand and foot, and had trussed up all but old Pop when the other two ruffians appeared in the doorway dragging the girl. Pop realized then what they were after, and with an oath, he leaped at the man nearest him. The man's gun cracked, and Pop slumped face down upon the ground. O'Brien pretended to struggle frantically with his bonds, cursing the Mexicans in a loud voice, and Martin sobbed with despair as he watched the men put Mary, who had fainted, across the leader's saddle and ride away.

The sun had climbed and was beating down blisteringly on their exposed faces when a small man on a gray horse rode into the clearing.

"Jack," wailed Martin, "they've got Mary!"

"An' the skunks have murdered Pop," cried Skinny.

The rider dismounted and, dropping to his knees, examined Pop. Then he freed Skinny and the other two. They carried Pop into the house and carefully dressed his wounds, then the little gunman turned to them.

"S'pose you tell me about it," he said.

Both Martin and Skinny broke into a voluble account. Abruptly Allen turned to Martin.

"Weren't you told not to bring any one here?" he asked.

"Yeah. Oh, I acted like a fool, but O'Brien teased me, an' — I deserve anything you do to me," he ended miserably.

"Nonsense!" O'Brien blustered. "Those Mexes have probably been watchin' the place."

"Yeah?" said Allen softly. "Why did you tease this fool kid into bringin' you out here?"

"So you still suspect me?" O'Brien said, trying to keep his voice steady. "After the other night, I sure figured you'd stop that foolishness."

"O'Brien's all right," said Martin impatiently. "Let's quit scrappin' and go after the Mexes."

"Me an' old Mud-in-the-face has been tracking them. We sees their tracks on the way out here," Allen explained and turned to O'Brien. "Why did you tease this kid into bringin' you here?"

"Heard she was a pretty girl. Look here, Jack, you —"

Allen interrupted, and though his grin was broader, his eyes were flecked with yellow.

"But I'm not Jack — I'm Jim," he said slowly.

Skinny cackled shrilly. Martin's eyes widened in horror, and O'Brien, white as paper, glanced wildly about as if seeking a means of escape.

"The Wolf! You're the Wolf? But he's dead," Martin gasped.

"Some folks call me the Wolf, but I'm plumb sure I ain't dead," Allen replied, and turned to face the Indian who had entered the door.

"Five meet one. They go north, go south, go east, go west — all go different," the red man grunted.

"There ain't no good chasin' them then. Reckon we'll find where they went nearer home, 'cause I figured Mr. O'Brien knows," Allen stated.

"Me? You're crazy. How —"

Allen silenced him. "Of course, you're the traitor Jack was tellin' me about. You fooled him, but you can't fool me, 'cause I knowed you when you had another name. Remember that little Indian boy that saved you the time you was lost in the desert? You knew he wasn't the kind that would kill an old lady, or he wouldn't have risked his life savin' you, but to get a measly two hundred dollars reward, you turned him over, an' he was hung. I know you, an' you're goin' to tell me where Quong took that girl."

"Try and make me," O'Brien flared.

"Martin, fetch that stake and chain from the shed there," directed Allen. "The rest of you get on hosses an' follow me."

A few minutes later, they all left the clearing. Allen zigzagged until the others had lost all sense of direction. At last he turned into a cleared circle in the center of which was a huge mound. They all knew what it was — an ant hill — but it was that which littered the slope of the hill that made them gasp. The bleached bones of a man were scattered there. Allen strolled forward, and, picking up a smooth skull, held it out to O'Brien.

"You know him?" he asked, and there was something horrible in his voice. "He was a gent by the name of Cutbill."

Martin cried out in horror, and O'Brien choked. The sight of the bleached bones had completely unnerved him.

"You betrayed him, and those devils tied him to that hill. I'm goin' to spread-eagle you there, unless you talk dang quick," Allen snapped.

"No, no!" O'Brien screamed. "I'll tell you everything, if you don't do that." He dropped to his knees, whimpering. Then he talked, told all that he knew and gave names and addresses. He was so abject that Martin almost felt sorry for him, but Allen's face was relentless.

"The girl will be taken either to the abandoned monastery in Santa Fe, or their place in Winton?" he asked at length.

O'Brien nodded fearfully. "They're goin' to use her as a bait for Jack," he stammered.

In a flash, Allen's mood changed. "Time's precious," he snapped. "Martin, ride to Gloster pronto. Get hold of Jack and tell him things. Tell him to watch the place in Santa Fe. You all can take the train. I'll have to ride, or they'll lock me up. I'll ride to Winton, see Charlie, and get the girl if she's there. When you get to Santa Fe, leave a message for me with Mike Casey at Torreno, just outside of Santa Fe. Got that all straight?"

Martin nodded and threw himself into the saddle, and the three returned at a gallop to the house, leaving behind O'Brien and the old Indian. As they were making their last preparations, Martin asked suddenly:

"What you goin' to do with O'Brien?"

"Nothin'," replied the little outlaw as he swung to the back of Princess. "Mud-in-the-face will take care of him. You see, he's the granddad of the little Indian boy I was tellin' you about." With that he was gone. Honey Boy following him like a dog.

Day came, then night, and then another day, but still Jim Allen pointed his course north. He rode the two grays turn and turn about, and they continued for miles like two machines. A short stop for water or grass and they were off again.

It was night when Allen finally reached Winton. He approached cautiously the house that O'Brien had told him of. There was only one light burning in an upper room. Like a shadow Allen slipped through a window and climbed the stairs. He crept along the darkened hall, until he came to a brilliantly lighted room, and peering in, saw Charlie, smoking an opium pill. The pudgy Chinaman squealed in terror, as Allen stepped into the room, and ducked toward another door. There was a steely flash, and Charlie dropped to the floor, clawing at the knife in his neck. A gun might have brought assistance, so Allen had used the silent weapon.

"Where's the girl?" the outlaw demanded.

"In Santa Fe — safe," gasped Charlie.

Without another word, Allen swung about and retreated the way he had come. He knew that there was nothing to be done for the Chinaman, for he would be dead in a few moments.

It was dusk of the following day when Jim Allen reached Mike Casey's in Torreno and found there a message from Jack that sent him spurring the grays toward Santa Fe, fifteen miles away.

"Come on, Princess," he pleaded. "That fool Jack is goin' to try an' get the girl to-night, an' that dang chink is usin' her as bait for Jack. Come on, old gal, shake your legs. I know you're tired, but we've got to get there."

He pleaded and urged, and Honey Boy as well as the mare responded with their mile-eating gallop.

CHAPTER THIRTEEN

A Harsh Fate

Jack Allen listened in some silence while Martin told his story, and as the young operative held nothing back and did not attempt to exonerate himself, Allen refrained from reproof and even stopped Bell when the old outlaw began to hurl oaths at Martin.

"We all make mistakes," Jack said quietly.

They quickly arranged a disguise for Bell, and then the three rode to the railhead and took the train for Santa Fe. They knew that they could hope for no assistance from the police in their rescue of Mary, for at the first sign of the law, Quong would arrange for the girl to disappear.

They located the abandoned monastery on the outskirts of Santa Fe, situated on the same street as the Sad Night Saloon. It was a big, gloomy building, encircled on the three sides by high walls. The fourth side was flush with the street, and contained only three windows, high up and heavily barred, so that there was no chance of entering through them.

Martin was all impatience and for making a frontal attack, but Allen vetoed this plan.

"Quong might have Black Steve and the whole gang in there," he said, shaking his head. "They'd simply down us, and Mary would be lost."

The three were crouched in a fringe of shrubbery opposite the windows, and even as Allen spoke, two men came slowly down the street, rapped on the big gate in the wall, and a moment later disappeared within.

"Them was Shanghai Pete an' How See," Bell said. "Reckon the whole gang is in there, an' we're in for a scrap." He rubbed his hands joyfully in anticipation.

An hour slipped by, and it was growing toward dusk when Allen espied a handkerchief being waved from one of the upper windows. A second later, a face appeared, and a folded note curved from the window and fell to the road. Allen restrained the others from picking it up before dark lest they be seen, and they waited impatiently for the coming of night. At last they slipped from their hiding place and retrieved the paper, then, retiring to a safer distance, read it by the light of a match:

> JACK: Quong's men arrive to-morrow and are taking me away from here by a secret passage. Come quickly and bring the police.

"It's her handwritin' all right," Bell stated positively.

"That means we got to get her out to-night, before the rest of the gang gets here," decided Allen.

They dispatched a message to Jim at Mike Casey's and waited several hours in various bars until close to midnight. Then they started again for the abandoned monastery. One by one, with the aid of a rope, they cautiously climbed the wall and dropped down on the inner wall.

"Gents, I'm warnin' you, if you like that girl, do your best," Allen pleaded.

The blackness within the courtyard was intense, and several times Bell and Martin stumbled and bruised their shins on piles of debris. They crept along the wall, examining various doors and windows, but everything seemed to be securely barred. They were feeling very despondent, when suddenly, rounding a corner, they came on a small window that had been left ajar.

Allen studied it carefully for a moment before he mounted on Martin's shoulders and pushed it gently open. He listened, peering down into the blackness, but there was not a sound. Whispering to his companions, he dropped down to the floor, where the others joined him. Then they crawled forward through the darkness.

From the moment she recovered from her faint after being carried off by the Mexicans, Mary Bell had comforted herself with the thought that somehow Jack Allen would save her. Even when she saw Quong's evil, triumphant face, she did not lose faith. They had forced her to drink a glass of water that tasted bitter, and then she knew nothing until she awoke in the abandoned monastery. She was waited on by a fat, dirty Mexican girl, who would only reply with a grunt to Mary's pleas for help. Then, on her second day of confinement, the Mexican girl became suddenly voluble.

"To-morrow Quong's men come take you away from here to marry Charlie," she said gutturally.

Again Mary pleaded with her, offering her money for her help, but parrotlike, the girl repeated her sentence and left the room. She had played her part.

Later Mary was taken to another room. She sat disconsolately on the edge of her cot, and for the first time since her abduction, gave way to tears. Forced to marry Charlie — no, it would be better to die She stood up and glanced through the barred window, looking up and down the street in search of some one to whom she could appeal for help. Then she saw the familiar figure of Jack Allen.

A surge of relief swept over her. She sprang down and searched for something to write with. At length she found a dirty scrap of paper and a stub of pencil, and hastily scribbling a message, was about to throw it from the window when Black Steve burst in and tore it from her hand. She saw with bitter despair that the note was passed to Quong, who read it with ill-concealed joy. Then, while Black Steve held her so that she could make no outcry, Quong refolded the note and threw it from the window. She struggled valiantly, but Black Steve only laughed at her futile efforts.

Then he carried her along corridors, through an old chapel, and into a room fitted out in the most gorgeous Oriental luxury. Here she was left alone, and once more the terrified girl threw herself down and gave way to tears.

* * *

As she sat in the darkness on the pillowed couch in Quong Lee's private quarters, Mary's fears were more for Jack Allen than for herself. She felt that he would manage to free her, even though he lost his life in doing so, and it was that thought that made her tremble. Time after time she circled the room exploring with her hands for a possible exit in the walls. Even when she was convinced that there was none, she continued her circuit. It kept her mind off Allen and what he must face when he entered Quong's stronghold.

Suddenly the faint sound as of muffled drums reached her ears. She knew only too well that it was the noise of Colts in some distant part of the building, and waited, as silently as though turned to stone. Jack had made his attempt and been caught — that she knew. She strained her eyes through the darkness, fixing them on the farther wall, where she knew there must be an entrance. Either Quong's men or Jack Allen would come through that door, and if it were the former, everything was over, for Jack would be dead.

Minutes slipped by, then suddenly she caught the faint sound of shuffling feet, and a yellow crack appeared in the opposite wall. It widened, and for a moment she was blinded by the light of the two brilliant lamps that appeared in the opening.

She dashed her hand across her eyes and stared at the group of men who crowded into the room, and tears began to slip slowly down her ashen cheeks. It was Quong Lee and his satellites who stood there. Her gallant Jack must be dead!

Quong held one of the lamps, and she saw that behind him Black Steve and Shanghai Pete were carrying a Chinaman. Then came Lily Joe and How See, who carried the other lamp. The girl watched the procession with a strange and calm detachment. She noticed, without any feeling of hatred or triumph, the blood on the wounded Chinaman's face, and realized that he was fatally injured. She felt numb, as though her emotions had died, leaving only her intelligence alive.

The two outlaws carried the wounded man across the room and through an opening which appeared in the wall when Quong pressed a carved knob in the wainscoting. How See placed his lamp on the table, and the three — the girl, the Negro and the Chinese — waited silently until Black Steve and Shanghai Pete reëntered the room and closed the panel behind them. Black Steve rolled and lighted a cigarette, and his thick lips split in a broad grin.

"Your sweetie, Jack Allen, has sure got nerve," he informed the girl.

She looked at him wordlessly, but her eyes held a question.

"Him an' your uncle an' that fool Martin tried to bust in here," the outlaw went on derisively. "Quong's a foxy old devil. He let 'em walk right into the trap he had fixed for them."

"Then just naturally blew 'em right to smithereens," Shanghai added with a chuckle.

"Just the same, Allen sure was fast an' put up a heck of a fight," said Black Steve grudgingly. "Them guns of his was like machine guns, an' when he hit the floor, they was both empty."

"Well, if that cousin of Quong's cashes, any of the three what is still alive down there to-morrow will be sorry," interjected Lily Joe.

The only thing that registered on Mary Bell's tired brain was that Jack Allen was not dead. Her cheeks flamed suddenly with color, and she seized Black Steve's arm. "Then — Jack isn't dead?" she inquired eagerly.

"Girl big fool. If him dead, all same good for him. A man may die a thousand deaths and cry aloud to his gods," chanted How See contemptuously.

"What does he mean?" muttered the girl.

"He means that if Allen is alive, Quong will stake him to an ant hill or somethin' pleasant," replied Black Steve brutally. "We didn't bother to see how bad he's wounded."

"No, no!" the girl screamed, covering her face with her hands.

Almost as if in answer to her cry, there came again that far-off sound as of muffled drums. The four outlaws spun about toward the slit in the wall that marked the secret door. For one brief instant, they stood in indecision, then as the sound of firing ceased, they sprang toward the opening. Lily Joe was the first to reach it, and thrusting his hands into the aperture, he slid the panel hastily back. Gun in hand he leaped through, and the other three jumped forward to follow, but the panel had been pushed back with such force that it bounded back and closed with a click before they could get through.

Growling oaths, they attempted to force it open again, hurling themselves against the wall, but the panel was solid and refused to give.

"How See, do you know how this thing works?" howled Black Steve.

The Chinaman shook his head helplessly, and the three stared at each other in bewilderment. Shanghai Pete was the first to recover his wits.

"Get Quong!" he yelled excitedly, but How See seized his arm.

"Ching very sick. You make noise, maybe he die, and Quong be very angry," he warned.

"That's so," said Black Steve doubtfully. He backed against the wall and looked at Pete. "What we goin' to do?"

"Nothing to do but wait," said How See philosophically and squatted on a mat in the corner. The other two at last calmed down, and Black Steve seated himself beside Mary on the couch.

"Quong's goin' to send you over the border," he told her with an evil grin.

Though his words were enough to make the girl shudder with horror, she paid no attention to them, for her eyes were fixed fascinatedly on the panel, which inch by inch was sliding noiselessly open.

CHAPTER FOURTEEN

Rescue

Jim-twin Allen reined in close to the monastery wall and sat for several moments listening. He had no knowledge of whether Jack had already entered or not, and was still undecided as to his best course of action. The place was like a tomb completely dark and still. He leaned forward finally and whispered a command in Princess' ear, grinning boyishly when the mare flicked her ears as a sign that she understood. Carefully he stood up in the saddle and grasped the top of the wall with his hands. A minute later, he was lying flat along the top, peering down into the court.

"Back up, old lady," he whispered to the gray. "Get goin' now, that way." Princess drooped her head, then followed by Honey Boy, walked away from the wall and vanished into the darkness. When she had retreated about sixty yards, she stopped and waited.

Allen twisted around on his perch and, dropping lightly to the ground, headed toward the building.

"I'm in now, but how in blazes am I goin' to get out if Jack ain't here yet?" he chuckled to himself as he cautiously approached the monastery.

His eyes shone through the darkness like pools of fire as they searched every foot of the wall for a means of entrance, and any one glancing into the court would have been certain that a wild animal had strayed in there. At last he found what he sought — a small window that was open and unbarred. Though Jim did not know it, it was the very window through which Jack and his companions had gone a short fifteen minutes previously.

The little outlaw was still debating with himself as to whether he should go in or wait there for his brother, when the muffled roar of many Colts reached his ears. Even as his brain signaled to him that Jack had already arrived, he had lunged for the window and squirmed through. He landed lightly on the floor and raced down a long, flagged corridor in the direction from which the shots had sounded. As he reached the end of the passage, the shots suddenly ceased, and he had nothing left to guide him. He swung to his right and tiptoed across a chapel, and was close to the farther end when the confused sounds of voices reached him. He saw the reflection of lamps dance on the wall, and a narrow door was framed in light. He crouched behind a pile of débris, and in a moment Quong, carrying a lamp, stepped through the door. He was followed by Shanghai Pete and Black Steve carrying a wounded Chinaman, and behind them came Lily Joe and How See.

Allen's guns leaped to his hands, but before he had drawn back the hammers, his impulse to wipe out Quong died. Far wiser to try to rescue Jack if he were still alive, than to get Quong and possibly bring more members of the gang to the scene. He waited till the group had crossed the chapel and vanished down a passage to the right, then made his way through the door they had entered and down the corridor until he heard the renewed sound of voices. Peering around a corner, he saw a lighted doorway a few feet away and slipped noiselessly toward it. Reaching it, he peered into the big, bare room where Jack and the others had been surprised a few minutes earlier.

The room was lighted by a big oil lamp hung from the ceiling, and though the wick was smoking and the light dim, Allen could distinguish everything. His eyes fell first on Kid Bell, lying flat on his back, his face drawn and white with pain. The old outlaw breathed with difficulty, for he was choking to death from a lung wound, but his eyes were open. Two burly outlaws stood close to the door with their backs to it, and to their left Dick Martin and two other motionless figures lay face down on the floor. Behind them lay two more corpses, while two wounded men leaned against a wall and swore at their companion who was dressing their wounds. At first glance, Jim did not see his brother, and he had to step farther into the room to find him. Jack was lying on his back, his head crimsoned, and his mouth gaping open. By his side stood a tall, skinny outlaw watching another as he searched the little sheriff's limp figure.

It was Kid Bell who first spotted Jim Allen. He stared in amazement, then his eyes sparkled, and his lips drew back in a grin as the fearless little outlaw advanced.

As Jim-twin Allen stood there for one brief instant, glancing about that room so like a slaughter-house, he was neither man nor Killer Wolf, but an executioner. There were five men on their feet and two who, though wounded, might draw a gun. They all had to die, for Jack, if he were still alive, needed immediate medical assistance, and there was the girl to be found. Jim could leave no living enemy in his rear when he went to find her and to face Quong and the rest of the band. Quickly the Wolf glanced around the room, planning which of them should die first.

None of Quong's men in that room possessed that sixth sense so necessary to men who live by their guns — that sixth sense which makes it impossible for a man to be taken by surprise and which controls his muscles and nerves without a message from the brain.

Allen's guns came up slowly, evenly. Two streams of red fire flowed through blue smoke, and the crashing double report smashed against the walls of the room. The two outlaws nearest the door toppled over and crumpled face downward on the floor, dead instantly. The thin man standing beside Jack and the kneeling fellow both swung around, but they were stunned with astonishment and fear, and neither had made a move toward his gun when Jim Allen's Colts swung slowly about and roared forth their message of death.

As the two crashed to the floor, the fifth outlaw, who had also been temporarily paralyzed with surprise, dropped the bandages in his hand and grabbed at his gun. It came up and spit forth fire, but its report was but an echo to Jim's right-hand gun, and the man had pulled the trigger at his moment of passing.

It was then that one of the two wounded men against the wall made his fatal blunder. Had he not snatched at a gun on the floor, Jim Allen would never have fired at them, but at that motion his terrible guns swung up, steadied for a fraction of a second, then smoke and death leaped again from their muzzles. Jim stood like a graven image, peering through the whirling smoke, then leaped across the fallen bodies and, thrusting his still-smoking guns into their holsters, knelt beside his brother.

Kid Bell had lived hard, and his fighter's spirit exulted at the awful destruction he had witnessed. "Seven bullets, an' seven gents accounted for," he gasped gleefully. "That was some shootin', Wolf."

Allen made no reply. He was desperately, yet skillfully examining Jack's wounds, and so absorbed was he in his task that he failed to hear the running feet in the corridor. His back was to the door, and he did not see Lily Joe when the black-faced outlaw blundered into the room. At first the Negro was blinded by the acrid smoke, and when at last he was able to see, he, too, was stunned at the scene before him. At first glance every one in the room seemed to be dead. Terrified, he looked from body to body, then his eyes came to Jim Allen. His hand was shaking as he raised his gun.

His hesitation gave Kid Bell a last opportunity to help square his account. Summoning his last ounce of strength, he raised himself to his knees and snatched the heavy knife from the Negro's belt. With a cry half triumphant and have savage, he flung his arm up and drove the weapon into the black outlaw's back. Lily Joe echoed that cry with one of fear and agony and swayed on his feet.

At the first sound from Bell, Jim Allen had leaped sideways and twisted around, and even as the black uttered his death cry, Jim sent a slug tearing into his chest. Lily Joe and the Kid fell to the floor together, and though the Kid's eyes were glazing fast, they still flickered with savage joy as he looked up at Allen.

"Dang you, Wolf, that's the first bullet you ever wasted. He was dead afore you fired," he said and choked with the effort of speaking. "There ain't nothin' to be done for me," he went on, dashing the red froth from his lips. "Get the gal. She's up front in Quong's room."

Mary's first reaction was one of intense relief as she saw the panel slide open, but when she knew that Allen — Jack Allen, she thought — was alone, she cried out sharply for him to go. He paid no attention to her, but advanced steadily into the room, and she realized suddenly that he had not seen the three outlaws. How See still sat in the corner, while the other two were listening at the second panel and debating the advisability of trying to attract Quong's attention. At the girl's cry they turned and stared, first at her, then around the room. But neither saw Allen for the same reason that he did not see them. The big lamp on the center of the table blinded any one looking directly at it, and it was not until the little outlaw had almost circled the table that the four saw each other.

Shanghai and Steve reached for their guns, but a cry from How See stopped them from drawing.

"No kill! Quong want him alive!"

"That's right," cried Black Steve. "Where'd you get them guns, you runt?"

Both of the big outlaws were confident that they could drop Allen at any moment they wanted to; hence they made no effort to bring the affair to a decision. They stood there, regarding him with crooked smiles, the attitude of each bespeaking arrogance and a supreme faith in his own invulnerability. Each thought it possible that his companion might go down, but that he himself would live.

"Quong — where is he?" Allen inquired in a flat, toneless voice.

"He's in the back room. Want us to take you to him?" jeered Black Steve.

Allen made no answer, and the girl noticed now how he was shifting his position like an animal that moves with no perceptible sign of movement. He continually edged to the right, and she saw with understanding that he was placing the two outlaws in a line with the Chinaman, who had got to his feet, but was still in the corner. Suddenly Allen tipped back his head, so that the battered felt hat no longer screened his eyes. The menace those eyes revealed was inhuman past all description; it was an omnipotent, avenging fury that glared from their depths.

Mary gasped and backed away. The smile left Black Steve's' face, and he stared in frozen silence at the little outlaw. Shanghai Pete leaned forward and peered into Allen's face, and he, too, stood rigid with terror. They knew now who it was that faced them, and they were unable to move. It was the Chinaman who at last broke the silence.

"His eyes — the eyes of a wolf," he said, and his thin voice had a touch of hysteria. "It is the ghost of the Killer Wolf come back!"

"He *is* the Wolf!" Shanghai cried.

The two big outlaws grabbed at their fleeting self-control. This was no ghost who stood there. Somehow Jim-twin Allen had escaped his fall over the cliff, and they understood now how he had been in two places in El Crucifixo.

Then Allen commenced to laugh — a terrible, crazy, mirthless laugh. Transfixed, the big men stared at him, and as they watched, they saw the yellow sparks in his curious, slanting eyes until they became pools of flame.

Suddenly the two burly outlaws went into action, and simultaneously their hands flashed to their guns. Fast as they were, and to Mary's eyes their hands were simply a blur, blue smoke and fire swirled from Allen's guns before their fingers had so much as touched their pistol butts.

Shanghai Pete staggered and crashed into How See just as the Chinaman fired. Black Steve swayed and his face set in a frightful grimace as he tried to raise his gun. Again Allen's Colts roared, and again Black Steve staggered, and How See squealed, his gun clattering to the floor, as a bullet tore through his shoulder. He groped for it with his left hand, then collapsed and lay still.

Still again Allen raised his guns and let the hammers fall, but two clicks told him that they were empty. Black Steve, his face ashen and twitching from pain, slowly raised his gun again, but before he could fire, Allen hurled his empty Colt straight into his face, and at last the big outlaw went down.

Mary Bell swayed toward Allen, and he caught her in his arms, letting his other gun fall to the floor.

"Everything's all right," he soothed.

She clung to him, and her sobbing hid from Jim the noise of the panel as it slid back. But when Quong glided through the opening, Jim swung about instinctively. The girl gave a choking cry and shrank away.

The Oriental glanced about the room, and his eyes were murderous when he looked at Allen. He held a long, gleaming blade in his hand now, and the sickening realization that Allen was weaponless suddenly came to the girl.

"You are —" Quong asked softly.

Allen's answer was to pull his battered hat from his head, revealing completely his flaring, yellow eyes — the eyes of a fighting wolf. Now as Quong swayed, Jim swayed, also, but as he did so, he moved almost imperceptibly backward.

Quong's face was distorted. Mary saw his hand tense, then the wrist flicked and a shaft of silver sped across the room. Then she saw Allen, his arm outstretched, the knife embedded in his crumpled hat. That was why he had backed away from Quong, to gain a second's time in which to catch the knife.

The expression on Quong's face was one almost of fear. He turned and ran toward the panel, but even as he reached it, Allen had retrieved the knife from his hat and sent it flying back across the room to bury itself in the neck of its master. Quong screamed once, then swayed through the panel and fell across the threshold of the other room. When Allen bent over him a moment later, a hasty look convinced the Wolf that Quong was done for.

Jim returned to Mary. The yellow flare had left his eyes, and he was once more a grinning, freckle-faced boy. He slipped his arm about her and led her gently from that room of the dead. They had reached the chapel when a heavy smashing came to their ears.

"Reckon that's the police," he said reassuringly. "Now don't you forget you're goin' to marry me, an' don't be surprised if the next time you see me I'm all covered with bandages. Guess they've busted open the door." He sprang across the room and opened a window. As he threw his leg over the sill, he turned and grinned at her again. "Don't forget what I tol' you," he chuckled.

When he had dropped from view, Mary ran to the window and peered out. Somewhere close at hand there came a shrill whistle, followed by the drumming of hoofs which faded into the distance. She turned back to the room as a crowd of rangers and police poured into it.

"What was all the shootin'?" some one asked her.

Brokenly she explained, and they scattered to search the place.

Much later, Jack Allen awoke in a white, hospital bed to find Mary Bell standing beside him.

"I understand now, Jack. It was Jim!" she cried softly. "That's what he meant by saying I'd see him in bandages the next time."

"Then he got there in time?" Jack asked weakly.

"And how!" exclaimed an orderly.

Mary Bell smiled down at Jack, and the corners of her mouth twitched mischievously. "But he didn't kiss me again."

CHAPTER FIFTEEN

An Avalanche

"Toothpick,' how'd yuh like tuh —"

Abruptly Jim Allen broke off his sentence when something ricocheted from the rock in front of him with a thin whine, and a report echoed in the canyon. Scarcely had the echo of the shot boomed from the mountain wall before he slipped sideways from his saddle and, rifle in hand, was crouching behind a big boulder.

Two more reports of different caliber boomed across the canyon, and the tall, lanky Toothpick slipped from his saddle and sprawled behind a covering pile of rocks. "Where are they? I can't see nothin'?" he cried.

There came a burst of rifle fire from the floor of the canyon, and the bullets spattered against the rocks like hail.

"Huh, they must be a bunch of Mexes, 'cause them slugs ain't comin' nowhere near us," Toothpick jeered.

But Jim Allen jumped to his feet, for he knew those shots were aimed at his horses. He let out a shrill, animal like cry as his gray pack horse snorted and jumped.

"Dang yuh, Toothpick! Come here an' help!" he cried as he commenced clawing and heaving at the giant boulder behind which he had sought shelter.

The two men had been following an old Apache trail high up on the shoulder of the canyon wall. Their position was such that they could easily beat off an attack, but there was no shelter for their horses, and the men below were deliberately trying to shoot down their mounts.

At last Toothpick understood what the little outlaw was trying to accomplish, and with a wild, reckless laugh, he sprang forward to assist him. Although Toothpick was not a burly man, he had the strength and steellike muscles of youth. He thrust his shoulder against the boulder and grasped its lower rim with his hands. His back bowed, and his muscles cracked. Slowly, very slowly, the rock moved. A bullet smashed against it and filled Toothpick's eyes with dust.

Then, at last, the boulder moved and started slowly down the slope. It moved majestically, at first, with a crunching sound; then, little by little, it gathered momentum, leaped into the air, and came down with a terrific impact on a large stone. Toothpick jabbered with excitement, astonishment, and awe, for the whole mountainside of loose rubble seemed to become fluid at his feet. A roar like that of a mighty tide filled his ears. He saw, down in the canyon, a man in a blue shirt, break from cover and race for the farther slope. A short, stumpy man followed, then, a second later, four other men, dwarfed by the great boulders which hurtled down the mountainside, sprang tardily from cover and started to run frantically. They had scarcely taken a step before a cloud of dust enveloped all of them.

Slowly the rumbling roar of the landslide died away, and the dust cloud drifted up the canyon. Toothpick was awed by the cataclysm he had unloosed by the rolling of that one boulder. He glanced at Jim Allen and watched the little outlaw trot to the side of his grays and examine them. Princess was untouched, but Honey Boy had a long gash across his chest.

Allen talked to Honey Boy and dressed his wound, appearing like some freckle-faced country boy fussing over a wounded dog.

"He ain't hurt bad," Allen said.

"You aimin' to go down and have a look-see?" Toothpick inquired presently.

Jim Allen nodded, and, rifle in hand, started down the slope. Toothpick gingerly followed.

"Why for you figger those gents shot at us?" Toothpick demanded.

Jim Allen did not reply immediately. He stopped and scanned the path of the landslide and the jumbled mass of rock that covered the floor of the canyon, then he turned and faced Toothpick.

"Yuh remember that chink I tole yuh 'bout?" Allen inquired.

"You mean Quong?"

Allen nodded as he again studied the floor of the canyon. "Reckon they was workin' for him," he said quietly.

"But Quong's dead. You left him with a knife through his yellow neck."

"I've been shot to pieces a couple of times, an' folks has left me for dead. But I'm still alive an' kickin', an' so is Quong."

"You positive?" Toothpick demanded.

"Plumb sure. I was certain he was dead that night I left him back in Santa Fe. But I was kind of hurried, 'cause there was a couple of officers tryin' to bust in, an' I had to hit the breeze afore they broke in. He played possum an' fooled me."

"You seen him?" Toothpick persisted.

"Nope. I wouldn't be trailin' him if I had."

Toothpick understood the grim significance that lay behind that statement. Then Allen answered the unspoken question in the puncher's eyes:

"I'm sort of used to getting shot at, so the first two or three times I didn't think nothin' 'bout it. But it got so I couldn't go nowhere without havin' a couple of gents try an' dry-gulch me. Then I started to figger things out, an' I savvies pronto that the different gents what tried to down me wasn't workin' for the reward on my head, 'cause every darn one of them thought he was tryin' to down my brother Jack, an' they plenty cussed the gent what had double crossed 'em an' sicked 'em on me without advisin' 'em who they was goin' 'gainst. These no-good border killers knows me, an' don't know Jack, so they figger he's easier than me.

"Well, that shows me that these here different homicidious gents was all being paid by some hombre what was darn anxious to get my scalp. Then a couple of 'em, afore they cashes, says they was hired by a gent called Sands. It got so I couldn't go nowhere without bein' shot at. The gent what was after my scalp sure was the head of a big gang, an' had darned efficient spies, 'cause he knew more 'bout my plans than all the sheriffs in half a dozen States. Then somethin' happens, an' I get a hunch that Quong ain't dead. I sends for Jack, an' we starts huntin' him. We never catch up with him, but we get near 'nough to be plumb sure Quong was the man behind this Sands person."

"How long you been huntin' him?"

"'Bout seven months. Let's be goin' on down an' look at them fellows."

Both Jim Allen and Toothpick were alert as they slid down the pathway of the avalanche; some men might still be living among that mass of rock. A short search convinced them that their fears were groundless, for they found only one who showed signs of life. The man in the blue shirt was still breathing.

Turning the man over on his back, Toothpick stopped and examined the dust-streaked face. "Figger I ought to know that gent, but I can't place him proper," he said thoughtfully.

"Yuh recollects when yuh an' me played at bein' sheriff up in Wyoming?" Allen inquired with a grin.

"Sure does. Your brother, Jack, was laid up with a broken leg, an' yuh stole his clothes, raised a beard, an' did his sheriffin' for him," Toothpick replied as he stooped and again examined the man in the blue shirt. Then he looked up at Allen with a stare. "Jumpin' jiggers, it's him — 'Bum' Rogers, the horse thief. But I thought he was in jail."

"He was — along with 'Bull' Morgan, that there gambler, Johnson, an' the rest. They all escaped a few months ago," Allen explained.

At that moment, Bum Rogers' eyes fluttered open. He painfully raised himself on his elbow and groped with his hand for his gun. Allen flicked it from its holster and tossed it away. The wounded man glared up at Allen.

"Yuh yeller hound!" he said. "Passin' yourself off as the Wolf an' chasin' gents like a bloodhound. But Bull —" He choked.

"Yuh mean Bull Morgan? So Bull's workin' for Quong?" Allen said with a shrug.

"You lyin' hound! Bull ain't workin' for no one. He's his own boss, even if the chink thinks different." Again he choked and gagged. With a desperate effort he aroused himself. "You lyin', yeller hound, passin' yourself off as the Wolf so you can —" His voice failed. He grimaced horribly, then suddenly was still.

"He thought you was Jack!" Toothpick exclaimed in surprise.

"Same as tothers I tole yuh 'bout."

"We know now for sure Quong is alive, 'cause Bum Rogers admitted plain he was workin' for him," Toothpick declared with conviction.

Allen grinned. "We knew it afore."

Suddenly Toothpick asked: "How did the chink know we was goin' to pass through this here canyon?"

Allen's strange eyes flickered with amusement as he countered: "Yuh recollect what 'Dutchy' used to tell yuh?"

Toothpick was silent for a moment while he considered, then his cheeks flamed red with embarrassment as he replied: "'Bout me diggin' my grave with my tongue?"

Allen nodded as he grinned broadly. "Sam Hogg give yuh a letter for me. Yuh stayed in Cannondale last night. Who did yuh talk to there?"

"Dang it, I never opened my mouth 'bout meetin' you. I didn't talk to a soul 'cept 'Tad' Hicks. Him an' me was talkin' 'bout the time we tossed you through the window in Ol' Mex."

"Yeah, an' I bet yuh tole him yuh hadn't seen me for a long time an' then acted sort o' mysterious 'bout your errand to-day," Allen accused good-naturedly.

Toothpick flushed guiltily, for he knew that he had deliberately aroused Tad Hicks' curiosity. He was silent for a moment, then he blurted out with a startled air: "But, gosh, you ain't suspectin' Tad Hicks?"

"Not any." Allen suddenly became grave. "I ain't accusin' Tad Hicks, but yuh got to remember that old chink is as clever as blazes. Remember what he said about himself: 'A clever man understands a nod, and words are the color of blood, and a whisper can bring on a war.'"

"Meanin', even if I didn't say nothin', some spy repeated my words to the chink, an' he put two an' two together, an' knew I was goin' to meet you up here?" asked Toothpick, who was disgusted with himself.

"Exactly. Those killers first trailed yuh, then, after yuh met me, they tried to bushwhack us."

"But if those killers trailed me out of Cannondale, Quong must be mighty close, or he couldn't have sent 'em as quick as he did."

"Yuh can go to the head of the class." Allen grinned as he thoughtfully rubbed the month's stubble on his chin. "Jack goes in for whiskers 'cause he figgers they make him look more like a man than a peanut."

"You mean to tell me you're lettin' yours grow apurpose?"

"Yep. I figger on doin' a little sheriffin' again like I done that time up in Wyoming," Allen explained. "Bum Rogers, here, was a-workin' for Bull Morgan. An' Bull Morgan figgers Jack is down here huntin' for him. Maybe he is. If so, there's goin' to be two of him."

Toothpick stared at Allen. "Darn it, you remember what Bum said 'bout Bull an' Quong. Gosh, that means the two is workin' together!" he exclaimed.

"Yep. Sure does. An' Bull is the cussedest gent I ever see, an' sure plumb full of brains," Allen admitted.

"That sure makes her a tough job, takin' on the two to once." Toothpick shook his head.

"Not any. Yuh is plumb mistook, 'cause it makes her plumb easy. 'Cause why? This here gent, Bull Morgan, ain't the sort to take no orders from nobody, an' Quong wouldn't take no orders from the devil hisself. So it's plumb certain the two will start fightin' among themselves, an' then they'll make a mistake, an' that's when I come in."

CHAPTER SIXTEEN

Plots

The L bar B ranch house was as square and flat-topped as a box thrown on the ground. Scattered about it were other boxlike houses. Two long bunk houses flanked it on the north and south, while on the east and west were the stables and cookhouse. "Old Man" Carver had built it with an eye to defense against raiding Apaches and Mexicans, rather than for beauty. On all sides the burned, desolate mesa, deep red in color, stretched many weary miles to the encircling, blue-tinted mountains. It was by far the largest outfit in the State, and sprawled over two counties along the border, flowing far across the line into Mexico.

Old Man Carver was a tall, gaunt, white-haired man with a hooked nose and kindly, deep-set blue eyes. Even at sixty-five his figure was erect. He cocked his feet on the porch railing and sighed.

"It's easy enough to talk, Sam, but don't be forgettin' Bill is my only son, and some day this whole outfit is goin' to belong to him."

He and Sam Hogg had been boyhood friends. They had fought Indians together, and loved and courted the same girl, and their friendship had continued even after

Carver had won her. Sam Hogg was a small, wiry man, with a thin, weather-beaten face, a bristling pompadour of snow-white hair, and fierce, penetrating black eyes, like those of an eagle. He was a silent man, given little to long speeches, so when he replied to his friend his words sounded brusque and almost rude.

"Quit babyin' him."

Old Man Carver sighed. "Yeah, maybe I do," he agreed. "But he is drinkin' too much and runnin' with a bad crowd."

"You an' me done the same, once." Hogg's black eyes traveled along the veranda, scrutinized two men who were dismounting before the bunk house, then turned back to Carver.

Old Man Carver glanced toward the two and grinned tolerantly at his friend.

"You don't like 'Big Montana'?" he queried.

"Nope, nor his friend," Hogg replied positively.

"Why? Both he and Silver are good cowmen," Carver pressed.

"Don't know why. They look good like a bad Mex peseta, but don't ring true." Hogg relaxed in his rocker as if exhausted by the effort of making this lengthy speech.

"Shucks, Sam, you was in the Rangers so long you look for crooks in every one." Carver smiled slowly, and then added slyly: "Funny how you swear by the greatest outlaw of them all. You never get tired of tellin' me 'bout this wonder, Jim Allen. Sort o' surprised me to hear an old Ranger praisin' a gent which everybody calls 'the Wolf.' "

"He's pure nerve and straight," Hogg explained.

"Reckon he must have nerve aplenty." Carver paused, and again glanced at Big Montana and Silver, who were slowly approaching from the bunk house, then he continued: "You was sayin' you had a letter from him askin' you to help him locate some chink. What does this chink look like? Maybe he's workin' for me, for I've got eight of the pigtails on my pay roll."

"Shut up, you fool!" Sam Hogg cried, and nodded toward Montana and Silver.

Old Man Carver considered the ex-Ranger's friendship for the noted outlaw, the Wolf, and their search for a Chinaman as something of a joke. He had always looked upon Chinamen as gentle, harmless folks much abused by the white cow-punchers, and he could not conceive of one who might be dangerous. He grinned amiably at Hogg, and nodded a greeting to Montana and Silver.

"'Lo, Big — 'lo, Silver," he drawled as he kicked a chair toward them. "Rest your feet."

Big Montana was a powerful, blond man of forty with a tremendous personality. He cultivated a heavy, bushy beard and mustache, through which could be seen his tight-lipped mouth. His cheek bones were rather high, his forehead broad, his nose big, and he assumed a hearty, friendly manner which was contradicted by his cold, expressionless eyes. With the sole exception of the expression about the eyes, Silver was his antithesis. He was a slender, sleek man, who took great pride in his personal appearance, and had a cold, impassive face. He seldom spoke, and when he did, his voice was as cold as water dripping from a glacier, while on the contrary, Big Montana had a deep hearty voice, and was garrulous in the extreme.

"Howdy, Mr. Carver — howdy, Mr. Hogg," Big Montana boomed.

Sam Hogg grunted a reply. Silver satisfied himself with a short nod as he sank into the chair pushed forward by Carver. The cattleman grinned at his friend, and then addressed himself to Montana.

"You ever see Jim Allen?" he asked amiably.

"The Wolf!" Silver snapped, as if the words had been jerked unwillingly from his mouth.

Big Montana's eyes flicked from Carver to Hogg, then, after a moment, he shook his head and laughed. "No, nor if what you say about him is true, do I want to."

Old Man Carver thought it would be a rare joke on Hogg to pretend to take up cudgels in defense of Allen.

"Tut, tut, I reckon if you had ever met him, you wouldn't talk that way. He is a real gent, and pure nerve. Didn't you never hear the story of what he did down in Old Mex? No? Well, he had himself tossed through a window into a room plumb full of border gunmen, downs the lot, and saves the judge from gettin' his neck stretched." He paused and grinned amiably, then chuckled inwardly when he observed the expressions on his listeners' faces. He believed they were incredulous as to Jim Allen's miraculous feats.

"Yep, he done that very thing, sure as shootin'. I don't blame you and John any for doubtin', but it's the gospel truth." He addressed himself to Big Montana. "An' what's more, he's comin' here."

"The Wolf! Comin' here?" Silver hissed.

"You kiddin' us?" boomed Big Montana.

"Sure is," Carver asserted, and glanced shyly at his friend.

He chuckled again when he observed the expression on Sam Hogg's face. It was as hard as granite, and his eyes were like gimlets as they traveled back and forth from Big Montana to Silver.

Both men were adept at concealing their fears and thoughts, but in spite of this, Sam Hogg saw a flicker of apprehension leap into their eyes. He knew by this that the knowledge that Jim Allen was to arrive was a body blow to them. Then simultaneously both relaxed, and Big Montana threw back his head and laughed genuinely in a deep voice. Even Silver's thin lips split into a fleeting smile, then his face was once more hard, expressionless, impassive. Sam Hogg was puzzled as to the reason for the two men's sudden mirth.

"What's bitin' you two?" Old Man Carver demanded. "You figure it's a joke about the Wolf coming here? Well, I'm telling you plain he's comin', an' he's lookin' for —"

One glance at Sam Hogg's face and Old Man Carver decided he had better leave his sentence unfinished. He grinned foolishly and lapsed into silence.

"You say the Wolf's a-comin' here a-lookin' for some one? Who's he lookin' for?" Big Montana asked indifferently.

"Nope, I was only foolin'," Old Man Carver replied unconvincingly. He bit off a piece of black plug tobacco and chewed on it reflectively for a few moments, then addressed Big Montana. "Things runnin' all right over the line?" he asked. "How's them chink cow waddies doin' you hired?"

Big Montana was foreman of the L Bar B line ranch over the border. Before he could reply, Sam Hogg cut in quickly.

"Chink waddies? How come?" he asked.

Big Montana's smile was genial, and his enthusiasm was sincere when he replied. "Don't wonder at your bein' surprised 'cause I never seen chink cow-punchers before those two turned up. But they sure know their business, and are right handy with their guns." He paused and looked at Old Man Carver. "How about sendin' that kid of yours over there? I wasn't right pleased when you first suggested it, but I've been thinkin' things over, an' now I figure it would do him a lot o' good to keep away from town, booze, and sort o' shake himself loose from that bunch of bums he's hitched up with. Besides, while tother side of the border ain't no place for a kid, I'll keep him close to me, and it'll give him a chance to win his spurs."

"That's right kind of you, Big, but I'm going to send him over to visit Mr. Hogg, here," Old Man Carver explained.

Big Montana became silent. For a while he sat absorbed in his thoughts, and stared out over the reddish mesa. Then he swung out one of his big hands and pointed to a rider who had just swung his horse around the corner of the bunk house and brought it to a sliding stop at the stable door.

"There's the kid, now!" he exclaimed.

"And stewed to the eyeballs," Sam Hogg grinned.

"Dang the whelp, I'll learn him!" Old Man Carver growled.

"A horse ain't no good if you break him with spurs," Hogg warned.

Old Man Carver ignored Sam Hogg and glared at his son, who grasped a post of the veranda for support and smiled inanely down at his father. He was a tall, clean-limbed youth of nineteen. There was something reckless and good-natured about his blue eyes, and something weak about his mouth, but the weakness was that of unformed youth rather than an inherent character blemish.

"So you're drunk again!" his father roared.

"You ain't got no right to talk to me that way afore folks," young Bill Carver replied angrily.

"I'll talk to you as I dang please!"

The boy was stung, his pride hurt at being treated like a child in front of these men. "Then I'll light out!" he flared up quickly. Swinging about, he returned unsteadily to where he had left his horse.

"You come back here now or you need never come back," his father said.

"He ain't no hired hand," Sam Hogg warned.

Old Man Carver glowered after his retreating son, then he turned to the other man and spoke sheepishly. "He's near as quick-tempered as I was when I was a kid."

"As you are now," Sam Hogg corrected. "Reckon I'll ride along after him."

Sam Hogg nodded a farewell to the three, walked swiftly across the yard to where he had left his own horse, leaped into the saddle, and spurred along the road after young Bill Carver.

"He's some sudden, ain't he?" Old Man Carver grinned.

"He sure is," said Big Montana. "If he started after you, you'd be wearin' wings afore you knew he was even mad."

The three men discussed the latest Mexican raid for a short while, then Big Montana and Silver took their departure. They declined Old Man Carver's invitation to remain to supper, and gave as an excuse that they had a fifteen-mile ride before them, back to the Casa Diablo, as the line ranch over the border was called, and that they preferred to return before dark.

The two rode silently for some distance along the trail to the Casa Diablo, then Silver turned in his saddle and looked questioningly at Big Montana.

"Yeah, things is breakin' wrong," Big Montana grunted.

"Sure is," Silver agreed swiftly.

"The whole thing is busted complete if Sam Hogg gets the kid out to his ranch. We won't be able to get nowhere near him," Big Montana rumbled.

"Right again. Sam Hogg ain't soft and easy-goin' like Carver, and he has a bunch of shootin', fightin', ridin' fools workin' for him," Silver said crisply. "What do you figger the old man was gabbin' about the Wolf comin' down here for?"

"Darned if I know," Big Montana replied shortly. "He must have been funnin', 'cause the Wolf is shore dead."

Silver was silent for a moment, and then said thinly: "Quong says he is, but I ain't so sure. There are plenty of gents that swear he never went off that cliff down in El Crucifixo."

Big Montana laughed and shrugged his shoulders. "Sure they do, and the world is full of fools. They see Jack Allen and think he's Jim, but Jim is eatin' cabbages by the roots sure."

"Well, we know that Jack Allen is down here somewheres, and if Jim was with him — well, I don't know," Silver grunted.

You ain't tellin' me no news, after what them twins done to us up in the basin. Cuss them, they're the only two that ever beat me in a game!"

"The key to this whole game is that kid, young Bill Carver," Silver suggested thoughtfully.

The two men again lapsed into silence. Suddenly Big Montana jerked his horse to a standstill and pounded his pommel with one of his heavy fists.

"I got it," he declared. He talked rapidly for a few moments while Silver stroked his small mustache and listened thoughtfully. When finally Montana finished, Silver nodded and bared his teeth in a grin.

"It works!" he cried enthusiastically. "But how about Quong?"

“This is my game, and no chink gets a cut in it,” Big Montana growled. “Once the kid is an orphan and receives us as his best friends, Quong will have to play our game whether he likes it or not.”

“Don’t be forgettin’ he ain’t no ordinary chink,” Silver warned.

“I ain’t afraid of Quong. Now you get started for town, and get ‘Big-foot’ or ‘Curly’ to escort that dang cub out to the ranch about eleven to-night. And don’t be forgettin’ to make him pass out when he gets there. When he comes to, he’ll be an orphan, and we’ll be his best friends — such good friends he’ll give us the ranch to keep his neck from being stretched.”

Silver’s lips again split in a thin grin. The two turned their horses into a wash, where Big Montana dismounted, but Silver put his horse to a gallop and headed toward town.

CHAPTER SEVENTEEN

Quong's Order

Sam Hogg did not ride hard when he left the L Bar B Ranch, because he did not figure it was absolutely essential that he overtake the boy, Bill Carver, before he arrived in town. He decided that it would be easy enough to locate him in one of the saloons; and besides, he thought it would be wiser to wait until the boy had a chance to cool off before he attempted to talk to him. When he trotted down Main Street, he saw the boy's horse tied to the hitch rack in front of the Red Queen Saloon. He himself dismounted before his brother's hardware store, and, having hitched his horse, turned across the street and entered the same saloon. He saw the boy standing at the bar with "Slick" Keen. Sam Hogg frowned. Slick Keen was not exactly a desirable companion for an angry, strong-headed boy.

"Dang half-breed chink," Sam Hogg growled to himself.

Slick Keen was both slender and young, not more than twenty-three or four. There was not another man in the county who would have dared affect the clothes he wore. But as some old-timer once remarked, Slick could appear in pink pajamas, and no one would rag him about it. He was dressed in a most gaudy fashion, wearing a soft white shirt, short, braided, blue jacket, and a wide, red-tasseled sash and trousers that flared from the knees down. The entire costume was decorated in the most likely and unlikely places with silver buttons. He was undoubtedly a handsome man, with a small mustache and red lips and olive-tinted complexion. It was his eyes which showed his mixed blood. These were typically Oriental, almond-shaped, and expressionless. He wore two broad, patent-leather crossed belts which were heavily studded with gold coins and which suspended two low-hung, holstered pearl-handled guns. Patent-leather, pointed-toed, high-heeled boots showed beneath his flaring trousers.

He had appeared in town some three months previously, and had bought the Red Queen Saloon, which had remained closed up to that time since the death of its former owner, Francisco Garcia, nicknamed the "Toad." Keen was a gambler by profession, and ran several games in the back room. Nothing was known of his past, and his face did not mark him as a desirable citizen. But after the sheriff had investigated his games and had been convinced somehow that they were run honestly, he was allowed to remain in town.

The old ex-Ranger paused for a moment in indecision, then he strode briskly forward. He nodded to Slick Keen and addressed Bill Carver. "Hullo, kid. How about comin' and havin' supper with me?"

Young Bill Carver tried to assume a superior air, but failed. He had consumed too many drinks. His eyes were truculent as he looked at the ex-Ranger. He knew Hogg to be his father's best friend, and was sure that he had been sent by his parent to drag him out of the saloon. "I ain't a kid," Bill Carver said with what dignity he could assume.

Sam Hogg laughed good-naturedly and said: "All right, Bill, I'll see you later." He knew it would be hopeless to try to talk to Bill Carver in the boy's present mood. His sympathies in this family quarrel were with the youth. A good jamboree would do the boy no harm, so Sam nodded again, and swung out of the saloon.

The boy watched him sullenly, then turned to Slick Keen. "I'm goin' to learn folks that I ain't no kid," he said.

A ghost of a smile flickered across the thin, hard face of the gaudy gentleman. He raised his hand and slapped young Carver genially on the shoulder. "You're talking now," he said. "You're full growed, or I wouldn't be standin' here talkin' to you."

Slick Keen's voice was a harsh whisper which never rose to normal tones, and which aroused the most intense antagonism in most of his listeners. But now young Carver found nothing disagreeable in it; he was too intensely flattered to find fault with the man's voice. Every one in town walked warily when in the presence of this flashy gentleman. Yet here Keen was making friendly advances to him; this naturally soothed Bill's ruffled vanity.

"Look here, Bill," Slick Keen said in his harsh whisper. "You know I am a gambler, and it's my business to read gents' faces, and I am tellin' you that I got you sized up for a four-square gent which has sand in his craw. And I'm your friend. Any time you want anything, you come to me."

The boy puffed out his chest and cast bloodshot eyes about the saloon as if searching for some one to witness this statement. Before he could formulate a reply, some one touched him lightly on his right hand, and he swung about to face Silver. He remembered that Silver had been a witness of his humiliation that afternoon, so he scowled truculently at him. But Silver replied with a friendly grin.

"I was a-lookin' for you, Bill," Silver said, "to tell you that I'm right sorry that you had that ruction with your dad this afternoon."

"He ain't got no right to talk to me that way," the boy mumbled.

"Of course he ain't," Silver agreed pleasantly. "But he don't savvy yet you're growed up. He don't savvy that you ain't a kid no longer, but man size."

Bill Carver blinked; it took some time for his fuddled brain to grasp what Silver had said. Then he swelled up like a pouter pigeon. Here was another famous gunman confirming his own estimate of himself. He must be even smarter than he had thought.

The two gunmen continued to flatter the boy as they plied him with drinks for some little time. Their lips always wore a smile when they glanced surreptitiously at each other. Each was wondering what the other's game was.

Then abruptly Slick Keen swung on his heels and walked into the gambling room back of the bar. Silver watched him until he disappeared, and frowned thoughtfully. Then he made his decision, and started to propel young Carver toward the outer door. But the boy resisted. Silver urged him to come and eat. He was in a quandary; he could not use force without running the risk of arousing the drunken belligerency in young Carver, so he urged and argued endlessly with him to eat before he had another drink. But the boy remained stubborn and insisted that he would not leave the place.

Silver was forced to give way. He ordered another round of drinks, and before the boy finished his, Slick Keen returned. Silver saw Slick Keen nod to two men seated at a table near the door. Silver knew them both; they were "Gloomy" Mason and "Stub" Porter, both tall and unshaven, and dressed in dirty overalls. They sauntered up to the bar and leaned against it directly behind him.

The significance of their movement was not lost on Silver. He would have faced Slick Keen or those two burly gunmen without a moment's thought, but the three of them together made the odds too great. So he turned to Slick and looked at him coldly.

"You gettin' ready to go to war?" he asked softly.

Slick Keen shook his head and whispered, "Not any, but the boss wants to see you."

So that was it. Silver swore softly to himself. There was no one he wanted to see less at that moment than the boss. But Slick's warlike preparations warned him that this was not a request, but a command from the boss. Silver would have to obey or fight. The odds were too great against him, so there was nothing for him to do but obey.

"Dang that old devil of a Chinaman, Quong!" he fumed to himself. "Who's he to be givin' orders to a white man?"

He put one arm around young Carver's shoulders, and said: "Bill, you wait here for me. I'll be right back, and then we'll feed."

"He'll be here," Slick Keen promised as he nodded toward Gloomy Mason and Stub Porter.

So that was it. Quong had some game which concerned the boy himself. Silver realized that he would have to watch his step in the presence of that wily old Chinaman. He was a hard one to deceive. Slick Keen and Silver walked side by side along the crowded bar and into the gambling room, which was at the left of the dance hall.

As the two men stepped into the gambling hall, Silver stopped just within the doorway and glanced keenly about. Silver's career had been a long and a bad one, and he had made many enemies; therefore, he was always on the alert and careful to look over a crowded room before he entered it. One brief glance satisfied him that there was no one there he need fear; there were only five or six men in the room playing faro, and all of these were strangers to Silver.

The two walked diagonally across the room to a door in the rear wall which supposedly led to Slick Keen's private quarters. They stepped through this into a short hall, and knocked sharply at a door at the farther end. A moment later, a panel in the door swung open, and a tremendous, heavy, fat, powerful, pock-marked Chinaman scrutinized them through the opening. A glance was sufficient, and he threw open the door. They entered another hall, which opened onto a stone flight of stairs, which they climbed, and at the top again knocked sharply at another door. Once again they were carefully scrutinized through a panel by another powerfully built Chinaman.

"He's sure well guarded," Silver mumbled to himself. "A mouse couldn't slip through his guard, much less a man. And I hear tell he's got a dozen exits to his burrow."

Silver's spurs rang musically as the two strode across the large, bare room to a door on the farther side. Slick Keen knocked once, twice, then once again on this door, then stood back and waited. After a short pause, the door opened noiselessly, and the two stepped through the doorway, and the door clicked behind them.

This was the first time that Silver had ever been in this particular den of Quong's, and he looked curiously about him. There were no windows in the room, and the air was heavy and rank with incense. It was also frightfully hot and close. The whole was a bit of exotic China cast in an American frontier town. Against the wall, on the farther side of the room, Quong sat on a couch covered with an embroidered shawl and piled high with cushions. He wore the robes of a mandarin.

One hand was concealed within the folds of the wide sleeve. The other held a scented cigarette in a long amber holder. The old Chinaman was apparently unarmed, but John Silver knew that Quong could throw back the folds of his robe, snatch out his knife, and hurl it with the deadliness, quickness, and sureness of a striking cobra.

Silver had no way of knowing why Quong had summoned him, but the fact that Slick Keen had called to his aid Gloomy Mason and Stub Porter to be sure that his command would be obeyed, convinced John Silver that, whatever the reason was, it might have a serious and fatal end for him unless he watched very carefully. He well knew that he had not a chance in the world of making a fight against this man. For even if he proved faster with a gun than Quong with his knife, there remained Slick Keen, and if he overcame the two, he knew that there were other eyes watching him. From two holes cleverly cut in the side wall, these watchers would blast him to death at his first hostile movement or at a nod from Quong.

With an effort, Silver steadied his nerves and forced the fear from his gray eyes as he lifted them and met Quong's coal-black, opaque eyes. For a long moment, none of the three men spoke. It was Quong who finally broke the silence.

"The next best thing to be born with wealth is to be blessed with brains." Quong almost lisped the words in his soft, singsong voice.

Silver stirred uneasily. It always bothered him when Quong spoke philosophically. He could not understand, so he made no reply. He simply stood there and waited.

"You have used your brains — you have a plan about young Bill Carver," Quong purred.

Silver had made his decision. He had a feeling that it would be hopeless to deny what he and Big Montana had planned to do with the boy. He had no way of knowing how Quong would accept his story, yet he intended to tell it. For John Silver had one virtue, and that was faithfulness to a friend. Never for a moment did he consider squirming out of the situation by throwing all the blame on Big Montana. Briefly, succinctly, he told what they had planned to do with young Carver. After he had finished, Quong was silent for a long time.

"And Quong — you did not consider him?" he said at last.

"We're partners in dope running and the catching of Jack Allen, but in other things we are free agents."

When the words left his lips, Silver resolved, if the worst came to the worst, at least to die fighting. He was no sheep!

"And after?" Quong demanded.

"We would have the ranch in our hands, and that would have made the other game easier," Silver replied.

"It is written to believe with certainty we must begin by doubting. I suspect a double cross — that you were planning something that would be to my disadvantage. But you were only seeking to fill your own pockets without thinking of mine. It is a good plan. I will become your partner in it."

A little quiver of relief raced up Silver's spine, but he swore to himself at the Chinaman's calm assurance in declaring himself in this game. Silver was irritated. He both hated and feared that yellow-faced statue with the evil eyes and cool smile. It was terribly humiliating to take orders from this man. He longed to open his mouth and tell Quong bluntly that he had no right to declare himself in on this game they were planning to play with young Carver, but discretion stilled his tongue. He simply nodded in agreement, and before either he or Quong could speak again, there came a brisk knock at the door.

Slick Keen, moving as silently as some animal, walked to the door and asked a question in shrill Cantonese. The reply came, which he passed on to Quong. A moment later, the door again opened noiselessly, and one of the huge Chinamen escorted a booted, spurred rider into the room who bore evidence of having ridden far and fast that day.

"Has the honorable pursuer of the men who sell the flower of the lotus flown away to join his ancestors?" Quong demanded.

For a moment, the rider was too overcome to speak, then with an effort he cleared his throat, and words rushed from his mouth.

"No, he ain't, an' it wasn't Jack Allen! We laid for him up in the canyon like yer told us to. I was back holdin' the hosses. He came along with a tall, skinny puncher. He was high up on the wall, following an old

Apache trail. But we figgered that we had him caught, and so we opens up on him. The boys didn't allow for shootin' uphill, so they missed him clean the first volley. Then him and that tall galoot started a big boulder comin' down the side of the mountain. It started the darnedest avalanche. It catches every one of the boys!"

At the news that his latest attempt to down Allen had failed as miserably as those that had gone before, Quong sighed. "It is repeatedly said that adversity is the path of truth," he almost moaned.

"So you bunked it up," Slick Keen whispered harshly. "Watcha mean, it wasn't Jack Allen?"

"Just what I say. It wasn't Jack, it was that darned brother of his, the Wolf!" the rider cried.

"The Wolf! He's dead," Silver snapped.

"Boss," the man said to Quong, "I know you're plumb full of brains, but you got this thing wrong. I'm tellin' you the Wolf ain't dead!"

Quong looked down at the floor. "Words are the color of blood, a whisper can bring on war," he murmured.

He raised his cigarette and made a cross of smoke. The dusty rider gave one shrill cry, then vanished through the floor. Silver leaped sideways and gazed fearfully at the gaping aperture in the center of the floor. He shivered, for he himself had been standing on that spot a moment ago, and he understood now that if he had failed to satisfy Quong, he would be down there in that pit where the rider was now. Slowly the trap in the floor came upward and clicked shut.

When Silver again faced Quong, the old Chinaman was regarding him closely. Silver sensed a new hostility; he was nimble-witted and he rapidly went over the events of the last minute. He reached the conclusion that Quong had deliberately killed the rider because there was one thing the rider knew that all the world did not know, and that was the knowledge that Jim Allen, the Wolf, still lived. Silver knew that he would follow the rider down that hole if Quong thought that this knowledge would make any difference to him.

"That proves my hunch," he said softly. "I always figgered the Wolf wasn't dead. I was willing to bet cards on it with Big Montana, but he's so darned stubborn he just got mad when I suggested the Wolf was still alive." He paused and looked thoughtfully at Quong. "That means we've got to move fast and catch the darned Wolf in a trap he won't get out of this time."

The belligerent glitter left Quong's eyes, and he nodded.

"The Wolf is still living. He is trailing me. Men fear him even more than they fear Quong. So I set a trap for him, and tell the fools who go to spring it that it is his brother Jack," Quong said.

"Huh! That's a hot joke. People figger they're trying to get Jack Allen when really they're trying to get the Wolf. And you dropped that hombre through the floor to keep him from talkin'," Silver declared.

"A man cannot talk from the sky," Quong said.

"Then you want Jim Allen and not Jack?" Silver asked.

Silver recoiled before the expression that leaped into Quong's face.

"No! Both! I must have them both. I would give my all — beggar myself — to make them suffer the 'death of a thousand knives.' "

There was something terrifying in Quong's hate, and Silver gaped at him. Then, with an effort, Quong conquered his emotion, and his face became expressionless.

"You two go and make young Carver an orphan!" he directed softly.

CHAPTER EIGHTEEN

Murder

When Sam Hogg left the Red Queen Saloon, he walked across Main Street to the Comfort Hotel and engaged two rooms for the night. Having signed the register, he strolled into the bar.

Tad Hicks, "Windy Jake," and "Kansas" Jones, three Frying Pan punchers, were lined up at the bar, celebrating.

"Hullo, boss," they called together.

The ex-Ranger's eyes flickered with enthusiasm as he looked them over. These three were his favorites among his men. Clean-limbed, hardy, eager-eyed, each one of them was prepared at any time to risk his life in defense of the Frying Pan Ranch.

"What will you boys have?" Hogg asked.

At this invitation, grins broke over their faces. But before they could give their orders, a voice from the doorway spoke:

"Hullo, gents!" Toothpick Jarrick greeted.

"Howdy, Toothpick! Hook your leg over the rail and have something," Sam Hogg invited.

Toothpick shook his head and looked at the three riders with intended scorn.

"Mr. Hogg, if you'll step up to the other end of the bar, I'll sure be proud to have a drink with you, but I don't like to drink with no mutton eaters."

"Look at the empty-headed mutt what is gettin' high hat," Windy Jake said derisively.

"Where you been?" Kansas Jones demanded. "From the looks of you and the dust on your boots, you sure been ridin' far an' fast."

"Me? Feller, you remember once afore I hit this town and played the messenger of Nemesis. This time I'm the messenger of destiny," Toothpick said gravely, and he nodded to Sam Hogg to follow him to the other end of the bar.

"Did you give him my letter?" Hogg asked when they were alone.

Toothpick nodded, gulped down a drink, then talked rapidly for a couple of minutes. As he listened, the ex-Ranger covered his mouth to hide his delighted grin. Toothpick handed him a list which he eagerly scanned. When he had read it, Hogg looked up.

"I got a brand-new pair of shiny boots which I reckon will fit him, and he can have my frock coat, which I got for my brother's wedding. I'll get a shirt, and tother things at my brother's store. So long. I'll be back pronto."

After Hogg hurried from the bar, Toothpick joined his three friends.

A short time later, Sam Hogg returned with a large bundle under his arm which he gave to Toothpick. The lanky rider accepted it as casually as he could, and sauntered from the hotel. A few minutes later, he was back again, and suggested that they all eat. He offered to stand treat, but before they had finished, he regretted his generosity. They were young and healthy, and when they had eaten everything on the entire bill of fare, they began all over again.

Windy Jake was leaning back in his chair with the satisfied air of a boa constrictor when a stir of excitement in the hotel lobby sent them all clumping out to see what caused it.

They saw a small man of about twenty-eight strut across the floor and drop a battered bag close to the desk. He wore a brand-new hat with an extra-high crown, high-heeled boots, and a black-silk shirt and tie. His suit was also black, with silk-faced lapels adorning a long-tailed coat.

As he leaned across the desk to sign the register, his coat fell back and displayed two enormous black-hilted guns tied down to his thighs. He scrawled a signature on the register and whirled it about for the clerk to read. The clerk's jaw dropped open.

Toothpick Jerrick approached the stranger, followed by the three riders. "Mr. Jack Allen, do you remember me? I knew you once up in Wyoming," Toothpick said.

"Sure I know you. You helped me catch a bunch of horse thieves," Jim Allen replied cordially. "Could you tell me where I can find the sheriff?"

"I sure can," Toothpick replied. "What's more, I'll take you to him."

He cast a superior grin at the three riders, then left the hotel with Allen. They went directly to the jail, where they found the sheriff and Sam Hogg waiting for them.

"Dang it, Jim," the ex-Ranger said as he slapped Allen on the back, "I'm plumb proud to see you!"

"But why for this disguise?" Sheriff Tom Powers inquired.

"'Cause if folks think I'm Jack Allen, I can walk around town without no danger of some fool tryin' to collect the reward on my head," Jim Allen explained.

He told them of Quong and explained how he had dedicated his life to running down and ending the career of that villainous old Chinaman.

"D'you figger he's holdin' up somewhere hereabouts?" the ex-Ranger asked.

"Sure do, an' he's runnin' as partner with Bull Morgan, the craftiest white man I ever knowed," Jim replied.

The four men sat and discussed various plans until far into the night. They were still trying to figure out where Quong might be hiding when a rider tore down Main Street on a sweat-covered horse and threw himself from the saddle.

Toothpick opened the door, and a white-faced puncher stumbled into the room. They all knew him as "Shorty," one of Old Man Carver's men.

"Some one's killed Old Man Carver!" he gasped.

"When? How?" Tom Powers snapped.

"The old man goes in his office about an hour ago. Me an' Fred sees the light in the window. We was wonderin' what he was workin' so late for, so we sneaks up and looks through the window. We sees him sittin' there, dead — shot in the back of his head."

The sheriff sent his deputy for horses, and ten minutes later, the four cantered down the street. The three Frying Pan riders, who had been waiting for something to happen, hopped on their horses and trailed along behind them.

When the cavalcade pulled up at the L Bar B Ranch, they found Fred waiting for them on the front porch.

He greeted the sheriff. "He's deader'n a doornail. Some skunk shot him from behind. I made the other boys stay clear of the place so's they wouldn't go trampin' up all signs."

"Good head, Fred," the sheriff commended as they trooped into the office.

The faces of Sam Hogg and the sheriff became grim and wrathful as they stared down at the murdered man. Both had been his lifelong friends. Old Man Carver lay slumped forward in his chair with his arms and head resting on the desk. Jim Allen stepped forward and looked down at him. He pointed to the powder burns on the silver-white head.

"Shot from behind, and at close range. Must have been done by somebody he thought was a friend, or the old gent would have never let him get behind him," Allen remarked thoughtfully.

Sam Hogg and the sheriff nodded and looked at Allen. Instinctively they waited for him to take command.

There was no moon, and the night was pitch black. Allen took a lantern and stepped out on the porch. A swift glance convinced him there was nothing to be learned there. He stepped off the porch and, holding his lantern low, commenced to zigzag back and forth. The others remained in the door and watched him.

Some hundred yards from the house he found the tracks of four horses. There was a story written on that area of earth, but a man had to be a born trailer or have Allen's eyes to read it. The horses had stood there for some time. From the boot tracks it was clear that two men had dismounted and gone to the house, while three had returned. Of the two going toward the house, one was considerably larger than the other. One man must have worn No. 9 boots, while the others were small and dainty.

Slowly Allen started to trace these tracks back to the house. Then he muttered to himself and shook his head. There clearly in the dust were the telltale marks where a man had laid on the ground, and there was a broad trail in the dust as if some one had dragged a body some distance. That mark disappeared, and Allen noticed that from there on the boot tracks seemed to sink deeper into the ground, as if the owner were carrying a heavy weight.

Allen returned to the porch and beckoned for the sheriff and Sam Hogg to follow him.

"If you don't read the signs as I does, you stop me. You see, four hosses stayed here quite a spell. Two gents hit the ground — a big feller from the size of his boots, an' one little feller. He wore pointed boots, so I figger as he was somethin' of a dude. They walked along here toward the house. When they gets this far, they lays down the gent they was carryin'. I reckon he must have been heavy, 'cause they decided to drag him a while. Findin' that won't do, they hoist him up again and start carryin' him. The tracks lead to the porch and disappear. Then three gents come off the porch. They come off after the other two stepped on, 'cause you can see easy where they stepped into big foot's tracks, as he was goin' toward the ranch. They all three goes back to the hosses and climbs into their saddles. Then all four hosses hit the breeze. What do you make of her?"

Sam Hogg and the sheriff shook their heads. Some of the signs they could understand only after Allen had pointed them out.

"Do you figger they killed the old man away from the house, then lugged his body in an' put it in the chair?" Sam Hogg demanded.

"Nope, not any; 'cause, if they did, the old man's clothes would sure have been right dusty, an' I looked careful for signs on that black suit of his," Allen said with a shake of his head.

"Then why for was they carryin' that gent to the house?" the sheriff asked, puzzled.

"Danged if I know," Allen replied with a ghost of a smile. "I reckon when we know that, we'll know who killed him. 'Tain't nothin' we can do now. We got to wait till it's light afore we can trail the coyotes."

Old Man Carver had been popular with his men, but they realized that Allen spoke sense and they agreed to wait for morning before starting to track down the murderer of their boss.

At the first streak of dawn, a band of fifteen grim-faced, heavily armed men rode away from the L Bar B Ranch. Jim Allen and Sam Hogg rode in the lead.

The trail first led due north, then, seven or eight miles from the ranch, it turned sharply and circled back toward the south. Where it crossed the road from Cannondale to the L Bar B Ranch, one rider had turned and headed for town. Sam Hogg carefully studied these prints and then announced that he would follow them into town. Allen and the others continued on the trail of the other three. They followed it to the border. There the trail ran across ground so sunbaked the tracks became indistinct, and no one could follow them but Allen. He took the sheriff aside and pointed to a well-defined road that led southwest.

"Them coyotes went down that road. Where does it go to?" he asked.

"The Casa Diablo Ranch," the sheriff replied.

"I'm tellin' the fellows we lost the trail," Allen said. "We're in Old Mexico now, so you ain't got no jurisdiction, and there's no use lettin' the coyotes know we trailed them home. We could never find the hosses they rode, so there's no use puttin' them on their guard."

The sheriff nodded and told the punchers they had lost the trail. Most of them declared that they intended to scout around and see what they could find. The sheriff, Allen and five punchers rode directly to the Casa Diablo. This was an old hacienda with a courtyard in the center. They clattered through the gateway and quickly dismounted.

There were three men at the other end of the courtyard. The largest of them jumped backward when he saw Allen, as though he intended to run for the house. Allen yawned indifferently and the big man relaxed.

"'Lo, Tom. What brings you this way?" Big Montana demanded.

The sheriff told him of the murder, and Montana appeared to be shocked. The latter went to the bunk house and questioned the men there.

"None of them seen any suspicious characters," he declared when he returned, then added carelessly: "You say you followed the trail across the border? How close did she come to Casa Diablo?"

"We lost her about five miles from here. Reckon the murderers went on south," the sheriff replied. Big Montana's relief was apparent to the sheriff. "This will sure be a knock-out blow to the kid. He got soused in town last night, so Silver brought him out here to sleep it off." Big Montana shook his head sadly.

The sheriff went into the ranch house to break the news to young Carver. When he reappeared, he wore a frown, and his face was very thoughtful. He and Allen, followed by the punchers, rode back toward the border and the Carver ranch.

Big Montana stood at the gate and watched them for several minutes. Silver joined him.

"Allen didn't know you with your beard," Silver suggested.

"If that was Jack Allen, I'd say yes, but if it was Jim, I ain't so sure," Montana replied thoughtfully. "an' if it was Jim, he didn't lose those tracks, neither, and he's wise."

"Then the sheriff knows, too."

"Quong hates Jim Allen enough to do anything to get even. We got to rig up a plan to get him started pronto, or we'll be in the soup."

"An' here's hopin' Quong will cash in the ructions what follow," Silver said hopefully.

"I'm plumb worried about that kid," the sheriff told Allen, as they rode back to the Carver ranch. "He didn't act right when I told him about his dad. He wasn't surprised at all."

"Has that big jasper got a side-kick what is sort o' small and dresses careful?" Allen asked.

The sheriff nodded.

"That big fella is Bull Morgan, and I bet his partner is Johnson, the gambler. Them's the two Jack is huntin' down this way."

"I hate to say it, but if that is true, it sure looks bad for young Carver. Shall I grab them the first time they cross the border?"

"Nope, leave 'em loose. Maybe they'll lead me to Quong."

Later that afternoon, when Allen and the sheriff returned to Cannondale, Sam Hogg told them that he had trailed the lone horse into town and that he was sure it was stabled behind the Red Queen.

"Jim, I got two pieces of news for you," he said. "There is a chink gunman named Hip Sing over in the Red Queen talkin' loud about you. He thinks you're Jack Allen. I sort o' inquired about this here feller, and folks tell me he's a darned nifty gunman, so you ought to watch yourself. The second news is that a couple of gals arrived on this morning's train and headed for my ranch. I sent Tad Hicks and tother two along with them to see that they got there safe. It's sure a funny joke, kid, your passin' yourself off as Jack Allen, for one of those gals is a little bit of a thing with blond hair and pretty as a doll. Do you happen to know what her name is?"

Jim Allen shook his head.

Sam Hogg chuckled. "She calls herself Mrs. Jack Allen."

Jim Allen stared at the old cattleman, then a broad grin lighted his freckled face, and his white teeth flashed in his black beard.

"Well, I'll be gosh darned! So the little runt has gone an' done it! A little blonde, huh? I bet that's Mary Bell, a gal I saved once."

"Can she tell you two apart?" Sam Hogg asked with a broad grin.

Jim Allen laughed. "Didn't used to, but I reckon she can now." Suddenly Jim Allen's face grew serious and he frowned. "Quong tried to kidnap her once, to get even with Jack, and I reckon he'll try it again."

"She'll be safe at my place. I got a couple of dozen of the fightin'est fools out there you ever seen," Sam Hogg boasted.

"Mebbe so, but you don't know Quong. I'm aimin' to go out there pronto."

Allen was about to ride away when he wheeled his horse and, riding close to the sheriff, leaned down.

"Mr. Powers, you watch your step. You don't know where Quong is, an' you don't know him. But I'm tellin' you he knows that you rode in with me. Don't be forgettin' this. Me an' you is the only two that knows the names of the two gents which was at the ranch when old Carver was murdered. So I'm tellin' yuh again, watch your step, or you'll be eatin' lead pills."

The sheriff nodded. He fully understood Allen's anxiety about the safety of Jack's bride. It was unfortunate that she should have chosen this time to visit Cannondale.

The sheriff strolled by the Comfort Hotel and seated himself in front of the hardware store. He rolled a cigarette and watched the group of loafers who were sunning themselves in front of the Red Queen Saloon. The place had always been a hangout for crooks and bad men; time after time it had been cleaned out. He knew it was like a rabbit warren with secret passages. Only a year before it had been the headquarters of the Toad and his Lava gang. What more likely than that this Chinaman should have moved in and made it his headquarters? His eyes narrowed as he remembered that the present owner, Slick Keen, was a mongrel Chinaman.

Suddenly the sheriff straightened and stared at a little man who swung around from Depot Street into Main. Allen had just ridden away and yet here he was coming down the street with a bag in his hand. The sheriff saw him hesitate before the swinging doors of the Red Queen, then, bag in hand, briskly push open the doors and enter.

The sheriff frowned. What was Allen going in there for? He recalled Sam Hogg's warning about the Chinese gunman, Hip Sing. His confidence in Jim's ability with a gun was tremendous, but that place might be filled with enemies who could overpower him by sheer weight of numbers. As these thoughts were running through his head, he saw several men dart from the saloon and then stand looking backward. The sheriff leaped to his feet and was halfway across the street when there came a bedlam of heavy reports. With an oath he snatched his gun and leaped into the saloon.

CHAPTER NINETEEN

A Puppet

Just when on the night that his father was murdered Bill Carver lost track of events, he never knew. When Slick Keen and Silver rejoined him at the bar after leaving Quong, he was already in a state of approaching unconsciousness. Later he remembered making some vague threats to them about his father. At the time the bystanders believed them to be nothing by the ravings of an angry, drunken boy and paid little attention to them; but on the following day, when the news spread that Old Man Carver had been murdered, they remembered these words, and in repeating them, magnified and completely distorted them.

"I tell you," Carver had informed his new-found friends, Silver and Slick Keen, "I'm aimin' to show the old man he daren't talk to me that way."

"How are you goin' to do it, Bill?" Silver inquired.

"Do it — darn him — do it?" Bill Carver asked maudlingly. "He'll never do it again."

Slick Keen's eyes met Silver's, and then they both nodded. They stepped forward, and each took one of the boy's arms. They attempted to lead him to the door, but he resisted. They then attempted to use force, but this aroused in him a drunken belligerency. Instantly they changed their tactics and began to argue with him. At last their efforts were rewarded, and they led him lurching, from the Red Queen Saloon.

Half an hour later, Gloomy Mason looked up from his game of cards and saw his boss, Slick Keen, sidle into the gambling room. Gloomy was acting as lookout for a game of faro; there were seven men seated around the table. Slick Keen watched the game for a few minutes in silence. Then he spoke across the table to Gloomy in a metallic whisper which could be clearly heard by all seven players.

"Gloomy," he said, "that fool kid, Bill Carver, is pie-eyed, an' is makin' threats about his dad. He started back for the L Bar B Ranch a while ago, and if he don't tumble off his horse an' break his neck before he gets there, I reckon he may do something he'll be plumb sorry for to-morrow. You get Stub Porter to take your place, take a broncho, and go and fetch that fool kid back here and put him to bed in the hotel."

These words caused little comment at the time. If the listeners thought about them at all, it was simply to wonder why a man like Slick Keen should be worrying about a drunken boy.

Gloomy turned over his chair on the lookout platform to Stub Porter, and clumped out of the room. Slick Keen stood for a moment longer, watching the game. Then he turned away. As he went, he called over his shoulder to Stub:

"I'll be in my office if anythin' turns up."

He spoke casually to several of the players as he strolled across the room, and vanished through the door that led to Quong's quarters.

Bill Carver remembered nothing from the time he left the saloon to the time he regained consciousness in his father's office. He had a sensation as if some one were beating him, then something jarred him into full consciousness. He opened his eyes and looked about. At first he did not know where he was. Then, little by little, familiar objects placed themselves in his mind, and he realized stupidly that he was sitting in his father's office, with his back to the desk. He looked down at his lap and saw that he was holding a gun in his right hand. His first rational thought was to get out of that office as quickly as possible. If his father caught him there, it would lead to a row. He lurched to his feet and rubbed his eyes with his hand.

Then something compelled him to turn around. He saw his father sitting with his head and arms sprawled across the desk. He stared dully at him for a moment. "Huh, the old man's drunk, too," he said with a drunken chuckle. He started to step toward the door, then remained frozen with one foot suspended in the air. He could not believe what his eyes saw. The shock completely sobered him. He shook once and turned and sought for help. He was still a little unsteady on his feet when he stepped toward the door and called for assistance.

Before he reached it, he heard two men step up on the porch outside. He halted as Big Montana and Slick

Keen walked into the room. The two stopped just inside the doorway and looked from young Carver to his father, and then back to the gun the boy still held in his hand. They said nothing, but simply stared at him. Their eyes questioned him, and there was something about the expression of their faces that disturbed the boy.

During the long silence, he had for the first time the sense of fear — a fear that had not completely formulated itself as yet. Desperately he sought back in his addled brain as to just how he had come there, but he could remember nothing, so he continued to stare dumbly at the two men in the doorway. "What is it? What are you looking at me that way for?" he demanded.

"Blazes, kid, what's been goin' on here?" Big Montana rumbled as he shook his head.

"Dad's dead. Somebody killed him," the boy replied with a shudder.

"That's plain enough," Slick Keen whispered.

"Kid, what have you done?" Big Montana demanded.

"Me?" Bill Carver replied stupidly. Then, following Big Montana's eyes, he dropped his own to the gun still held in his hand. From there his eyes switched to his father; a spasm of horror, grief, and despair swept over him. He dropped the gun to the carpet and collapsed into a chair, burying his head in his hands.

Again there was that terrible silence in the room. This was broken by Slick Keen's metallic whisper. The gunman's words rasped against the boy's nerves like a file on steel wire.

"Kid, I was scared that something like this was goin' to happen. You was talkin' loud in town. We followed you out here to try to stop you."

With an effort Bill took his hands from his face and looked stupidly about the room. He saw Big Montana stoop and pick up his gun from the floor. The big man twirled the cylinder and then ejected one empty shell, which he handed to Bill Carver.

"Silver is waiting for us outside," said Slick Keen, "so we'll have to tell him about this. But he's a square hombre, and knows how to keep his mouth shut. No one else knows nothin' about this, so listen, let's all promise to keep it to ourselves. The kid, here, when he done it, didn't know what he was doing, and he ain't responsible."

"Sure he didn't," Big Montana agreed. "But maybe the jury wouldn't see it in the same light."

"You're right there; the jury would be for hangin' the kid sure," Slick Keen cut in quickly. "But it'll never come to that. You and Silver take him over to the Casa Diablo. We'll all swear that he stayed there last night and never came to this ranch at all."

Big Montana nodded. "We'd better move pronto. Come on, kid."

Young Bill Carver was bewildered; his reasoning faculties were numbed. Otherwise he would have realized that his only hope of ever convincing people that a horrible accident had happened while he was sleepwalking was to arouse the ranch and confess then and there. But his mind did not work clearly If the murdered man had been any one but his father, he would probably have stayed and taken the consequences. It was not the rope he feared, or a jail sentence; he lacked the moral courage to face his father's friends and admit that while drunk he had killed the old man.

Young Carver did at first refuse to go with them, and wanted to arouse the ranch. But the two men were both older than he, and they both insisted that it would be an act of madness. They appeared to be his friends, and were trying to help him out, so in the end he accepted their advice and allowed them to lead him from the room to where Silver waited with the horses.

He was so stupefied that he started that ride with no idea of what direction they took. He was across the border into Mexico, close to the Casa Diablo Ranch, before his mind could again formulate coherent thoughts. When they arrived at the Casa Diablo, Big Montana and Silver plied him with liquor until he relapsed into a drunken sleep. It was only on the following morning that he realized his terrible predicament.

"Of course, kid, Big Montana and Slick did what they did because they wanted to help you," Silver said coldly. "But I'm tellin' you that you made a fool play, for now if it ever comes out that you killed your dad, you'll hang sure. No one will believe that you were drunk when you did it, after runnin' away like you did."

These words of Silver's stunned young Carver. He was sick with despair and grief. His father, up to a year ago, had been more a pal than a father, so the boy's grief was greater than the fear of consequences. Yet the two combined seemed to overwhelm him so that he lacked all will-power and became a mere puppet in the hands of Silver and Montana.

So when the sheriff arrived at the Casa Diablo in his search for the murderers, Silver forced the boy to see and talk to the officer of the law. He knew that he was in no state to play a part. He knew that when the sheriff told him of his father's death, Bill's actions would arouse suspicion. But that was what they wanted. They wanted talk about the boy. They wanted people to suspect him. In that way he became more firmly theirs. For the more people talked, the more surely would the boy realize that his fate rested in the hands of Big Montana, Slick Keen, and Silver.

When Tom Powers told him that his father was dead, Bill attempted to simulate surprise. He made a miserable failure of it. He had a panicky feeling when he saw the man look curiously at him. "This thing has knocked me off my legs," Bill muttered. "I'll be over to the ranch later."

Again that veiled look of suspicion leaped into Tom Powers' eyes, but he only nodded, swung about, and rejoined his men. They mounted, and the boy watched them as they rode slowly back toward the L Bar B Ranch.

Toward noon, Gloomy Mason, riding a sweaty horse, thundered up the draw, swung into the courtyard of the Casa Diablo, and threw himself from the saddle. He shouted a question and dashed into the house. A little later, Big Montana, followed by Gloomy, stepped out of the house and walked across the courtyard to where the boy was sitting, staring stupidly out across the mesa toward his home ranch.

"Kid," Big Montana boomed, "we got to hustle into Cannondale."

"I ain't goin'," the boy replied with a show of spirit. "I'm goin' home."

Big Montana's face hardened. He looked at the boy for a moment, and then, when he did speak, his voice was harshly authoritative.

"Kid, I helped you out of a mess last night. The time has come when you must help pay back that debt. You're comin' to town with me now."

That was the first time any of the three had snapped the whip. It brought a flush of anger and resentment to the boy's cheeks. He leaped to his feet and glared defiantly at Big Montana. "I tell you I won't go to town. I'm goin' home!"

"Kid," Big Montana said slowly, "you'll either go to town with me and help me out of a mess, or when I get there, I'll be goin' straight to the sheriff's office and tell him what I know."

Fear leaped into Bill's eyes. He gave a panic-stricken glance at Gloomy, who was standing a short distance away, saddling some horses. Then he looked at Big Montana and shook his head. His action showed as clearly as words that he was afraid that Gloomy might overhear Big Montana. The big man laughed loudly.

"You sort o' scared he might hear me and get wise?" Montana demanded sarcastically. "If you're scared about him, how about the sheriff?"

The boy blanched and shivered. He could already see the scornful faces of his father's friends. No, he would never be able to face that. Weakly he consented to go to town with Big Montana.

Arriving at Cannondale, Bill for the first time fully realized the pit he had fallen into; there was no escape for him. On the ride to town he had been silent, but both Big Montana and Gloomy were loquacious in the extreme; they talked endlessly about a man named the Wolf and his brother, the sheriff, Jack Allen. They related story after story about the twins. Little by little their words penetrated Bill's numbed brain, and he started to listen with a show of interest. It seemed impossible that any human being could have done the things that Big Montana and Gloomy swore the twins had done.

"Two fellers I know," Gloomy said, "see this here Jack Allen up in Wyoming shoot down three kids. They were the Stetson boys, and it was just before election; Allen was runnin' for sheriff again. A bank had been held up, and a lot of folks figgered that Jack Allen had done it himself, so he had to go out and get some prisoners. These Stetson boys were sort of wild and freelike, so he picks on them. He goes out to their ranch and lines them up and starts to ride back to town with them. But they never got there; at least, they wasn't alive when they got there. He swore that all three had tried to escape and he had to shoot them down. Two friends of mine was hiding in the brush and sees the four of them come riding along. Jack Allen sort o' dropped back and yanked out his gun and started shooting without saying a word."

"Yeah, I heard that story afore. He's sure a dirty coyote," Big Montana said furiously. "This here outlaw, the Wolf, is just like him."

"Sam Hogg swears by him," Bill Carver cut into the conversation. "He told me about that time the Wolf had himself thrown through a window into the old mine building across the border and helped clean out the Toad and the Lava gang."

Big Montana brushed this away with a wave of his hand. "'Tain't nothin' in that, kid. The truth of that story is that the Toad and the others down there was his friends. They let him come through that window, 'cause they thought he was goin' to help them. Then, when he gets inside, and they wasn't lookin' he starts shootin' right and left. Then Sam Hogg comes along with his punchers and knocks the doors down, and every one there thought the Wolf was plumb heroic."

"If that's the truth, this Wolf person must sure be a skunk," Carver said.

The three riders did not enter the town along the south trail, but circled it, and approached from the east. This was the Mexican quarter — several blocks of tumble-down, squalid, adobe shacks. Close to the center of this quarter, Big Montana turned down an alley and then entered a yard.

"I got to blindfold you here," Big Montana said as the three dismounted. Then, before Bill could protest, he took a large handkerchief from his pocket and bound it about Bill's eyes. Gloomy and Montana each seized an arm and led him into a tumble-down shack. They mounted a flight of stairs, and then it seemed to the boy that they walked an interminable distance through complete darkness. They climbed stairway after stairway, until at last the handkerchief was snatched from his eyes, and he found himself face to face with the Chinaman, Quong.

The lights were dim in that room, but even so they temporarily blinded Bill Carver. He blinked his eyes to accustom them to the light, and glanced about. He was startled and amazed at what he saw. It was like some "Arabian Nights" tale. Then his eyes became fixed on the withered old Chinaman who sat cross-legged among the cushions on his couch.

The boy gaped at the yellow face of the old Chinaman. There was something so indescribably sinister about Quong that little prickles of fear raced up and down Carver's back. He looked about and saw that he was alone in the room with that silent, immovable figure. Big Montana had gone. It leaped into the boy's mind that the man sitting on the couch was not real, but some kind of a mummy, or even a corpse. Then he saw Quong's eyes, and he knew that this was not true; those eyes were alive, horribly alive.

Bill Carver stared at them, and the terrible silence added to his alarm and tortured his jangled nerves. He licked his dry lips and tried to speak.

"You are Bill Carver. You are a friend of Sam Hogg," said Quong.

Bill nodded stupidly.

"There is no joy to the soul like when one returns a favor. Big Montana saved your neck last night. Big Montana has an enemy. You will help him to escape this enemy. The heavens will rejoice that you have paid your debt."

This was so much gibberish to Bill Carver. He could not understand it, so he simply stood and stared.

"You want to help Big Montana?" Quong queried.

Bill Carver nodded again.

"You have heard of Jack Allen? You know him? You like him?" Quong demanded.

"Nope, and if what I hear of him is true, I don't want to know him. He must be a sort of yellow coyote," the boy muttered.

Quong's eyes lighted with joy, and he smiled to himself. So Big Montana had already planted the seed of hatred, and very cleverly.

"Jack Allen tricked Big Montana once. Cheated him out of money, then framed him and had him arrested as a cow thief. Big Montana was sent to prison but escaped. Jack Allen is down here now, looking for him. If he finds him, he will either kill him or send him back to jail. Now, if you will do this, you will help Big Montana and aid justice."

Bill Carver nodded eagerly.

"Then go to Sam Hogg's ranch, make friends with Jack Allen's wife and stay there and wait, then do what my messenger tells you." Quong was silent a moment. When he next spoke, his voice was no longer friendly, but was hard. "Big Montana is not asking much, but if you don't do it, you'll hang."

Bill Carver's face blanched at these words. The door behind him slid open, and Big Montana appeared in the entrance and beckoned to him. Bill stumbled from the room.

"Gosh!" the boy breathed when the door shut behind him. "You know, that old chink scares me. Certainly I'll help you out, Big."

The boy's eyes were again blindfolded, and he was led down the stairs and along the passage, finally returning to where they had left the horses. They swung into their saddles and turned into the trail that led to Sam Hogg's ranch.

The trail split a short distance from the ranch, and the south fork led over the border to Casa Diablo. Here Big Montana said good-by to the boy.

CHAPTER TWENTY

Two Girls

Fifteen miles to the southwest of Cannondale there was a great barren waste of lava rock. It extended for miles southward over the border. It was utterly devoid of vegetation; even cactus could not find root there. It was cut in a blind maze of deep ravines and sheer-walled canyons, and its smooth, wind-swept slopes were as slippery as glass. The old Lava gang had used it as a hide-out. Even shod horses left practically no mark on its flintlike surface, yet Jim Allen had managed to trail the gang to their hiding place and had ended by driving them over the border. The Frying Pan Ranch was to the west of this rocky waste.

Sam Hogg and Jim Allen covered the distance from Cannondale to the ranch at a rapid gallop. Both were nervous and apprehensive for the safety of the two girls at the ranch. Sam Hogg had told Allen the name of only one of the girls. He had intended to name the other, but it had slipped his mind at the time. Now he felt that it would be a good joke on Jim Allen to hold it back and surprise him when he arrived at the ranch.

"You say, Jim, that your brother Jack's wife mistook you for him once?" the old cattleman inquired as they galloped along.

Jim Allen grinned broadly. "Yeah. It was down in El Crucifixo that Jack first met her. He fell hard for her, but was plumb scared to say anything, so I sort o' helped him along."

The two rode in silence for a moment, then Jim Allen chuckled aloud at the remembrance.

"She thought I was Jack, and just as I was riding away, I stooped down and kissed her. Then I told her to ask me why I had done it the next day. So when she sees Jack she asks him about it. He was plumb flabbergasted, and went on the prod when he learned what I had done."

The ex-Ranger chortled and slapped his knee. "Do you reckon you could do it again?" he asked with mischief in his eyes.

"I'm aimin' to try," Jim Allen replied with a broad grin.

As the two dismounted in front of the ranch house, a girl appeared in the doorway. Mary Bell Allen was as pretty as a picture as she stood there on the porch. She looked at Sam Hogg for a moment, then called to some one who was in the house. Jim Allen stood close to Princess and kept his hat pulled down over his eyes. Once she saw him, the girl gave a glad cry and ran toward him.

"Jack! Jack! So you're safe!"

Jim flung open his arms, and she leaped into them, then he gave her two resounding smacks full on the lips. Apparently she sensed something wrong the moment his arms closed about her, for she started to struggle and push him away so she could see his face. But he held her firmly and again kissed her. Sam Hogg shouted with mirth and started to dance a jig. Then, as the second girl appeared in the doorway, he stopped his dancing and prepared to enjoy the second joke.

Snippets McPherson was of medium height and slender. She had a quantity of wavy, black hair which was drawn back in a tight fold off a smooth, high forehead. Her face was oval and her mouth firm, her nose rather large, and her eyes wistful and dark.

Sam waited eagerly for Allen to look up and see Snippets standing there while he kissed another woman. He thought it would be a rare joke, but when Allen did look up, Sam Hogg regretted what he had done.

Mary Allen had struggled free from Jim and was looking at him with scornful eyes. It was then that Allen saw Snippets McPherson for the first time. He ignored the little blond girl's angry reproaches. He simply stood and stared at Snippets. There was something terrible about the intensity of his gaze. Both of them stood there too moved to speak, but their eyes spoke volumes. As Sam Hogg watched them, he swore softly at himself for the unfairness of his joke. He remembered that these two were no ordinary sweethearts. They were separated by a gulf too deep for either one to cross. Jim-twin Allen was an outlaw with a fabulous price on his head. Fate had made him a desert wolf; he, like a gray lobo, was condemned to travel always alone.

"Oh, wait until I tell Jack on you. He'll fix you. What he did the last time will be nothing to what he'll do now!" the little blond scolded. Then, as she caught sight of Jim's face, her words came to an abrupt halt. She glanced from the little gunman to Snippets, and instantly understood. Pity welled up in her heart for those two.

With a desperate effort, Jim Allen summoned a feeble smile to his lips. He attempted to appear nonchalant and at ease. "So it's you, Snippets. What you doin' here?" he asked stupidly.

"Jim Allen, what do you mean dressing yourself up to look like Jack?" Snippets said severely, but here eyes were smiling.

"Oh, shucks, I gets tired of goin' around lookin' like a scarecrow, an' I gets the notion to sort o' try an' make myself appear man-sized, so I wears eight-inch heels and whiskers that are big enough for a giant, an' that sort o' makes me think I ain't no peanut. Yep, folks, when I'm dressed this way, I'm just like Jack, plumb full of dignity and vanity."

This broke the tension, and both Snippets and Sam Hogg laughed, but Mary was indignant.

"How dare you make fun of the best, bravest man in the world?" she said witheringly.

"Sure, he's all of that, or I wouldn't have made fun of him," Jim Allen said seriously.

Mary recognized the sincerity in his voice and promptly forgave him. The four stood in silence for a moment, then the two girls returned to the job of house cleaning.

Allen and Sam Hogg went to look for Windy Jake, Tad Hicks, and Kansas Jones, whom they found seated in the shade of the bunk house.

"Boys," Sam Hogg addressed them seriously, "Allen, here, has got somethin' to say to you, and he's speakin' for me, too."

"I don't know if you know the reason I'm down here, but anyway, I'll tell you," Jim Allen began. "Jack Allen's after a couple of fellers, Bull Morgan and Tom Johnson, what broke jail up in Wyoming. Both of them is plumb dangerous critters. But they've hitched up with a chink what is twice as bad as a thousand rattlesnakes. We busts up this chink's gang some time ago and kills the chink's son. That was before Jack was married. That time the chink steals Mary Bell and we got her back after a fight. He sure hates the Allen twins, and he'll do anything to get even, so I figgers he's goin' to try and steal Mrs. Allen again. I want you boys to promise you'll never let her out of your sight. If any stranger comes to the ranch, watch him close, and keep your guns loose."

It was Tad Hicks who replied for the three. "Allen, don't you be worryin' now. Mrs. Allen will be safe, or we'll all be dead."

Allen grinned widely at them. "Thanks, fellows. I know I can trust you, but remember this — it won't do me no good to have yuh dead, so keep your eyes peeled an' see that that chink doesn't get his hands on her."

Allen and Sam Hogg walked back toward the house, and the three punchers watched them go. Then Tad

Hicks pushed back his hat and scratched his ear thoughtfully.

"Fellers," he said at last, "that's darned funny. Did you notice Allen kep' talkin' about 'we' an' 'Jack'? It was Jack this and Jack that, as if it was Jim talkin' an not Jack."

"Now you recalls it to me, it seems plumb curious," Windy Jake said.

It was late forenoon when young Bill Carver rode up to the ranch. Sam Hogg ran down the lane to meet him, and walked along by his side to the house.

The two women's hearts went out at once to the young fellow, for his handsome face was strained, and there was a haunted look about his eyes. Allen gave the boy one swift glance and then ignored him, but he took the first opportunity to examine young Carver's horse's tracks. After he had studied these for some time, he arose to his feet and whistled tunelessly. He called Sam Hogg aside.

"Mr. Hogg, what kind of a kid is he?"

"He's a darned nice kid; a little wild — but we was all wild when we was his age," Sam Hogg defended.

"Is he yeller? Is he honest? Would you trust him?" Allen demanded.

"Sure, I'd trust him with anything I've got," Sam Hogg replied warmly. "That kid's got good blood in him; his kind would rather die than do a mean thing." The old cattleman was silent for a long time, then he sighed, and into his eyes there came a far-away expression. After a time he continued: "You see, Jim, now that his dad's gone, I feel like he's my son. He doesn't know it, but ever since he was born he's been my heir. He — Oh, shucks, Jim, let's you an' me go an' have a nice big drink." He led the way to the cellar, followed by Allen. From a barrel in the corner he drew a tin pannikin of whisky, from which he and Jim drank.

Allen was now convinced that Bill Carver was the fourth man in that party which had ridden away from the ranch after the murder. He had only been in town a short while that morning, but it was long enough for him to have heard a little of the gossip which was floating around about the threats the boy had made the previous night. He knew that people were already talking. He knew that men were already pointing the finger of suspicion at Bill Carver. And Allen also knew that the boy was in some peculiar way connected with that murder. He looked at his friend, Sam Hogg, and shook his head, resolving then and there that he would never take another step to unravel the murder, for he was certain in his own mind that if he did he would bring sorrow to the old ex-Ranger.

After supper that evening Allen wandered off by himself and sat on top of the corral fence and talked to his grays. They were always his confidants. When he ceased speaking, they rubbed their soft muzzles against his pockets, looking for sweets. Finding none, they showed their resentment by shrill squeals. He was sitting there talking to his two pets when Sam Hogg joined him.

"What's the next step in catchin' them jaspers what murdered Old Man Carver?" Sam Hogg demanded.

"I ain't got nothin' in mind," Allen replied evasively as he thought to himself that one of the murderers was at that moment under Sam Hogg's roof. Then suddenly he remembered how two men had carried and dragged a third to Old Man Carver's house, and he whistled softly. Was he jumping at conclusions too rapidly?

"I got to go to town pronto," he said.

"Why for?"

"To ask some questions." Allen grinned broadly and added: "You remember when we was after the Lava gang, I finds one of the back ways to get into the Red Queen? I reckon I'll use it again and see what I can find out."

"Jim, you watch out. You figure that's the center of Quong's web, an' if that chink is as wily as you say he is, he'll nab you if you go foolin' around in there," Hogg warned.

"I know, but it's got to be did."

"Then I'll go with you," Hogg declared.

"Nope, I goes alone," Allen replied positively.

Before Sam could make further protest, a wolf shattered the night with his mournful cry. It quavered, rose high, then slowly died away.

"When I hear a lobo like that, I always feel plumb sad," Sam said. He saw that Allen was not listening, but was staring in the direction from where the call had come. Hogg saw his white teeth flash in the darkness. His eyes were also shining.

Then, from the opposite direction, another call came. Allen swung about and looked into the darkness.

"That one sounds sort of phony," Sam Hogg muttered.

"That last one was Jack. He's out of practice," Jim Allen replied. "I'm aimin' to answer him, so don't get scared."

In spite of the warning, Sam Hogg jumped when Allen threw back his head and gave a perfect imitation of the wolf's plaintive call.

"If I hadn't seen you do it, I'd have sworn it was a real wolf," Sam chuckled.

"Don't get scared, 'cause I'm goin' to show you a real one," Allen said with a happy laugh. He placed his fingers to his mouth and whistled shrilly, then stood listening.

From the night there came a faint murmur of swiftly moving, padded feet stirring up the sand. Then Sam Hogg jumped backward and dropped his hand on his gun as a big gray desert wolf materialized from the darkness and stopped close to Allen. The beast stood silent and looked at Allen with large, luminous eyes.

" 'Lo, King," Allen greeted. "I was wonderin' if you'd show up."

He stooped and stroked the big, shaggy head. Instantly there came a volley of deep-throated growls.

"That's his way of tellin' me he plumb loves me," Allen laughed happily. He adopted me a couple of months ago. I reckon he's part dog. He can follow my tracks even when they're two days old." As Allen talked he saddled his gray mare. "You tell Mary Bell I'm comin' back pronto, and aim to do what I did this afternoon."

"You mean that tother wolf was Jack, and he's out there waitin' for you?" Hogg demanded.

"Yep. Don't forget to tell Mary Bell."

The older man chuckled as he remembered the scene of the morning. Then he grew serious. "Jim, I don't like the idea of you prowling around those secret passages in the Red Queen."

Jim Allen made no reply to this. He swung into his saddle and, followed by the wolf, trotted quietly away into the night.

CHAPTER TWENTY-ONE

Hip Sing's Finish

For a month, Jack-twin Allen had trailed the two escaped prisoners, Bull Morgan and Tom Johnson with almost as much patience as his brother, Jim Allen, would have employed. His search took him for many a weary mile up and down along the border. He had ridden over two hundred miles to run down the slightest clews, and never once, when they proved false, had he grown discouraged.

Now, little by little, he had narrowed the circle and knew that the men he sought were within a short distance of Cannondale. It was for that reason that he had allowed Mary Bell to accept Snippets McPherson's invitation to visit the old bachelor, Sam Hogg, who was an old friend of Snippets' father. At the time Jack gave his permission, he knew nothing of the presence of Quong in the neighborhood. Having been married only three months, he jumped at this opportunity to have his wife near him.

He arrived on the train at Cannondale in the forenoon. Bag in hand, he left the station and walked up the street, looking for a hotel. He had heard the story about how Jim had cleaned out the Lava gang, and he looked curiously about as he walked. It was partly through curiosity to see the interior of the place that had played such a prominent part in that fracas, and partly to quench his thirst, that he decided to visit the Red Queen Saloon.

He stepped briskly through the swinging doors and dropped his bag close to the bar rail. Jack Allen was a man who always carried his life in his hands, so he glanced keenly about for a possible enemy. His eyes traveled along the bar. They found no one he knew, no one his intuition told him he need fear, until they rested on a group of three standing at the other end of the room.

Then his sixth sense warned him to be on his guard. He noticed that the men who lined the bar between him and the group of three sauntered away with assumed carelessness, and took a position farther away, where they turned and watched. Jack ordered some beer from the bartender and then watched the three men in the mirror. The fellow in the center of the group was a short man with a powerful torso and long, gorillalike arms. After studying him a moment, Jack realized that the man was a Chinaman. Jack looked curiously at him, for Chinese gunmen were very rare; in fact, this was the first Jack Allen had ever seen. And the man was obviously a gunman, for he not only carried two guns, but his two companions were obsequious. They fawned upon him and plainly showed that they feared him.

Jack Allen gulped down his beer thirstily. He had finished it and pushed the glass toward the bartender to be refilled when the Chinese gunman swung about and saw him for the first time. Instantly the Chinaman's eyes narrowed to mere slits. Then, slowly and unobtrusively, he edged away from the bar. Even if Allen had not been watching him intently, he couldn't have got away with this, for the instant his two companions saw Allen they ducked around the corner of the bar and dropped to the floor. This warned Allen that the Chinaman was not only his enemy, but had boasted of it.

Conversation stopped, and silence fell on the room. Every one was watching Allen and the gunman at the other end of the bar.

The Chinaman saw that Allen was watching him, and therefore it would be impossible to surprise him. His abnormally long arms and short legs made him look like a gorilla as he swung toward his enemy.

Jack Allen remained in the same position. His right arm was hooked over the bar with a glass of beer in it. The other hung carelessly by his side. His face was serene and untroubled, but the watchers saw that his eyes never left the squat man for a minute.

The Chinaman halted within ten feet of him, slowly raised his hands and crooked his arms, till his fingers were almost touching the black butts of his guns. "What's your name, runt?" he growled.

"Jack-twin Allen," the reply came softly. "What's yours?"

"Hip Sing," the other replied. "So you are the famous sheriff? I've been hopin' that no one would knock your horns off before I met you."

Allen knew that Hip Sing was deliberately picking a quarrel and would kill him if possible; still he continued to lean carelessly against the bar, his mouth split in the faintest of smiles, and his white teeth flashing in the midst of his heavy black beard. “Glad to meet you, Hip Sing,” Allen said quietly. “Why for was you hopin’ that nobody’d knocked my horns off?”

Allen’s coolness nonplused Hip Sing. A little voice warned him, but he had gone too far now to back out. So now his fingers stiffened and became like the claws of a bird as they hung close to his pistols.

“Because I aim to clip them horns myself!” Hip Sing growled throatily.

Scarcely had the words left his lips when his hands clamped down on the butts of his guns. Bystanders saw Jack Allen’s left hand move like a blurred streak. His long coat flipped up, and there was a resounding, smashing roar. Both of Hip Sing’s guns echoed that single shot of Allen’s, but their owner was practically dead when he pulled the trigger, and the leaden slugs dug into the floor at Allen’s feet. Allen had fired only once; he knew that shot was fatal.

Hip Sing’s hands dropped to his side, and his guns clanked to the floor. His vitality was terrific, else he would have crashed to the floor the instant the slug tore through him. His wide eyes had the appearance of a man who has received a tremendous solar-plexus blow, but the Chinaman tottered to the bar and gripped the rail with his hand. He nodded weakly to the white-faced bartender, who, with a trembling hand, filled a glass of whisky and pushed it across the counter to him.

Jack Allen whirled as the swinging doors burst open, and Sheriff Tom Powers ran into the saloon. Allen saw his drawn guns and raised his own, then he saw the man's star and relaxed.

"It's all right, Jim," the sheriff called.

Allen nodded, and then half pointed his gun at Hip Sing. Twice the Chinaman made a desperate effort to grasp the whisky, but each time he was forced to catch at the rail to keep himself erect. The third time his hand closed about the glass, but he never raised it to his lips, for before he could do it, his last spark of vitality was drained from him, and he went down to the floor like a pack of cards.

"You got him, Jim," the sheriff said.

Jack nodded and returned his gun to its holster.

"Some of you fellows cart that chink over to my office," Tom Powers directed the bystanders, and turned to Allen. "Come on, I got something to tell you."

Out in the street, Tom Powers took Allen's arm, and they started off briskly toward the jail and the sheriff's office.

"That was Hip Sing, Jim, the feller that Sam Hogg was tellin' you about this afternoon," Powers stated.

"That's the third time you called me 'Jim.' How come?" Jack Allen demanded.

The sheriff stopped dead and gazed at the little sheriff, then he cried out in amazement. "Well, I'll be hot frazzled if you ain't Jack Allen instead of Jim. Well,

I'm sure right glad to meet you, Mr. Jack. I'm a good friend of your brother's."

Jack Allen thought swiftly, then he asked grimly: "Then Jim's hereabouts, and he's playin' he's me. How come?"

"Come along to my office, and I'll explain things to you."

Once the two men were alone in the office, Tom Powers related what Jim Allen had told him about Quong, and how the two men Jack was looking for were partners of the wily Chinaman. Then he told Jack that his wife had arrived that morning and of Jim's fear for her safety.

Instantly Jack Allen asked for a horse so that he could ride out to the Frying Pan Ranch, and the sheriff said he would go along with him and show him the trail.

It was nearly dark when the two men approached the ranch, and Jack halted and suggested that he should call Jim. He thought perhaps his untimely appearance might interfere with Jim's plans. It was then that Jack Allen uttered the wolf call. He was answered by another wolf, and a few seconds later by another. Jack grinned at the sheriff in the darkness.

Presently Jim Allen trotted up to them, flung one leg over the pommel, and held out his hand to Jack.

"Well, yuh cockeyed wampus on stilts, how be yuh?" he demanded.

"Huh, I hear tell you're down here plumb ruinin' my reputation," Jack said disgustedly. "And a friend of yours, Hip Sing, tried to gun me before I was in town a half hour. Mary Bell get here all right?"

"Sure." Jim Allen chuckled heartily as he replied. "An' she's waitin' for you on the corral fence."

Jack relaxed, and favored Jim with a searching look. "Tom Powers, here, sort o' hinted that you know where I could lay hands on Bull Morgan and Tom Johnson," he said inquiringly.

Jim Allen was silent for a moment, then he shook his head. "Can't be did. Jack, them two is workin' for Quong. I figger they'll lead me to him, and he's the one I'm after. I don't care nothin' about them two galoots, but Quong has got to be got."

Jack Allen's eyes narrowed with anger. "Jim, you darned fool, don't you know I've been trailing them two for months? And here you know where I can lay hands on them and you won't tell me."

"Jack," Jim Allen replied slowly, "I knows how you feel, but I'm tellin' you straight, you've got to trail along with me and make Quong the end of the trail, or I won't throw in with yuh. But if yuh do that, after we get Quong, if Bull Morgan and Tom Johnson gets clear, I promise to hunt them down and deliver them to yuh, trussed up like a couple of calves for branding."

Jack Allen argued, pleaded, threatened, but Jim was adamant.

"All right, Jim, then you and me is goin' separate ways," Jack said at last.

"I'm sorry, Jack," Jim said softly. But there was no yielding in his voice.

Followed by the wolf, Jim Allen swung his horse toward the town and trotted off to his intended exploration of the Red Queen Saloon. Jack Allen and the sheriff rode silently to the ranch house.

CHAPTER TWENTY-TWO

When Thieves Fall Out

About two hours after the two brothers, Jim-twin and Jack-twin Allen, had separated and gone their different ways, Big Montana and Silver, followed by four other riders, picked their way through the dense brush that lay along the southern edge of the lava field. The four men who trailed them rode in complete silence. Their leaders conversed in whispers.

"You done a wise thing in refusing to meet Quong back of the Red Queen," said Montana. "He has things fixed there so you ain't got a chance if you disagree with him."

"Darn the wild-eyed old devil! If it had been any other place 'cept there, I sure wouldn't have let him in on the game we was playin' with Bill Carver," Silver said softly.

"I'm aimin' to learn him that he ain't the boss!" Big Montana cried. "An' I'm namin' the place where we'll meet hereafter."

The two men became absorbed in their own thoughts. The only sound that broke the silence of the night was the creaking of stirrup leather, the jingling of bits, and soft pad of the horses' hoofs.

Big Montana brought his hand down with a resounding slap on his horse's neck. "You say that Quong's hate of Allen is plumb poisonin' to his system?" he asked eagerly.

"It sure is. That chink don't think of nothin' else. I sure would hate to be in the Wolf's shoes if Quong ever catches him."

"They say he's better than an Apache at makin' a man holler and then keepin' him alive so he can make him holler some more," Montana observed. "And that's the thing we got to play on; we got to figger out a way to catch Jim Allen. We'll wise off Jim, and when he and the chink gets down to cases, let's hope they both do for each other."

"But without Quong, that dope business wouldn't be any good," Silver objected.

Big Montana laughed shortly, scornfully. "To blazes with that stuff. The L Bar B Ranch is worth close to a million dollars. I'll be satisfied with that for my cut."

"And with Quong out of the way, Bill Carver will sure have to give it to us."

For the next hour, while their horses picked their way along the trail through the high brush, the two men eagerly discussed ways and means by which they could both trick Allen and the Chinaman. They thought of plans which would be fatal to both. First one and then another was discarded. Neither of these men were fools; they knew that one false step would be their end. Finally they hit upon a plan which by its very simplicity would probably work.

The lava fields were split by a giant fissure which ran almost due north and south. When they came to this, they headed north. The footing along the floor of this fissure was extremely treacherous for horses. In places it was as smooth and slippery as glass; in others it was splintered, and the projections were as sharp as steel daggers. Sometimes they had to dismount and lead their horses.

They had covered about five miles when they took a trail to a broad shelf. Here they dismounted and proceeded on foot. Silver whistled softly several times. Finally an answering whistle came from somewhere ahead of them. They advanced, and presently a light flashed from a natural cavern on their right. They turned into this and found Slick Keen, with a lantern.

Keen looked sharply at the four men who followed Big Montana and Silver. He hesitated for a second, then turned and led the way along the floor of this cavern to a smaller one which branched off in the rear. He pulled aside a heavy curtain, disclosing a lighted cavern, and beckoned for them to enter. They hesitated, then Big Montana stepped forward and walked across to where Quong sat on a pile of cushions. He was followed by Silver and the other four.

The cave was furnished to a degree; there were some rough tables and chairs, and several cots were ranged along the wall. It was lighted by a dozen large candles.

Quong's black eyes clouded as he saw the four men who followed Montana and Silver, two of whom were Chinese and the other two American.

"Why do you bring those others here?" he demanded, and his eyes glittered dangerously.

Big Montana shrugged and said bluntly: "You told us to bring Fah Woo and Charley May, so I figgered I might as well bring Big-foot and Curly. That sort o' makes things equal, in case we choose to disagree."

At this blunt challenge Slick Keen swung abruptly about and fell into a slight crouch in front of Silver. The two Americans became alert, and the Chinamen regarded them with suspicious glances.

Only Quong remained unruffled. Slowly the anger died from his eyes. "Suspicion is the father of hatred," he chanted.

Again Big Montana shrugged. "I figger it's time for a show-down."

"Show-down?" Quong purred. Again the two factions tensed themselves and waited for the sign that might send them at each other's throats.

"Yep, show-down," Big Montana repeated calmly. "You an' me are partners in this deal, Quong. There ain't no boss. An' you ain't my boss, savvy?"

Quong allowed his heavy lids to droop and cover his black eyes, hiding the gleam of anger that flamed in them.

When he next looked up, his face was bland and his eyes expressionless. "Words of truth are wisdom; it is written that two heads are better than one."

Big Montana nodded and smiled inwardly. He was satisfied that he had called the Chinaman's bluff. The tension in the room relaxed, and the Chinese and American punchers seated themselves out of earshot at one end of the cavern, while Quong, Big Montana, Silver, and Slick Keen, gathered about a table at the other.

"You know that Jack Allen is in town; I mean Jim Allen, posing as Jack?" Big Montana said.

Quong nodded. "Hip Sing met him, and is now conversing with his ancestors."

"Yeah, I heard tell of it. I hear Hip Sing was sort o' surprised," Silver commented. "He seen Allen ride out of town and started to talk big, and there is Allen right by his side again!"

"Allen only pretended to leave," Slick Keen whispered harshly.

Quong nodded and again veiled his eyes with his heavy lids. He knew that the Allen who had ridden out of town had not returned. Others might be mystified by that sudden return, but the wise old Chinaman knew that there was not one Allen, but two, in Cannondale. But this he decided to keep to himself. To know more than others was the secret of success. In the coming duel of wits with Big Montana that little bit of knowledge might turn to his advantage.

Silver told them of the plan that he and Big Montana had concocted to trap Allen. When he had finished, Slick Keen laughed harshly.

"It won't do. The Wolf is too wise for that," he whispered.

"The wife of Jack Allen is kin to the Wolf. The man who is blinded by a woman will follow her into a trap. The trap will be set for a wolf, the jaws strong and sure." Quong's eyes were venomous with hate.

"Then when Bill Carver has caught the girls, we'll use them as bait for Allen."

"Girls? Are there two of them?" Slick Keen questioned.

"Sure," Silver replied easily. "There's Jack Allen's wife, and a gal called Snippets McPherson."

"Snippets McPherson!" Big Montana cried excitedly. "That's the gal Jim Allen's sweet on!"

"Then truly the gods are kind," Quong murmured, and his voice shook with excitement. "If we catch them both, truly will the Wolf follow to the uttermost depths of hell."

"And we'll slam the doors and see that he don't never come out no more," Big Montana said with satisfaction.

They eagerly discussed the rest of the plan. Little by little they arranged the details. This time there would be no failure. When at last they had finished, Big Montana looked at Silver with triumph in his eyes. Quong looked at Slick Keen, and there was unholy joy in his. Each pair was confident that by this plan they would kill two birds with one stone — destroy a hated enemy and get rid of an unwelcome partner.

Later, when Big Montana and Silver were returning to Casa Diablo, Silver turned to his friend and said with a harsh laugh: "You know what's goin' to happen if Quong steals those two gals?"

"I sure does. The chink thinks he's plumb smart, but he don't savvy Americans. The minute the news gets out that he's kidnaped a couple of white gals, the whole countryside is goin' to rise up."

Silver looked at his friend and chuckled. "An' us sittin' across the border with a lieutenant of the rurales as our alibi to prove we had nothin' to do with it."

Twice within the following days Jack and Jim Allen met, but neither referred to the subject over which they had quarreled. Each knew that it would be useless to try to change the other's viewpoint.

Old Man Carver's funeral was held on the third day after the murder. The whole countryside attended it.

Bill Carver was a tragic figure. He was no longer the carefree, wild youth of a few days before. He had aged during the last seventy-two hours; his face twitched, and his eyes were sunken and bloodshot. He was like a haunted man. The people at the funeral regarded him with mixed feelings; some looked at him with open scorn and made no effort to hide their suspicion, others had pity for him. Sam Hogg became openly belligerent if any one dared voice the suspicions that were flying over the countryside about the boy's responsibility for his father's death.

It was late afternoon, when Sam Hogg, Snippets, Mary Bell, and Bill Carver had returned to the Frying Pan Ranch, that Jim Allen introduced his wolf to Snippets for the first time.

The others looked at the great, heavy-fanged beast with fear and awe, but from the first, Snippets showed no fear of him. Perhaps she had greater confidence in Allen's judgment, for when he told her she had nothing to fear from King, she treated the big wolf with the same carelessness she would a pet collie. At first the wolf resented her attention, but after Allen had spoken to him and told him to be still while Snippets fondled him, he accepted her caresses and divided his affections between her and his master.

During the days which followed, Allen spent a great deal of time searching among the lava beds. On these trips the wolf accompanied him, but when Allen went to Cannondale, he left King with Snippets.

"Look here, King, stay with her an' don't let no one touch her," he would command as he rode off toward town.

The three inseparables — Tad Hicks, Windy Jake and Kansas Jones — took their job of protecting Snippets and Mary Bell with extreme seriousness. Never for a moment did they allow the girls to stray from the ranch without them. They went about armed to the teeth, and their ferocious air and extreme seriousness always filled Snippets with mirth. They all three admired Mary Bell's looks, but they waxed enthusiastic when discussing Snippets.

All three resented the fact that Jim left the wolf as an additional guard. They did a lot of grumbling about it; it was as if he doubted their ability to protect the girls. But they were very careful about approaching Snippets when the wolf was there. Once Windy Jake stumbled and fell against her when passing. Like a flash King was by her side, hackles up and eyes flashing. The wolf's ferociousness made even Snippets a little breathless.

The twins were never at the Frying Pan Ranch at the same time. The Frying Pan riders were vastly puzzled at Allen's ability to be in two places at the same time, but they never suspected the truth. Sam Hogg himself found it difficult to tell them apart.

It was on the third day after the funeral that Silver rode up to the ranch. Watching from a convenient place, he had seen Allen ride away, and he figured it was safe for him to visit the place.

"Mr. Hogg, I wonder if any of your men have seen a pair of piebalds on your ranch," Silver said to the owner of the ranch as an excuse for his visit. "They was Big Montana's pet hosses, and they got out of the corral somehow and are roamin' free and easy."

Sam Hogg went off to question his men, and at the first opportunity Silver drew young Bill Carver aside.

"Bill, the time has come for you to pay that debt to me and Montana," he said bluntly.

The boy's face blanched, and he sought desperately to regain his lost will-power, but he had not the strength to stand up before the hard-eyed Silver. "What do you want me to do?" he stammered.

"Quong has figgered this thing out. You know that chink has a long arm!" Silver said softly.

Young Bill Carver caught the underlying threat beneath these words. He nodded dumbly. He had not forgotten his visit to Quong; that Chinaman was an ever-present nightmare in his dreams. "There is no need to threaten me with Quong, Silver. I want to help you and Big," Bill Carver said quickly.

Silver talked rapidly for several minutes. As he listened, the boy's face grew distressed. When Silver had finished, he looked at him and there was real rebellion in his eyes. "I won't betray those gals," he said, and there was stubbornness in his voice.

Silver shrugged and smiled thinly. "I give you my word they won't be harmed. We only want to use them to get Jack Allen."

"You promise that?" young Carver asked earnestly.

"Word of honor as a gentleman," Silver replied seriously.

Bill Carver might have asked himself what such an oath had to do with Silver, but it satisfied him. He had decided that Mary Bell was altogether too attractive to be married to such a coyote as he believed Jack Allen to be. After Jack Allen had met his just deserts, she would soon learn his true character and be really grateful to the man who had helped her to be free from him. With an effort young Carver downed his last shred of doubt and agreed to do as Silver asked. Then he suddenly remembered Snippets bodyguard and asked what was going to happen to them. Silver smiled and took a package of cigarettes from his pocket and handed them to the boy.

"Quong thinks of everything. You give them hombres one of these things to smoke, and they'll just drop down and sleep peaceful for twenty-four hours," Silver stated. "An' don't be worryin' for they won't do them no harm at all."

As the two walked slowly toward the house, young Bill Carver quivered with humiliation and shame. His conscience and better nature told him he was not playing the part of a man. The thing for him to do was to go to Sam Hogg, his father's friend, and confess fully. But horror and excitement had so jangled his nerves that he no longer had the strength to do what his conscience dictated. Just as Silver was about to swing into the saddle, the boy was struck with a sudden thought. "They tell me the sheriff, Tom Powers, has disappeared. They ain't nothin' happened to him that you know of?" he asked with anxiety.

John Silver's eyes flickered, but he shook his head in denial. He knew that Quong had Tom Powers, but he thought it just as well to keep silent.

"Nope, don't know nothin' about him," he lied easily. "Kid, as I told you, we're only goin' to take the girls so as to get Jack Allen over into Mexico. The fellows what take the girls will take you along with them a ways. Then you come back and catch Allen alone and tell him you escaped. Tell him the girls are in a cave on the east side of that split through the lava fields. Say you hung a handkerchief over the entrance when you escaped, so he can find his way there alone."

Silver talked for several minutes, giving details of his plan and minute directions as to how to find the cave; then, satisfied that the boy understood, he prepared to leave. He was about to swing into his saddle when the faint click of a shod hoof reached his ears and he looked up sharply. He swore, for there, not fifteen feet away, rode Jim Allen, with his wolf by his side.

Silver was momentarily panic-stricken. He dropped his hand to his gun, then the idea struck him that Allen might not recognize him. Common sense told him to wait. With an effort he banished the fear from his face and looked carelessly at Allen. He made some inconsequential remark to the boy, and, dropping his head so that his hat covered his face, he carefully rolled a cigarette. Jim Allen nodded a greeting to the boy and rode on unconcernedly. Silver breathed a sigh of relief. He watched Allen enter the house, and was about to swing into the saddle when Sam Hogg hailed him from the veranda.

"Say, Silver, do you mind comin' in a minute?"

Silver walked slowly toward the porch. He wanted to get away from the ranch before Allen recognized him, but he could not disregard the old cattleman's summons without creating suspicion. Hogg took him by the arm and genially led him into the living room. Silver saw no sign of Allen. Then his eyes came to rest on Mary Bell.

"I want you to meet Mrs. Jack Allen," Sam Hogg said jovially. "An' I want you to try a new bottle of whisky I just got. Think it might do you good on that long ride to Casa Diablo."

Silver accepted the glass of whisky and looked with admiring eyes at the little blond girl. He refused a second drink, and hurriedly made his excuses to get away. Bowing to the girl, he left the room and rode away.

Jim Allen watched him from the corner of the house. When Silver had vanished over the rise, Allen strode over to Bill Carver. He did not miss the look of apprehension and fear that leaped into the boy's eyes. "That fellow a friend of yours?" Allen asked carelessly.

"He works on our ranch," the boy replied surlily.

"Suppose he came to see you about ranch business then?" Allen said indifferently.

As he put the question, he was watching Bill Carver from the corner of his eye. The boy flushed and then paled. He struggled for words, but none came, so he ended by swinging around and walking rudely away. Allen's eyes were grim as he watched him.

A little later Sam Hogg buttonholed Jim Allen and demanded: "What did you want me to get that jasper in the house for?"

Allen grinned broadly as he replied: "So I could put a little aniseed on his horse's hoofs. The wolf can now follow him through a stampede of cattle, can't you, King?" As Allen finished, he stooped and patted the big wolf's head.

CHAPTER TWENTY-THREE

Double Cross

"Kip" Moore had run a small bakery in Cannondale for years. Sheriff Tom Powers had known him from the time he had first arrived in town. He considered him a spineless sort of creature, the last man in the world to be a member of Quong's gang. If asked, Powers would have said contemptuously that the man was a white rabbit, without either the nerve or the urge to do anything doubtful. Therefore, when Moore came to him with a message purporting to be from Jim Allen, he accepted it without question.

That same afternoon he and Jim had explored the cleft in the lava fields in an effort to find Quong's hiding place. The search had been rewarded with a certain measure of success. Allen's keen eyes had spotted a faint trail in the bewildering maze of crevasses, but he had insisted that they give up their search. They were so near the end of it that he was afraid they might be seen and cause Quong to abandon the place.

When the sheriff received the supposed message from Allen that evening, he obeyed instructions without a single suspicion. He saddled his horse, and, without telling any one where he was going, rode to the northern entrance of the crevasse. Here he dismounted, and walking to a rock which had been mentioned in the message, prepared to wait for Allen. He was completely off his guard when two men leaped from the shadow of the rock and threw themselves upon him. He was knocked flat at the first onslaught. His struggles were futile, and he was soon tied up. They threw a sack over his head and hoisted him on a horse.

The sheriff rode through darkness for what seemed to him to be hours. At last he was roughly hauled from his horse and pushed up a steep incline. He counted the steps as he went along, and after he had walked about three hundred, the sack was jerked off his head, and he found himself in a lighted room. He blinked his eyes and glanced about. There were four men in that room, all of them Chinamen. Two of them he had never seen, but he instantly suspected the other two of being the much-talked-about cow waddies from the Casa Diablo Ranch. The sheriff's spirit drooped when he saw Slick Keen, for he knew that if they ever intended to let him leave here alive, Slick would never have appeared.

Tom Powers was a noted figure along the border. For years, as a Ranger and sheriff, he had upheld the law in that turbulent country. He had fought Indians, rustlers, gamblers and common killers, and not once had his courage been questioned. But when he saw the fourth man in that cave, he felt a shiver of apprehension in spite of himself.

He knew the man at once from Jim Allen's description. It could be none other than Quong, and as

Powers looked at him, he understood Jim's determination to exterminate him or die in the attempt.

"A wise man knows when to speak. Only a fool waits to have the words torn from him," said Quong gently. "What did you and the Wolf discover today? How much does the Wolf know about the Carver murder?"

So that was it. They had been seen!

"We got lost, and we was danged lucky to get out of the place again," Powers said.

The moment the words had left his lips, he knew that Quong was not deceived. It was almost as if his eyes, those black pools of evil, could read into a man's soul.

"Many men have the fortitude to die one death for a friend; none have the strength or will to die a thousand. It is written that only a fool is stubborn. So speak now, and answer truly, before your tongue is loosened at your hundredth death," Quong chanted, and waited.

The sheriff knew what that meant. In the old days he had seen men after the Apaches had finished with them. The memory of them had caused many a nightmare. He offered a silent prayer that he would be able to stand the torture with fortitude and keep his tongue tied. He had great faith in Jim Allen; he was certain that sooner or later the Wolf would find the place and rescue him. He already knew its general whereabouts. Powers knew that if he spoke now, these Chinamen would abandon the cave, and he and Jim would lose all chance of exterminating them. Therefore it was up to him to bear the torture and remain silent.

Tom Powers had the fortitude of an old frontiersman, and he needed it in the twenty-four hours that followed. Slick Keen acted as chief executioner, and they spread-eagled the old sheriff in one corner of the cavern, with lights arranged so that every movement of his tortured flesh was visible to their watching eyes. But in spite of the horrors they inflicted upon him, they failed to wring from him the information he guarded behind grim, locked jaws.

Powers lost all count of time. After what seemed all eternity of suffering, Silver strode into the place, and he could have blessed him. His appearance gave a temporary surcease to the frightful pain. Silver's face paled, and his mouth shut in a hard line as he looked down at the wretched sheriff. He muttered something to himself and turned to Quong.

"The thing is fixed for to-night. The kid is going to ask them to take a ride with him right after supper, when it will be nearly dusk. They'll go to Indian Head Bluff to see the moon rise. I gave him the cigarettes like you told me, so there will be no warning shots fired."

Quong's face was a mask of cruel, devilish pleasure.

Silver left the cave. His hatred of Quong increased every time he saw him. If things broke right, they would be rid of Quong and the Wolf at the same time. Out on the shelf, Silver stopped and listened. No one followed from the cave. He took a white-silk handkerchief from his pocket and fastened it to a long branch above the entrance. After he had satisfied himself of its firmness he stood looking up at it. A little smile of contentment flickered over his lips as he turned and descended to his horse. The handkerchief would remain undiscovered until darkness, and would eventually lead the Wolf to

Quong. When the two met, if it did not relieve Big Montana and himself of the Wolf, it would at least dispose of a dangerous partner. He swung into his saddle and rode rapidly out of the crevasse. Out of the lava fields, he made through the brush at a headlong gallop, straight for Casa Diablo.

He was close to the ranch before he discovered that he had lost one of his guns. He always wore two — a .45 single-action low on his right hip and a pearl-handled .38 in a holster above his belt line. It was the latter that was gone. For a moment he considered returning for it, but he decided he had lost it while climbing up to attach the handkerchief above the cave; in any case, there was no great harm done, so he rode on.

As he rode into the courtyard of Casa Diablo, Big Montana came out to meet him.

"Things is all set," said Silver. "I fixed the handkerchief above the cave, an' now all we got to do is get the Wolf to go down there lookin' for it, and I figure we can say good-by to Quong. If the Wolf goes alone, then they'll both cash."

"Where's Quong goin' to take the girls afterward?" Big Montana asked.

"I don't know, unless he takes them to the cave."

"Well, we got to find out and see they get back safely, not because I'm sentimental, but this country won't be safe for no one with them gals stolen."

John Silver smiled thinly with complete satisfaction. "Don't worry none, Big. If the Wolf don't get 'em, we'll get 'em, and then we'll be the heroes!"

Silver's satisfaction would not have been so complete if he had known where his gun was. Hardly had he left when Slick Keen handed it to Quong.

"I flicked this out, an' he never felt nothin'," Slick whispered.

"It is a pretty gun," Quong purred, "and has dealt death often."

"And it will deal two more deaths to-night," Slick Keen said.

Then, followed by Fah Woo and Charlie May, he left the cave and descended to their horses. They were on their way to keep the rendezvous with Bill Carver.

That evening Sam Hogg was sitting on his porch, trying to convince himself that his friend, Tom Powers, had not come to grief. Jack Allen was with him.

"How you comin' with your plans?" the ex-Ranger asked suddenly.

Jack Allen laughed. "I reckon I know where to find my men, and when I get them, I bet I'll also get the murderer of Old Man Carver. Here's some one comin' fast from town."

The two listened in silence to the drumming hoofbeats of a hard-ridden horse. It swung into the lane and headed straight for the ranch. In the gathering dusk they saw Toothpick Jarrick. He brought his horse to a sliding stop and leaped to the ground. He peered at Jack Allen and frowned undecidedly.

"I'm Jack." Allen grinned.

"You're all sort o' puffed up with vanity. You got some news?" Sam Hogg asked with a chuckle.

"I reckon I have. I been foolin' around the Red Queen, an' back of it, in that old Mex cantina, I seen several pack horses leavin' the lane. Looks as if Quong was movin'," Toothpick spoke importantly.

"If he's movin', he's gettin' ready to strike," Jack Allen said.

Toothpick glanced around and asked, "Where are the gals?"

"They went to look at the sunset with young Carver."

"Say, Mr. Hogg, didn't Jim tell you not to let them gals out of your sight, to-day special?" Toothpick demanded.

"Yeah, but Windy Jake and tother two are with them. They're all right."

"Just the same, if Jim said that, I reckon I'll join them. Jim never shoots off his mouth for nothin'," Jack Allen said decisively, and hurried toward the corral to saddle his horse.

Sam Hogg also became alarmed, and five minutes later the three started rapidly for the bluff. It was quite dark now, except for the light of the quarter moon. As they neared the bluff, they saw the blurred shape of three horses cropping grass at its base. Jack Allen raised his voice and shouted, but no answer came. Again he shouted, then all three hallooed loudly. They stood waiting, and when no answer came, their eyes filled with anxiety. They scattered to search. Jack Allen swung from his saddle and started to climb the bluff. He was stopped by a shout from Toothpick.

“Hey, fellas! Here’s Windy Jake and tother two, and they’re all three dead!” Toothpick yelled.

Allen ran to Toothpick and saw the three riders lying on the grass. He dropped to his knees and examined them. “They ain’t dead, they’re drugged,” he said.

He leaped to his feet and began searching the ground. A little farther on they came to a place where the ground was trampled as if from a struggle. The girls’ footmarks were clearly visible in the soft ground. There were also the tracks of three men. Sam Hogg lighted a match and carefully examined one of the prints. The owner had a small foot and wore a pointed boot. Hogg rose to his feet. “It’s the same gent that helped kill Old Man Carver!” he said.

Jack Allen’s eye caught a shining object lying on the ground. He stooped and picked it up. It was a pearl-handled .38. He held it out at arm’s length to Sam Hogg. “Do you know that gun?” he demanded.

“Sure do! It belongs to Silver. There ain’t another in the country like it,” the old cattleman said furiously.

“Go back to the ranch and get help,” Jack Allen snapped to Sam Hogg. “Me and Toothpick will start trailin’ them buzzards. Hustle!”

Sam Hogg needed no urging, and before the words had left Allen’s lips, he was on the back of his horse tearing toward the ranch. Jack and Toothpick had scarcely covered two miles when Hogg was back, every available man from the ranch with him.

“Jack,” Sam Hogg growled, “we know Silver had something to do with this, so let’s get goin’ toward Casa Diablo!”

Allen agreed, and the whole troop put their horses into a gallop. They were a grim band of horsemen. Every capable man at the Frying Pan had seized weapons and followed Sam Hogg, even a fourteen-year-old boy. They swept across the border and down the road that led to the line ranch. When they sighted the lights of the ranch, they dismounted. Hogg appointed a few to remain with the horses, and the rest moved forward on foot, led by Allen and Sam Hogg.

As they entered the courtyard, they halted in surprise. Seated about the large fire were some twenty Mexicans in the uniform of the rurales, dining with the Casa Diablo riders. Allen saw the men he wanted seated at a table with a lieutenant of the rurales. He and Sam Hogg walked forward slowly. Their men poured through the gateway and formed a half circle around the fire.

Big Montana was the first to see them. Casting a hasty glance over his shoulder, he rose slowly to his feet. "What you gents want?" he demanded.

"You!" Jack Allen replied bluntly.

"What for?"

"For kidnapin' my wife and Snippets McPherson to-night!" Allen spoke slowly; his eyes caught and held Silver's cold stare.

The head of the rurales stepped forward and held out his hand authoritatively. "Señor, who are you? What do you mean by entering Mexico with a troop of armed men?" he asked sternly.

Allen explained, but the officer's expression did not relax.

"Señor, let me tell you that it is impossible that Señor Silver would have had a hand in the kidnaping, as he was dining here with me at the time it took place." The lieutenant's voice was courteous but firm.

A howl of anger went up from the line of American riders.

"The Mex lies!" some one shouted.

Jack Allen swung about. His face was stern and his eyes were snapping with rage. "The next man that speaks out of turn answers to me!"

Both he and Sam Hogg knew that the lieutenant was telling the truth. The rurales were the one body of men in Mexico who were incorruptible. They entered the service for the love of fighting and not for graft. Allen was completely disconcerted, yet he was positive that Silver and Montana had had a hand in the kidnaping. He debated with himself for a moment, then he made his decision. There was nothing else for him to do. He bowed courteously to the lieutenant.

"Señor," he said gravely, "I ask your pardon for invading Mexico. I am sure you will understand that we meant no disrespect to your country, but were simply moved by the desire to catch the scoundrels who kidnaped my wife."

"Truly, I understand, senor." The lieutenant bowed. "And now —" He left his sentence unfinished, but his meaning was clear.

Jack Allen knew that the only thing for him to do was to withdraw with as much dignity as possible from an impossible situation. He ordered the punchers to depart, then he drew Big Montana and John Silver aside. He drew out the pearl-handled gun and held it out to Silver.

"I found that where the girls were kidnaped," he said, and without waiting for a reply, he added: "I know you both, you're Bull Morgan and Johnson."

"Even so, what're you goin' to do about it?" Big replied with a sneer. "These rurales ain't going to let you do anything to us in Mexico!"

Allen knew that this was true.

"I'm offering you a trade," he said. "Bring back those girls unharmed, and I'll forget I ever saw you."

Montana and Silver exchanged fixed looks.

"It's a go," Silver said quickly.

"You got twenty-four hours," Allen said sternly.

They nodded. Allen swung on his horse and followed the Frying Pan riders.

When the two returned to the fire, they saw the Mexican officer regarding them suspiciously. They were both relieved when he and his men departed a short time later.

"Damn Mex," Big Montana growled.

"He's wise that we used him as an alibi," Silver stated.

"He sure is, but if he hadn't been here, those Frying Pan riders would have strung us up pronto."

"Just what that double-crossin' chink hoped when he planted my gun back there."

"Lucky for us we outsmarted him," laughed Big Montana. "We'll go see him pronto and act suspicious and sore about that gun, then we'll tell him he's got to give us the girls, or we won't be safe hereabouts."

"Ain't you forgettin' we arranged to have Carver send the Wolf to meet Quong?"

"Not any. It will take him four hours to get to the Frying Pan and be sent back to the cave. So we got plenty of time to see Quong and be gone before he gets there."

If Silver and Montana had known it was Jack they had been talking to, and that Jim was at that moment talking to Bill Carver, their satisfaction would not have been so complete, as they, followed by five riders, started out to visit Quong.

As they neared the entrance to the first cave, they were challenged sharply. Big Montana gave his name and Silver's, and the party was allowed to proceed. At the heavy door which led to the inner cave another guard stopped them and would only allow Big Montana and Silver to pass inside. Their men would have to sit in the larger cave. As the five Casa Diablo riders stood in doubt, the first guard approached them.

"Why don't you fellas go in the little cave where it's warm? The cook's just gettin' breakfast."

He led them over to a smaller cave. As they ducked their heads to enter, the guard stopped them.

"Say, there's only five of you. With the two that went inside, that makes seven." The man frowned in perplexity. "I could swear that I counted eight when you came in, and where's your dog?"

One of the five shook his head.

"We didn't have no dog with us."

"I tell you I seen him," the man replied with a touch of anger.

"Shucks, you're dreamin'. First you count eight of us then you start talkin' about a dog."

"Just the same, I swear there was eight of you and I seen that dog," the man, Gloomy Mason, said doubtfully, and he shook his head as he returned to his post.

As Big Montana and Silver entered the inner cave, they saw Slick Keen warming his hands over a brazier.

"Darn these caves," he said. "They're as damp as the grave." He watched the two with apparent indifference, but in his lap, under his hat, he had his gun in readiness.

John Silver frowned and asked: "Where's Quong?"

"In the little cave asleep, dreamin' sweet dreams of vengeance on the Wolf," Slick Keen said jokingly. He was quick-witted and knew that the chances were that Silver and Montana had been visited by a posse and knew about the gun he had planted at the scene of the kidnaping. Therefore, he said to Silver: "Say, Silver, I'm plumb sorry. I found your gun and then lost it again."

"Where did you find it?" Silver demanded.

"On the path leading to the bottom of the split," Slick replied easily.

"An' where did you lose it?" Montana growled.

Slick Keen shrugged. "I don't know."

"Well, some one found it," Silver said softly, and his eyes bored into Slick Keen. "You dropped it right where you kidnaped them gals."

"Gosh, maybe I did. Them gals sure put up a fight; that tall one was like a wild cat."

Big Montana and Silver stared at the handsome, sleek-haired Keen. They knew he was lying, but they did not wish to start a fight.

"We'd been dead men if a bunch of rurales hadn't been at Casa Diablo when the Frying Pan riders arrived," Silver said.

So that was how they had escaped Quong's trap, thought Keen.

"It's like this — now we're suspected, we got to give up the gals or we don't live long," Big explained.

"You could disappear until it blows over," Keen suggested.

"And leave you and Quong to take our share," Silver sneered.

The eyes of all three grew cold and hard. They did not trust each other. Then the latch of the door clicked, and they swung about. What they saw made them once more allies. For death to all three stood by the door.

Tom Powers was still spread-eagled in the corner of the cave. He twisted his head and stared unbelievingly for a moment. He was weak from torture, and his voice trembled shrilly, as he screamed exultantly: "Wolf the coyotes! Wolf 'em, Jim!"

CHAPTER TWENTY-FOUR

A Confession

Perhaps if Jim Allen had not been so absorbed in his determination to exterminate Quong, he might have warned Snippets not to leave the house that night. He was convinced that John Silver had brought Bill Carver some message. As it was, he merely called the three — Windy Jake and his two fellow guards — aside and gave them an earnest warning to be especially on the lookout.

King, the wolf, was unlike a bloodhound inasmuch as he never bayed when following a scent. He was a true wolf, hunting silently as a ghost. Allen showed him the footprints of Silver's horse and ordered him to follow them. The wolf found no difficulty in trailing these tracks scented with aniseed; in fact, the two followed so rapidly that once Allen had to halt for fear of overtaking the quarry. Where Silver's trail entered the lava fields, Allen decided it would be safer if he followed on foot. Accordingly he dismounted and, having hidden Princess in the brush, tramped down the crevasse at the heels of the big gray wolf.

As he had expected, the tracks left the floor of the crevasse and started to zigzag up one of its banks just about where he and the sheriff had turned back the day before. He cautiously climbed the other side, and soon discovered the opening which he knew must lead to a cave. There he again descended to the floor of the crevasse. For a long time he stood in deep thought. If he could only be certain that Quong was now in the cave, he would follow Silver, and no matter what the odds against him, he was satisfied that before he fell, he would bring down the Chinaman. But he was not sure, and if he attacked and did not find Quong, it would simply mean a week's work wasted. For Quong would naturally abandon that hiding place.

He concealed himself behind a jagged pillar of rock and watched the entrance to the cave. He had been there scarcely five minutes when he saw Silver come out and fasten a white handkerchief above the cave mouth. While he was puzzling over the meaning of this, he saw Silver mount his horse and ride south of the crevasse.

"Well, he's goin' back to the Casa Diablo, so we'll let him go. But what the devil has he fastened that handkerchief above the cave for?"

It was close to six o'clock before Allen returned to where he had left his horse. He decided to head toward Cannondale for two reasons; first, to see if Toothpick had heard any news of the missing sheriff, and, second, to have another try at those secret passages back of the Red Queen.

It was dusk when Jim arrived at Cannondale. He went straight to the Comfort Hotel.

The proprietor told him that Jarrick had gone to the Frying Pan Ranch immediately after lunch. "Toothpick acted right important and in some hurry when he forked his bronc," he said.

When Toothpick acted important, it meant he had some news. That decided Allen to ride immediately to the ranch.

It was long after dark when he arrived. The place was practically deserted. A glance at the bunk house convinced him that every man on the place had saddled his horse and gone. He raced for the house in alarm, dashed in the front door, and called: "Snippets! Snippets! Mary Bell! Mary Bell!" But the only answer was the echo of his voice.

He tore through the house, and it was only when he reached the kitchen that he found anybody. There was the cook, too old and fat to ride. He gaped at Allen.

"Did you catch 'em?" he gasped.

"Who?" Allen snapped.

"The fellas who got the girls. Didn't you go chase 'em?" The cook was bewildered.

Before he could get any information, Jim had to convince the stupid cook that he was not Jack Allen. Then the cook told his story.

As he brought his rambling account to an end, both men heard a stumbling footstep in the passage outside. They swung about and faced the door.

Young Bill Carver stood there, pale and exhausted. He started when he saw Allen, and swallowed convulsively several times.

"Where you been? Where are the gals?" the cook stuttered.

"They took me, but I escaped," the boy stammered.

Allen took him by the arm, shoved him into the sitting room, and shut the door in the cook's angry face.

"Tell me about it, kid," Allen said softly.

The boy flinched before those quiet eyes and mumbled something inarticulate. Then he shivered as he remembered Quong, Montana and Silver. Desperately he started the story Silver had rehearsed him in. Allen listened in silence until he had finished.

"Then you think if I go to that cave pronto I may be in time to save the gals?" he asked.

The boy nodded, and his face grew white and strained, as Allen picked up his hat and started for the door. He knew that Allen might be going to his death. Fascinated, he watched him. Then his nerve broke.

"No! Don't go! It's a trap!" he cried.

"I'm glad you said that," Allen answered. "If you hadn't, I'd have taken you out and hung you to the first tree."

"Hung me!"

"I knew you was lyin'," Allen said mercilessly. "They told you you had killed your dad and threatened to expose you unless you played their game."

"But I was drunk."

"Shucks, you didn't kill him. I'll prove it to you later. I've got to go now."

For a moment the boy was too overcome with relief to reply. Curiously enough, he never doubted Allen for a moment. "Where you going?" he asked at last.

"To that cave to get Quong."

"But it's a trap!"

"Sure, Silver set it for both Quong and me."

"They'll kill you!"

"Don't make no difference, if I get Quong first."

Before the boy could reply, the door slammed and Allen was gone. Bill stared at the empty doorway a moment, then sprang to his feet. Here was a way to redeem his manhood. He would go with Allen and fight and die by his side. He rushed out, threw himself into the saddle, and rode furiously after his deliverer. But there was no overtaking Princess as Allen rode her that night.

Jim Allen had made many a famous ride, but never before such a one as he made that night; never before had he had the motives that now drove him on. He rode like an avenging fury; Princess ran like a tireless machine. She seemed to understand the need for haste. Even in the darkness she was as sure-footed as a cat, and moved as silently as a shadow flitting through the night.

Twice during that wild ride Allen passed bands of grim-faced searchers, for the whole countryside had been aroused by the kidnaping. The searchers would be aroused by the click of a horse's hoof; then they would catch a momentary glimpse of a racing mare, a small figure crouched on her back, and a big wolf running by her side. The apparition would be gone like a blurred shadow and swallowed by the night before they could be sure whether what they had seen was flesh or spirit.

Allen did not check his headlong speed even when he swung into the cleft through the lava fields. The treacherous floor of the cleft offered such footing that no one but a madman would race a horse over it even in daylight. Twice the gray mare slipped and nearly fell. Each time she managed by a tremendous effort to keep her feet and continue the headlong run.

When at last he reached the path that lead upward to the cave in the wall of the cleft, Allen slipped from the saddle, and, concealing the heaving and blowing Princess behind some rocks, then slipped up the trail to the shelf above. Here he paused and listened. He made King lie down in the dense shadow close to the wall. Then he saw a man standing in the black outline of the cave's entrance.

There was no entering while that man stood there. It was impossible to slip by him, yet Allen must enter. Quong was somewhere in that cave.

Allen dropped down and started to edge along the inner wall toward the sentinel. He had no way of knowing how many guards Quong had about him; the only thing he was sure of was that Quong was somewhere in that cave.

From what young Carver had confessed to him, Jim understood that Big Montana and Silver meant to double cross Quong. Silver had marked the entrance to the cave and then had instructed Carver to send Allen there. Just what was behind this, Allen did not know. It might be a trap for him, but he was inclined to believe that Silver was working a double cross, by which he hoped Allen would rid him of a partner of whom he was afraid. Probably he also planned to drop Allen after Quong was dead. That to Allen was not important. If he reached Quong while he still had life enough to pull a trigger, what happened to himself afterward was of little consequence.

He was close to the unsuspecting man at the entrance of the cave when a sound stopped his advance. He heard the murmur of voices and the sound of several horses below in the path. Then he heard men scrambling up the trail. He slipped back to where he had left King and crouched down beside the wolf. "Quiet, now! Quiet!" he whispered.

Just when the men were opposite where Allen lay hidden, the sentry challenged them.

"It's us, Big Montana and Silver. We got to see the boss pronto," the leader of the gang replied.

A light flashed from the cave. The sentry inspected Big Montana and Silver, then stepped aside and beckoned them to enter.

Allen came to his feet, and with the wolf by his side, dropped in behind the last man of the gang. He held his breath as he came abreast of the sentry, but the man allowed him to pass without question.

The moment he was in the cave Allen slipped away from the others and vanished from the circle of light cast by the lantern. He heard Big Montana, Silver and the guard clump across the floor to the rear of the cave. There they were challenged by a second guard, and after a brief parley a door swung open, and Montana and Silver passed into the second cave.

The rest of the men trooped across and vanished behind a curtained cave close to the outer entrance. Allen heard the first guard return to his post, then he started to creep toward the man who guarded the entrance to the inner cave.

Five minutes later there was a muffled thud, and the second sentry slumped to the ground. Again Allen listened, but nothing stirred. He pressed the latch on the door and opened it a crack. Then he and the wolf slipped through. He cast one rapid glance about, then shut the door behind him, and slid home the bolt. He muttered something when he saw the sheriff's pain-racked face. Then he faced the three gunmen who had swung about at his entrance. From the corner of his eye he saw the sheriff lift his head slightly and stare at him. Then Tom Powers screamed:

"Wolf the coyotes! Wolf 'em, Jim!"

After that shrill, exultant cry, Powers became silent and was so absorbed in watching, that he even forgot his pain. He had known Allen for a long time, but he had never seen him in action. Now, as he watched, he understood why he was called the Wolf. All signs of the freckle-faced boy had gone. Allen's face looked old. His big, loose-lipped mouth twisted into a snarl, revealing his big teeth like the fangs of a beast. His eyes flamed.

He moved across the cave very slowly, walking stiff legged, like a fighting wolf. There was something about his slow advance that even appalled the sheriff. It was implacable, relentless, and yet there was something impersonal about it. He would deal death as surely and impersonally as the desert itself. As he moved forward, King, the big desert wolf, moved with measured tread by his side.

"Two wolves," Tom Powers murmured.

They were indeed that. Allen, at that moment, was as much of a wolf as the beast at his side. The three gunmen stood motionless, rigid, as he walked toward them. Their eyes became slits. All three were noted for their cold nerve, their speed and skill as gunmen; yet, even in spite of the odds in their favor, they had no confidence in the outcome of this meeting. There was something about Allen that forbade that — something inhuman, a destroying force that discounted the odds of numbers.

Silver and Big Montana, still unaware that both Jim and Jack Allen were in the country were puzzled and surprised at Allen's appearance. They could not understand how Jack Allen could have returned to the Frying Pan Ranch, seen young Carver, and then arrived at the cave in two short hours.

"How did you get here so soon?" Silver demanded.

Allen ignored this and demanded flatly: "Quong?"

"He's inside there," Montana replied, and jerked his head to the rear of the cave.

"You ain't forgettin' that you promised to let bygones be bygones if we helped you find the gals?" Silver asked.

"So! You was plannin' a double cross!" Slick Keen whispered harshly.

The other two ignored him and continued to stare at Allen, who nodded toward the tortured sheriff.

"I ain't Jack, and ain't havin' no truck with the coyotes what had a hand in deviling the sheriff."

Allen's voice was flat, expressionless, yet its very flatness carried a terrible menace.

Startled, Silver stared at Allen. The blood drained from his face and left it ghastly white as he cried: "The Wolf!"

The sheriff laughed hysterically as he twisted his head to watch the three gunmen.

Big Montana and Silver knew that no words of theirs could ever explain away to the Wolf that spread-eagled figure in the corner. The tortured sheriff damned them forever in the eyes of the Wolf. They would have to fight. It was a question of kill or be killed. They both had iron nerve, and the moment they knew they could not avoid the fight, they became cool and calculating. Acting on the same impulse, they commenced to edge away from Slick Keen, who was between them.

But Allen saw and understood the maneuver. "Gents, I'm counting three," he called softly.

At that all four men went for their guns.

The cave was lighted by large candles in brackets along the walls. The lights from these flickered from the concussion of the heavy reports, which were like thunderclaps in the cave. Jagged streaks of red flame pierced the swirling blue smoke. Continuous streams of fire flashed from Allen's two guns.

Big Montana was a marvel of speed. His two big hands clamped on his pistol butts, jerked them from the holsters, cocked and fired in one blurred, continuous motion. But fast as he was, just as he leveled his guns, a heavy slug caught him full in the chest with the impact of a sledge hammer. He convulsively pulled both triggers as he staggered backward. Before he could fire again, two more slugs crashed into him and threw him against the wall of the cave, where he slumped down on his face.

Silver never even drew his guns. No sooner had his hands closed on them than a bullet caught him squarely between the eyes and tumbled him over backward.

Slick Keen had a cold and crafty nerve. He prided himself on his skill and speed, but he had no intention of testing it against the flaring-eyed man who faced him. He knew that the first two men to draw would be the ones to receive Allen's first fire. So he delayed his own draw for a fraction of a second, hoping by this trick to get a free shot at Allen. His scheme would have worked except for King, the wolf. It is doubtful if Keen knew of the wolf's presence before the beast, with a terrific roar, launched himself straight at his throat.

His guns were out, but the sight of that big, blazing-eyed, white-fanged beast made him flinch, and he ducked without firing. The wolf's fangs missed his throat, but clamped shut high up on his shoulder. If King were part dog, he did not fight like it, but attacked like a true wolf. He made no effort to shake his prey; when his fangs clamped shut, he allowed his momentum to tear them free.

His first attack jerked Keen sideways and threw him off balance. Before he could steady himself, the wolf turned in mid-air and leaped in again. King ended his part of the fight almost as quickly as Allen did his. At his third rush his fangs found their mark, and the light of the world went out for Slick Keen.

The echoes from Allen's heavy guns were still vibrating from wall to wall when Slick's last despairing cry punctuated the bedlam. Then there was silence — sudden, complete.

The sheriff saw Allen stoop to peer beneath the swirling smoke clouds, then eject the empty shells, and thrust new ones into his guns.

Without speaking, Allen cut loose the sheriff's bonds. "You got to wait — Quong comes first," he said slowly.

The sheriff looked up at Allen's wrinkled face, those strange, flaring eyes, his twisted mouth, then switched his gaze to the wolf, who, with stained jowls, was watching Allen. And again Powers told himself that the two were akin.

"All right, Jim, get Quong; he done this to me," the sheriff said weakly.

Then, from the outside, there came the hoarse shouts of several men, the muffled boom of shots, and a voice called: "Jim! Jim! Where are you?"

Allen leaped to the doorway and threw it open. Three men leaped through the door, and as Allen slammed it shut behind them, several bullets spattered into the heavy wood.

CHAPTER TWENTY-FIVE

Trail's End

Jack Allen did not trust either Big Montana or Silver. He did not believe they had nothing to do with the kidnaping. But he did believe a sense of self-preservation would make them do the best they could to return the girls. His promise to forget the past if they recovered the girls would make them force Quong to free Snippets and Mary Bell. Or, at least, they would attempt to make him do so. It was Jack's belief that they would not lose any time visiting Quong, which motivated his actions last night.

He did not feel there was anything to be gained by charging aimlessly about the country. The Frying Pan riders were impatient and craved movement, so he decided to let them go and work by himself. He would wait behind and watch Casa Diablo. If Silver and Big Montana had made no move by dawn, it would be time enough to start tracking the kidnapers. Besides, he had the feeling that Jim would be on the trail by this time, and he was the only one Jack knew who could follow a trail in the dark with any measure of success.

At the first opportunity, Jack Allen pulled his horse off the trail and allowed the others to pass him. He thought at first he had made this maneuver without being seen. But a few minutes later Jarrick materialized from the darkness and joined him.

Jack Allen flared up with quick anger. "Get goin' and join the others!"

"Me? Not any," Toothpick replied coolly. "If you want to play a lone hand, then I'll do the same."

Jack Allen respected Toothpick's fighting ability. He was a good man to tie to.

"Right. What was you aimin' to do?" he asked, mollified.

"Last year, when Jim was huntin' the hangout of the Lava gang hereabouts, he quartered the lava fields pretty thoroughly," Toothpick explained. "From something he said tother day, I figgers Quong is holin' up somewhere along the big split through them. So I figgered to ride along that split and see what I could see."

Jack Allen nodded. He said he intended to watch the Casa Diablo that night. If Big Montana and Silver left the ranch, he intended to trail them in the hope they would lead him to Quong.

"If they don't succeed in making him give up the girls, maybe I'll have better luck," Allen finished grimly.

The two chose a place close to the entrance of Casa Diablo and settled down to watch. They saw and heard the rurales clatter from the doorway and take the trail to the east. Then, half an hour later, several other horsemen left the ranch and followed the rurales.

"Silver, Montana, and five riders," Allen whispered.

"Here's hoping they're visitin' Quong," Toothpick replied softly.

The two trailed behind the Casa Diablo riders in complete silence. They had ridden nearly an hour and a half when Montana and his men swung sharply to the left and headed north through the lava fields.

"They're goin' up the cleft I told you about. A dollar to a doughnut they're headin' for Quong's hideout!" Toothpick said excitedly.

Jack Allen nodded. He was silent for a moment, then pointed at a high mountain to the south of them. "Look at that light!" he said.

Toothpick saw a light halfway up the mountain about five miles from them. This flickered about five miles from them. This flickered on and off. He watched it with amazement for a moment, then turned excitedly to Allen. "Some one's signaling!" he exclaimed.

"Morse code," Allen replied. "They're spellin' out 'Help!' over and over again. There it goes again and this time it's in Spanish."

"Come on, let's go see who it is!" Toothpick cried, and swung his horse about.

"Nope," Allen checked him. "Our best bet is to follow Montana and Silver. Besides which, those rurales has eyes like lynxes and will be sure to spot that light and investigate."

Rather unwillingly Toothpick followed Allen down the cleft. They rode rapidly at first, then slowly when they again neared Montana and his men. Hearing the seven dismount, they pulled up and saw the vague shapes of the men mount the steep path, then vanish high up on the face of the cliff. Jack and Toothpick stood for a moment undecided. Then they heard the drumming of a hard-ridden horse coming from the north. The sound grew louder and increased to a crescendo as the horse neared them.

A rider pulled up with a jerk and stared at the bunch of saddled horses.

"It's young Bill Carver!" Toothpick cried.

" 'Lo, kid. What you doin' here?" Jack Allen greeted.

Bill Carver peered at him through the darkness. "Hello!" he cried at last. "So you ain't gone in the cave yet?"

"I'm Jack Allen, not Jim," the other replied quickly. "What's this about Jim going in the cave?"

"Quong's there. They set a trap for your brother. I wanted to go with him, but he wouldn't wait. He said if he got Quong, he didn't care what happened to himself!" Carver said breathlessly.

So Jim intended to attack Quong single-handed! While he was wondering if he were too late, Jack was thinking out a plan. "Kid, you ride hard, straight through the cleft. When you get out of here, start shootin' and hollerin'. There's a bunch of rurales over there. You make enough noise so they hear you, then bring 'em here pronto."

The youth protested. He wanted to remain and go with them to rescue Jim, but Jack was adamant and drove him away.

Then Jack Allen and Toothpick hastily climbed the trail to the shelf. Just as they reached it, the muffled roar of guns floated from the cave.

"Jim's started!" Jack shouted.

The two, guns in hands, dashed forward. As they reached the entrance to the cave, a blurred shape leaped forward to block their passage.

A stream of orange fire leaped from Allen's gun, and the way was clear. They leaped over the body just as some one lifted a curtain from before a smaller, lighted cave to their left, and several men poured out of the opening.

Both Allen and Toothpick halted these men by firing at them.

"Jim! Jim! Where are you?" Jack called.

Ahead of them they saw a door swing open and they saw Jim Allen framed in the doorway. They dashed through it, and Jim slammed it behind them. They gave one quick glance around them and relaxed. They saw the still bodies of the gunmen and the mutilated body of the sheriff.

Toothpick swore feelingly as he crossed to the sheriff. "Them gents was worse than Apaches. Is he hurt bad?"

"They hurt me plenty bad, but I reckon I'll live," the sheriff answered faintly.

"You got all three!" Jack said admiringly.

Jim Allen shook his head and pointed to Slick Keen's slashed body. "No, King got that one."

Toothpick shivered. He backed away from the big wolf that stood close to his master.

"Quong and the girls?" Jack Allen demanded.

"Quong's in there," Jim Allen nodded toward the end of the cave.

The men outside were beating and hammering on the front door.

"It's solid and will hold 'em until we dig out Quong," Jim said.

Jack took one step toward the end of the cave, then the back door swung open, and Quong appeared in the opening.

"Quong is not a rat to be destroyed in a pit. You could break in to me before my men could break in to you, so I come out and defeat you with wise words," he chanted.

He was dressed in a magnificent jet-black robe, elaborately embroidered. A gorgeous dragon was etched in gold across his breast. His eyes were bland, expressionless; they gazed out of his evil face triumphantly. There was no defeat there. Surprisingly, he seemed to feel himself master of the situation.

Jim Allen slowly raised his guns.

"Wait! For if you kill me, you will never see those girls again," Quong purred. His words were unhurried.

"Where are they?" Jack Allen demanded.

"Where you will never find them — unless I walk out of that door free."

A frozen hand clutched at Jack Allen's breast. There was silence in the room. It was the dying Bull Morgan, otherwise Big Montana, who broke that silence. He laughed and choked horribly, because of the wound in his chest. His face was distorted with hideous mirth as he looked at Jim Allen.

"You got me, Wolf, but I'll go knowin' Quong will live to send you to join me," he gloated. "You bested him twice, but the third time he'll get you!"

"There'll be no third time," Jim Allen said tonelessly.

At these words Toothpick switched his eyes from Quong to Jim Allen. He was startled at the change in him. Allen's face was a pasty yellow beneath his tan, and the freckles looked like faded drops of paint. His eyes were like those of a dead man, dull and glassy in hollow sockets. He seemed to have shrunk, to have grown smaller. Toothpick was stunned at the portent of Jim's words. This thing could not be. Hard, remorseless as he knew him to be, it was impossible that he contemplated sacrificing Snippets and Mary Bell.

"Truly a man who becomes tangled in his own web is like a child," Quong mocked. He stood immovable as a statue, his eyes sparkling with unholy triumph.

"Words will not stem a torrent," Jim Allen said flatly.

"All things move and change. Quong is not a fool. He and the honorable brother of a wolf will make a pact. The girls will be returned unharmed and then the Wolf will allow Quong to go unharmed, or —" His lips split in a fleeting smile, and he gestured.

That "or" was like a death knell. Each man understood its significance. Suddenly full comprehension came to Jack Allen. His agonized eyes darted from Quong to his brother's corpselike face. Jim Allen shook his head.

"You mean you won't accept?" Jack cried.

Again Jim Allen shook his head.

"But, my God, Jim, you know what will happen to them!" Jake almost screamed.

It was Quong who replied. "They will go across the border. I say no more; a clever man understands a nod."

"Shut up, you yellow devil!" Jack Allen raged.

Quong's face was inscrutable. He bowed blandly, but there was something mocking in the glance he directed at the Wolf.

Jim Allen stood with lowered head. To Toothpick he seemed to be a man whose soul had departed and left behind a shell which spoke, breathed, and acted without feeling. Then he spoke, and his voice was weary. "Jack, you got to listen to me. Quong has already sent many girls across the border, and if we let him go, he'll send many more. Look what the devil done to the sheriff. He cashes now!"

"I ain't sayin' he don't need killin' bad. But I'm tellin' you, Jim, if we got to let him go to get those gals back, then he goes free!" Jack cried passionately.

"No," Jim replied shortly.

"You mean you're going to sacrifice those girls?" Jack asked, his voice brittle and hard. "I always figgered you loved Snippets and you'd —"

Jim's dead eyes met Jack's blazing ones, and he nodded.

"I'm tellin' you, I won't let you! Quong goes free!" Jack cried.

Jack's words had the wild force of a tempest, but they broke futilely against Jim's rocklike will.

"Jack," Jim said slowly, "once I found a feller out in the desert what was lost. He was a teacher in some kind of college. He tole me about a disease what he called leprosy. It's plumb fatal, and they don't know no cure for it. These here people what get it have to be kept shut up on an island. He tole how nice gals and doctors an' other folks goes to them islands and live there always so's to find out a cure for it so's they can cure other folks what will get it years from now." Jim spoke as if every word was an effort. "I reckon you're right about Snippets," he continued. "Her an' my hosses is about all I hanker for in this world. But I'm tellin' you, we got to be like them doctors and nurses and play this game straight. You got to remember that a heap of women won't go across the border if Quong cashes now. So I says he stops lead."

Jack Allen's mouth tightened, and his eyes were pools of ice. "An' I says he doesn't!"

"Then you got to kill me, or I'll kill him," Jim said flatly.

Jack's face turned pale at this. Then he shook himself, and his face grew hard.

Toothpick gasped, "Jim, you don't mean that!" But he knew that Jim Allen would carry out his threat at no matter what cost. From the corner of his eye he saw Quong's hand creep upward to the fold in his gown. He knew that the Chinaman must have a knife concealed there, but he stood fascinated, confused thoughts swirling in his brain, knowing not what to do. It was Jim Allen who ended his dilemma.

"Quong, drop your hand and shake that knife to the floor!" he commanded.

Quong's eyes flickered with hate, but he flipped his gown open, and the long, thin knife tinkled on the floor. Jack Allen kicked it aside, then like a flash placed himself in front of Quong.

"You'll have to shoot through me to get him," he said coldly.

Toothpick gasped and turned away. He threw one arm over his eyes. Jim Allen had twice saved his life, so now, although he sympathized with Jack, he could not interfere.

"Stand aside, Jack," Jim said clearly. "We ain't got the right to sacrifice a thousand gals to save two."

"No," said Jack shortly.

Toothpick could hear the two men breathing deeply. Bull Morgan's terrible laugh filled the cave.

Then suddenly a hurricane of shots crashed out in the outer cave. There were shrill cries of fear and pain. Some one pounded on the door. Toothpick recognized the voice of the lieutenant of rurales. With a moan of relief he threw open the door, and the lieutenant and young Carver entered.

"The girls are safe!" Carver cried.

"You got 'em! You saved 'em?" Jack Allen cried.

"No, señor, I did not save them. I cannot claim that honor." The lieutenant smiled and bowed to Jim Allen. "Señorita McPherson proved herself the true mate of a wolf and saved herself."

Toothpick explained the events that had happened in that room. The lieutenant's eyes were hard as they looked at Quong.

"The señor is an officer. We are in Mexico. I claim his protection," Quong shrilled.

Jim Allen pointed to Tom Powers' horribly mutilated body. "He done that," he said simply.

"So!" the lieutenant cried, then he added: "Officially, I am not here."

He swung about, and his spurs rang musically as he walked to the door. Without looking back, he passed from sight.

Quong knew he was doomed when he heard the girls were safe. After his appeal to the lieutenant failed, he resigned himself. "Even a monkey sometimes falls from a tree," he murmured. "My mouth has a bitter taste as I go to join my ancestors. Those were his last words. His face seemed to shrivel; his eyes became sunken pools of bitterness.

His end was merciful and quick.

Jim Allen's guns came out so quickly that they were throwing a double stream of death at Quong before any one had seen his hands move. The force of that stream of bullets kept Quong upright against the wall until Allen's guns were empty, then he softly slid to the floor and lay still.

Jim Allen never once looked at Quong after he had ceased firing. Without pausing to reload his guns, he dropped them into his holsters, swung about and, with his wolf, passed out of the cave to where he had left Princess.

Men saw him riding through the dawn, down the cliff, and watched him vanish around a bend. He had finished his job and he was going home.

Later they carried Tom Powers back to the Frying Pan Ranch. The doctor who had been summoned said that in time his frightful wounds would heal, and he would be as well as ever, but he would carry the scars of his experience to the grave.

It was Mary Bell who told about the kidnaping. They had been confined in an old hacienda built on the edge of a cliff. They were guarded by Charley May and Fah Woo and his wife, who lived there with their infant son.

Mary Bell spent most of her time in tears, but Snippets watched for a chance to escape. Finally she thought of a plan to aid them. The first time the guard was relaxed, she snatched up the baby and raced to the roof of the building. When Fah Woo and his wife pursued her, they saw her standing on the balustrade on the edge of the precipice.

"Go back! Or I'll jump, and the baby goes with me!" Snippets cried.

They drew back in terror at her threat. The child was their first-born. Holding the infant, Snippets had stood there hours signaling with a lantern. Finally the rurales had seen the light and secured them. Later Carver had brought the rurales to the cave.

Young Bill Carver made a full confession to Sam Hogg. The ex-Ranger was silent for a long time after the boy had finished, then he sighed.

"Kid, you wasn't full growed," he excused.

"I acted yellow. I got to prove I ain't yellow all through. I was hopin' to get a chance last night, but the Allens do things by their lonesome."

Hogg's eyes glittered, and there was regret in his voice when he spoke.

"I wish I was young and could go with you. There's one way you can prove you ain't yellow." In answer to the question in the boy's eyes, he explained: "Join the Rangers. If you make good with them, folks'll know dang well you ain't yellow. I reckon I could get you in."

"I'm starting pronto!"

Within an hour the boy had gone, and Sam Hogg had nothing but envy for him, for he was young.

It was on the following day when Toothpick and Sam Hogg were discussing the fight in the cave, that Sam Hogg demanded:

"An' do you figger Jim would have really shot his brother if the rurales hadn't come?"

Toothpick answered this by asking another. "Do you figger Snippets would have jumped with that kid?"

Sam Hogg sighed and scratched his head. "I dunno," he said. "He's a wolf, and she's sure a true mate for him!"